DEAD
RUNNING

CAMI
CHECKETTS

Other books by Cami:

The Fourth of July
The Broken Path
The Sister Pact

A portion of the proceeds from *Dead Running* will be donated to The Child and Family Support Center. For more information on this worthy cause – www.cachecfsc.org

www.camichecketts.com

DEAD RUNNING

Birch River Publishing
Logan, Utah

CAMI CHECKETTS

This is a work of fiction. Names, characters, places, and incidents are either the product of the author's imagination or are used fictitiously.

ISBN: 978-1475166606

Dead Running

Published by Birch River Publishing
2925 North 1000 East
North Logan, Utah 84341

Contact information: camichecketts@yahoo.com

Cover design by Janna Barlow

Edited by Nancy Felt Nancy_felt@yahoo.com
Cover Design by Janna Barlow
Cover Copyright Camille Coats Checketts
Typesetting by Heather Justesen

Published in the United States of America

Dedication

To all of my boys. I love the five of you more than you know.

To Richelle, the best running buddy a girl could ask for. Thanks for helping me solve the world's problems as we pound through the miles.

Learning to Run

I inched down another stair, hoping the soft creaks wouldn't give me away to whoever was arguing in my living room. My dad was visiting me this week, gathering medical supplies for another one of his projects. I'd been gracious and allowed him to host his meetings in my living room. The support from the medical community in our little corner of Northern Utah was actually impressive, but did one of the doctors have to show up in the middle of the night?

I was in that luscious almost-asleep phase when I heard the banging on my front door and crawled out of bed. Irritation turned to fear as I listened to the conversation. The man threatening Dad wasn't one of his supporters.

"You interfered with the wrong shipment this time."

"*Shipment?*" Dad asked. "These are human beings, not some profit margin."

I reached the bottom step and peeked around the wall. My dad stood near the fireplace with a mixture of shock and revulsion on his sunburned face.

Just inside the front door, a man peeked out from the shadow of a hooded sweatshirt. He yanked out a wicked-looking blade. I covered my mouth to stifle the scream. My stomach knotted. My legs felt like ice. I didn't know if I could move, let alone help.

The knife sailed through the air. My father darted to the side. The blade jabbed into his upper arm. Dad yelped. The pain in his face lodged in my own gut. He grabbed at his arm and yanked the knife out, spraying the wall with blood. My dad's blood. Help. I had to *do* something.

The hooded figure closed the distance and wrenched the weapon from dad's fingers, lifting it above his head.

1

"No!" I leapt from my hiding spot, grabbed a heavy picture frame off the end table, and smacked the man with it.

"Cassidy!" Dad inhaled quickly, hazel eyes widening.

The attacker knocked the picture frame out of my hands and pointed the bloody knife my direction. Dark eyes swept over the skin not covered by my t-shirt and cut-off sweats. I squirmed, his look scaring me as much as his knife. I backed up a step, eyes focused on the blade.

My dad planted himself between me and the man.

The man's white teeth flashed against leathery skin. "She's beautiful, Doc." His tongue darted across his lower lip. "The dark hair and pretty brown eyes. Looks just like her mom."

Dad held up his uninjured arm and shoved me behind him, his breath coming in ragged gulps. "Leave her out of this, Panetti."

Panetti cocked his head to the side. "I'm supposed to kill you, but I could bring her in alive for some extra compensation. How old are you, sweetheart?"

I glared at him over my dad's shoulder. "Twenty-one and going nowhere with you. Get out of my house before I call the police." It was a lame threat since I was visibly shaking and had no clue where my phone was.

The man threw back his head and laughed. "I like her, a bit of attitude. Ramirez and I will both enjoy her."

I swallowed the sickening taste of his threat. Sweat trickled down my spine. I clung to my injured dad, who was currently no match for this psycho. How could I protect either of us?

"You'll never touch her." Dad pushed me toward the kitchen doorway. "I can't believe you would betray the children for Ramirez."

"Not for Ramirez. I betrayed the children for lots and lots of money." Panetti revealed his perfect teeth again.

Dad looked back at me. "Run," he whispered.

I swallowed, trying to catch my breath. No matter how scared I was I couldn't leave him.

"Run, Cassie!" He shoved me and faced the madman.

Panetti let out a warrior cry and lunged with the knife. Dad ducked. The blade sliced air instead of flesh, throwing Panetti off balance. Dad plowed into the man's abdomen, knocking him into the front door. I screamed, running towards them to try to help.

"Get out of here," Dad yelled.

Stumbling away from the fight, I slammed into the wall. A yell of pain from my dad forced me to keep moving. I ran into the kitchen and nearly collapsed with relief when I saw my phone. Placing all my hopes and prayers on three numbers, I stilled my trembling hands enough to dial: 9-1-1.

The call connected. "A guy is trying to kill my dad!" Grunts and the sound of bodies slamming into furniture reassured me Dad was still alive. I told the dispatcher my address, but then she started asking more questions.

"I've got to help my dad."

"Officers are en route."

"Good!" I clung to the phone but stopped listening as I sprinted back into the living room. Dad was on top of Panetti. The knife was on the floor, Panetti reaching for it. I covered the last couple of feet, kicked the knife farther away, and stomped on his hand with my bare foot. Pain radiated up through my leg but I heard a crunch that hopefully meant I did some damage. How awful that I really wanted to hurt him.

I held up my phone. "The police will be here any second."

Dad strained to keep Panetti pinned. "Go back to the kitchen."

"I am *not* going to the kitchen while you fight for your life."

"Cassidy," Dad groaned. "For once in your life listen to me."

Panetti shoved Dad off of him. Dad banged his injured arm against the sofa, blood mingling with the leather finish as he yelped in pain. Panetti leaped to his feet, pushed me out of the way, and ran for the front door. Dad struggled to stand up. I regained my footing and hurried after Panetti, but Dad grabbed my arm before I got outside, allowing Panetti to disappear into the darkness.

"We should go after him," I said.

"Not tonight." Dad shut the front door and slid to the floor, clutching his bleeding arm. "I'll find him." The sheer determination in his eyes made me glad I wasn't Panetti.

"That guy wasn't one of your Mexican orphanage supporters."

Dad laughed, patting the floor next to him.

I clenched my hands together to stop the shaking. A few more deep breaths and I might feel like I wasn't going to pass out. "You need something for the blood."

He reached up a hand to me. "I'll be okay. It's you I'm worried about." I sank next to him and threw my arms around his neck. My entire body was trembling now. Dad patted my back and whispered that I was safe. It was exactly what I needed to hear, but still had a hard time believing. Several minutes later I could hear sirens approaching the house. I wiped at my nose and bit my lip to hold back more tears. "Someday you're going to tell me what that was all about."

Dad shook his head. "Hopefully you'll never know."

4

The First Race
(Four Years Later)

Step after excruciating step, I slammed one foot after another into the ground. My uneven stride rattled my dental fillings. I prayed for the pain to end, but no, voluntary torture just doesn't work that way. How had Raquel talked me into this?

"You gonna make it, Cassie?" Raquel asked.

I scowled at my pregnant sister-in-law. She ran effortlessly by my side, up this mountainous 5K route that somebody at the starting line had the gall to claim was an easy race. "I'll hop on your back and make it just fine." The words distorted as I sucked in air.

"The turn around is just around this next bend," Raquel said, "and then we get to fly downhill." She actually had the nerve to flap her arms. "You're doing great. Remember how Dory helped you on our training runs?" Raquel continued in a singsong voice, "'Just keep running, just keep running, run, run, run, run, run.'"

"Shut it, on the Dory," I yelled. Within milliseconds I regretted my words—not the rudeness, but the irreplaceable loss of oxygen. I gasped and saw black, but somehow kept putting one foot in front of the other while *Finding Nemo* pounded through my eardrums. Teach me to mouth off.

"Okay, no Dory," Raquel said, but she kept humming the tune.

How could she run, talk, not get irritated with me, and look fabulous? She was four months along and still running me into the pavement.

"Look at the bright side." Raquel grinned. "You're almost to the mile and a half mark and haven't thrown up on anyone yet."

Not appreciating the reminder of my high school humiliation, I didn't respond.

"Here's the turn-around," Raquel said.

I followed her in a U-pattern, and thanks to someone in heaven who was interested in Cassidy's well-being, we started going downhill. I thought it would get easier, but that would be asking too much of my guardian angels.

We ran faster.

The rushing of the nearby river urged me on. Raquel's pace wouldn't allow me to slow down. Other runners streamed past me, battering my pride. I had a degree in exercise science, for heaven's sake, I couldn't let a pregnant lady and a sixty-year old man show me up, but my legs screamed that if we didn't break into a walk soon they may never produce forward momentum again.

I lengthened my stride to try and lessen the discomfort. My leg knocked into a runner coming up fast behind me. I lost my balance and flipped forward. Asphalt rushed up to greet me, thrusting my hands out did little to break my fall. Skin meeting pavement trumped the agony of my 140-pound frame slamming into the ground. Pinpricks of pain screamed from my hands to my knees.

"Cassidy!" Raquel cried, pivoting back to me.

Choking on my own saliva, I rolled over and sat up. Ugly road-rash covered my hands, forearms, and knees. A beefy palm gripped my stinging elbow, jerking me onto my feet without consent. "You okay?"

I stared into the scarred face of a Nasty Muscle Man, from his bald head to his thick fingers he looked like he could easily pick me up and drown me in the river. Scarier still, he looked like he wanted to.

"Um, yeah." I shook off his hand with a grimace.

"Are you all right?" Raquel asked.

I nodded, terrified by the way the big guy, with scars on his face that were probably made by sharp knives, and his lanky buddy, who looked like he'd slicked his hair with nonstick cooking spray, were studying me. Hunger radiated from their eyes. Escape was my only desire. Bloody abrasions forgotten, I threw my legs into motion.

Raquel was by my side in seconds and we sprinted until my legs felt like limp noodles. Sweat rolled into open wounds. My hair escaped from the ponytail. Yanking the mass loose, I tried to refasten my wad of dark hair. The extra effort cost me more energy than the annoyance was worth. "Are they still," I caught a quick breath, "watching us?" I needed to stop and nurse my wounds, but couldn't face those men again.

Raquel glanced back. "They're gone. That's weird."

I looked over my shoulder. The spot where I'd tripped was still visible but the men were not. Where could they have disappeared to?

"You want to stop?" Raquel asked.

"No. I'd rather spew on my high school fantasy again," I took a quick breath and then spit out, "than have those two stare at me again."

Raquel laughed. "Gotcha."

A man buzzed past us, all sinewy legs and broad shoulders. Fine-Looking Runner Man almost erased the pain of my recent injuries. How had I missed this perfect specimen on the way up the canyon?

I found enough air for a soft whistle and a muttered, "Nice calves."

He glanced over his shoulder and gave me a grin and a wink before racing down the road.

I increased my leg speed. The cuts in my knees only stung a little. "Catch . . . him."

Raquel chuckled. "Honey, even if you could catch him, you couldn't beat him."

Not comprehending, I stared at her.

"He's running the 10K not the 5."

"Seriously?" My mind whirled trying to make sense of it. We were barely past halfway. My little incident had taken some time and there'd been a few people passing us. Well, more than a few, but no one who had to run twice as far up the canyon before they turned around. I groaned and tried to increase my pace.

Fine-Looking Runner Man powered up an incline that I would need climbing ropes and grappling irons to conquer. My heart stopped. I pointed. "Do we have to . . . ?"

Raquel laughed. "No. That's how I knew he was running the 10K. We run back down the canyon to where we started."

I exhaled. "Thank heavens." I took a large breath and then shot out the words, "I was prepared to strangle you."

"Glad we avoided that." Raquel gestured to the green boughs sagging over our heads. "Isn't this beautiful?" she said. "Do you see why I love running this canyon?"

"Yup," I muttered, thinking anyone who ran this incline twice in their lifetime was insane. The agony obliterated the enjoyment of hills covered with greenery, natural shelter from the sun, and silence from traffic and people.

Raquel surveyed my injuries while we ran. "Are you okay?"

"I'll live." The scratches weren't deep. Although I wanted her to feel guilty for getting me into this misery, I was more worried about those men finding me again.

Ritzy homes, hidden by the canyon foliage, shrunk in stature and appeared more frequently. I remembered this spot from the run up the canyon. Hope spiked. Somebody in heaven did love me. Minutes later, the finishing tunnel beaconed. My mouth watered at the sight of it. A hundred more feet and my aching body would find solace.

"Finish strong," Raquel said. "Let's see those horse legs in action."

I dug deep, pumping my arms and lengthening my stride into full sprinter mode. Trees and people flew by as I gasped for air and pushed myself onto glory. I could hear Raquel's loud breathing behind me. Raquel was behind me? The mere thought gave me energy. I dashed through the finish-line tunnel, enjoying the claps and hoots from the onlookers.

Raising my hands, I crossed the white line and allowed myself to slow down. Walking was bliss. I did a bow for my admirers, climbed over the low fence that surrounded Mack Park, and collapsed onto the grass.

Raquel appeared above me seconds later. Hands on knees, she gulped deep breaths and drummed up a smile. "Good job. I always knew you had horse legs."

I lay there, sweat dripping down me. I'd just beat myself up for sport. Odd that I also felt pretty darn proud. "You know it," I said. "I had to use 'em so I could kick your tail." Never mind the fact that Raquel had held back to stay by my side.

Raquel tossed her highlighted twists of brown and gold. She smirked at me. "Try the race next year when I'm not pregnant."

I groaned and pushed to a seated position. "If you ever get me to run another race, I'll do it in Princess Leia braids."

She giggled. "*That* I'd like to see."

I was distracted by a well-built man with deeply-tanned skin approaching us. His dark hair was just long enough to curl slightly and make me want to touch it. He reached out his hand and lifted me the rest of the way from the ground. I teetered as I gawked into deep brown eyes and a smile that made me feel like I was sprinting again.

"Are you okay?" he asked.

The depths of his baritone rolled over me, rendering me speechless.

He arched an eyebrow, leaning closer. "Ma'am?"

"*Ma'am?*" I choked on the word. "Do I look like a ma'am to you?"

A grin crinkled his olive skin and I decided he could call me anything he wanted to. My eyes trailed from the strong planes of his face along his upper body. The well-toned muscles of his arms were plastered with tattoos.

9

One or two tattoos? Could be attractive. Not an inch of flesh showing through the ink? A bit much for me. I swallowed hard and met his gaze.

He'd noticed my reaction, his eyes cooled from hot fudge to obsidian. "I'm a surgeon," he said, "I was going to offer my services."

"As long as it's not as a tattoo artist." I bit my lip the instant the words escaped.

His eyebrows shot upwards. "Excuse me?"

Raquel caught my gaze and shook her head. She waved to someone, fleeing the uncomfortable silence.

"Sorry," I mumbled to the ground. Someday I would learn to control my tongue. "I'd love to have you doctor me."

Dr. Tattoo gently grasped the un-bloody part of my arm and escorted me to the first aid tent. His hands were the beautiful male kind with tan, strong fingers. His face definitely had a rough edge to it, but was gorgeous nonetheless. But his body? I shuddered. I'd never been a huge fan of draping a healthy body with artwork. This professed doctor's appearance screamed bad boy, but his kind eyes warred with the image.

We didn't speak as he bandaged my scrapes, his warm fingers doing a number on my hypersensitive skin. Sadly for me, he finished, threw the wrappings in the garbage, and lifted his eyes to mine. "All better?"

If I focused on his face, I could've thrown myself at him and never looked at another face again. I swallowed and whispered, "I would be if I hadn't offended you earlier."

He glanced down at his multi-colored arms then back at me. "It's understandable."

I nodded, wanting to ask why he hadn't stopped after the first twenty tattoos. "Thank you," I murmured, standing and pivoting away.

Dr. Tattoo stood with me. "Hopefully I won't see you again."

I spun back. "How am I supposed to take that?"

10

He grinned, his dark eyes sparkling mischievously. "I'm a plastic surgeon and you obviously don't need any work done." He gestured to me and I reddened with pleasure.

"Okay, then." I reached out and shook his hand. The pressure of his grasp made me wish I did need "work" so I could see him again, though he obviously wasn't my type. "Here's to never seeing you again."

He winked. I walked away on unsteady legs that had nothing to do with my road rash.

Raquel and I sprawled under the shade of the bowery at Mack Park. After one of the most painful half hours of my life I was entitled to sip water and munch on Great Harvest Bread. I hadn't seen the Nasty Muscle Man who I tripped on during the race. At the moment I was safe and satiated.

A woman with a cheap megaphone called out, "It's time to annou . . . the prize win . . ." or something like that, her voice was so garbled I missed half her words.

Raquel dragged me closer to the picnic tables in hopes of hearing better.

Race Organizer Lady gave away a treadmill, gift certificates to iFrogz and Mio Global watches (crap, I wanted one of those), and a year of free ice cream from Casper's Malt Shoppe (shoot, I *really* wanted that one).

I kicked at a clump of grass clippings. Same old routine. I never won anything. Then like a miracle, I heard it.

"Cassidy Christen . . . has won, garble, garble, garble."

I shrieked and grabbed Raquel. "I won!"

Raquel faced me, eyes wide. "You *won*."

We locked onto each other's forearms and jumped up and down as if I'd just won the Idaho lottery. "You won," she screamed.

"I won," I yelled louder.

A tall brunette next to us asked, "What did you win?"

"I don't know," I laughed, gleeful in my ignorance.

A middle-aged, miniscule man chuckled. "Glad you're so happy about it." He pushed back his baseball cap and scratched at a tuft of blond hair. "You won the entrance into the St. George Marathon."

Raquel's mouth dropped open. A loud guffaw emitted from her pink-stained lips. I stopped jumping. My eyes widened. My heart fell to my running shoes. "A marathon entry? What kind of a stupid prize is that?"

Raquel released her grip on me, her entire body shaking with laughter. "A marathon? Why would *you*," cackle, cackle, cackle, "enter your name into a drawing for a marathon?"

I dug my toe into the dewy grass, extending my lower lip. "I didn't know it was for a marathon. I entered every drawing there was. I wanted the year of free ice cream from Casper's."

"And you got a marathon." Raquel laughed so hard I was afraid she would hurt my future nephew. "Wait till Jared hears this," she said. "Our Cassie. Running a marathon."

A beautiful, hard-bodied redhead, in a sports bra and what could have passed for running shorts, if you added six inches of cloth to the backside, sidled up next to me. "I'd buy the entrance from you."

I whirled from my cackling sister-in-law to look down at the woman trapped in a teenager's body. "Why would you waste your money?"

A soft dimple appeared in her lovely face. "I didn't get into St. George and I really want to. Actually, I'm desperate to get in."

"I'd feel like a piece of trash selling you such a stupid prize." I turned away, more frustrated with myself than the redhead. Raquel smirked at me and sauntered towards the refreshment table.

Hot Redhead rushed around in front of me. "You don't

understand. The lottery for the marathon entries is over and my name didn't get pulled. Races like this," she gestured around with her hand. "Are my only hope." She smiled, revealing perfectly straight and whitened teeth. "I have a really big reason for wanting to run St. George."

"Which is?" I demanded. I needed to know all the facts. Maybe I should be aching to run this race too. Maybe—if I was a raving lunatic.

She tilted her head towards the end of the pavilion. A gaggle of women in shorter shorts than my new friend flittered around Fine-Looking Runner Man, the same perfect specimen who sailed past Raquel and I earlier this morning.

"*Damon* is running St. George," she caressed his name like he was royalty.

Damon. I let the name rest in my brain. It was perfect. *He* was perfect.

I rolled my eyes at Hot Redhead, showcasing my lack of interest. "What a pathetic way to try and snag a guy."

Hot Redhead glared at me. "He's offered to train with any locals running St. George. It would mean hours with him." She sighed. "And depending on who else gets into the St. George Marathon," her voice lowered conspiratorially, "possibly hours *alone* with him."

"Aha. It's a fabulous strategy for picking up a man." I tilted my head to the side, studying her. No guy would turn down a woman that perfect. "Why don't you just ask him out?"

Her copper-tinged lips curled into a pout. "I just met him this morning. I'll wait for him to ask."

I clucked my tongue and pointed at the horde of women hanging on Damon's every muscle. "Well, good luck with that one. He's desperately searching for some female who holds back and waits for *him* to ask."

Race Organizer Lady, an exotic-looking woman with her dark hair in cornrows, approached me. Thankfully, she carried the megaphone instead of screeching through it. "You're Cassidy Christensen?"

"Yes." How did she find me so quickly? I searched for the person who had ratted me out. Raquel grinned, gave me a thumbs up, and took another bite of bread. She was going to pay for that.

"Congratulations," she gushed. "You're going to love this race." Her almond-shaped eyes and wide lips tilted upwards with excitement. "You'll need to fill out the paperwork and then I'll give you the address to send in the fee." She offered a clipboard.

"Whoa, hold up." I stepped back. "What fee are we speaking of?"

"The eighty dollar marathon fee."

"Eighty dollars?" I gagged on the words. "Wh-what?" The sparrows twittered through the oak trees, adding their chirping laughter to my confusion. I frowned at the inconsiderate birds. "Reverse a bit. You said I won the marathon and now you're trying to make me pay for it. Something is messed up here."

Race Lady rolled her dark eyes. "You just won the *right* to enter."

"The right?" I blinked at her. "And people are excited about this prize?"

Hot Redhead tugged on my T-shirt. "I'm excited about it. Why not let me buy the entry?"

Race Lady was getting impatient. She pointed at me. "*You* have to pay for the marathon and you can't transfer it as I'm sure you read when you filled out the entry."

I hadn't read anything or I wouldn't be in this mess. "Seriously?" This woman was crazy. She couldn't force me to run a marathon.

"I'll give you a hundred bucks for it," Hot Redhead whispered into my ponytail.

I glanced back at her. "I think you want it more than that. One-twenty five."

14

"I just told you that you can't transfer it," annoyed Race Lady said.

"Uh-huh," I said. "Give us a second."

Hot Redhead stared at Damon and sighed. "Okay, one-twenty-five."

I glanced at Damon and his gang of feminine admirers. I wondered if they had a club. Maybe I could join up and buy me a Damon T-shirt. Nah. I'd never been much for organized man-chasing.

At that moment, Damon glanced over a blonde Barbie's head and smiled at me. My stomach fluttered. It was a feeling I wouldn't mind experiencing again. I guess I could understand why Hot Redhead was so intent on getting into this marathon.

Race Lady folded her arms across her chest, the megaphone dangling from her fingertips. "I'm *waiting*."

"One-fifty," I whispered at the woman hiding behind me.

"What?" Hot Redhead gasped. "You can't raise your price."

"I'm the one with my name on that entry," I said, poking at the clipboard in my hands. I jerked my head in Damon's direction. "I'm going to be the one training with Fine Damon. One-fifty or you can watch me drip sweat all over him."

Race Lady slapped her megaphone against her thigh. I don't think she found either of us comical. "The entry is non-transferable. I can't believe anyone would try to sell this."

"Sure you can." I offered her a cheeky smile and a discreet wink. "Now I'll give you a cut, say twenty-five bucks if you pretend you pulled her name out of the hat instead of mine."

"That's obscene." She jammed the clipboard into my ribs. "Fill out your information here."

"How do you spell your last name?" I whispered to the petite redhead.

"R-a-n-d-,"

Race Lady whipped her megaphone to her mouth and pressed it against the side of my head. "You *can-not* transfer it."

Agony raced from my eardrum, spreading throughout my nervous system. I bowed forward, clapped my hand to my ear, and writhed in pain. "Did you seriously just do that?"

Race Lady dropped the megaphone, stole the clipboard from my hands, and printed C-a-s-s-i-d-y C-h-r-i-s-t-e-n-s-e-n. I watched helplessly. My head ringing. My eardrum splitting.

Race Lady gave the clipboard back to me. "Fill it out. If you didn't want to run the marathon, you shouldn't have entered your name."

Hot Redhead leaned in. "Please." It was a simple but heartfelt request for my tormentor to have some pity on our situation. Hot Redhead's luminous green eyes were pretty convincing. I might have fallen for them.

"Get out of here," Race Lady shooed away my shadow.

My mouth dropped in despair as the girl pivoted and scurried away. "She would've given me a hundred and fifty bucks," I muttered. "Now I have to pay eighty and run an entire marathon?" Dang, this cruel Race Lady. She didn't even have the courtesy to look apologetic about my hearing damage.

"You'll love the St. George Marathon."

Was that her idea of sorry? "I wanted the ice cream."

She jabbed a long finger into the paper. "Get writing. I'll be back."

I slowly scratched in my address and phone numbers just to get her off my back so I could think for a minute. Maybe it would be fun to run a marathon and train with Fine Damon, or maybe I could throw the papers in the recycling when I got home and forget the whole thing. I shook my head and pressed several fingers against my eardrum. The ringing wasn't going away.

I glanced around for an escape route. If I ran now Race Lady wouldn't be able to track me down. I scanned for gaps in the crowd. My eyes landed on Dr. Tattoo. Yum, he looked good. His own mob of feminine admirers fought for attention. He caught my eye and smiled before refocusing on the tall brunette at his left. What would Nana think if I brought him home? Doubtful the plastic surgeon bonus would overshadow the dozens of visible tattoos. I wondered if he had any hidden tattoos. Even covered in ink, his chest would be worth a peek.

I forced myself to continue my search for Race Lady's position. She stood amidst a group of official-looking people under the bowery. Holy crackers. Was that the mayor? Race Lady nudged him, pointing in my direction. Several other members of her entourage turned to stare, obviously shocked that a girl had attempted to sell *the* marathon entry.

I couldn't run away with the mayor looking on. He had police backup. Was there some kind of law against not accepting a Health Day's prize? I rounded my shoulders and scratched at the entry form. Why had I been cheering a minute ago? I'd finally won something. Fabulous.

"Hey, I'm entered into the St. George Marathon too," a male voice said.

"Whoopee for you," I muttered, printing my identity for anyone to steal.

"Maybe we could train together," the deep voice interrupted again.

"Maybe," I drawled, obviously this guy was too thick to realize I wasn't interested in him or this stupid race. "*If* you could keep up with me."

A sharp jab in my abdomen jerked my eyes from the paper. Oh great, my sister-in-law had returned. "Ouch, wha . . ." My voice trailed off as I stared in awe. Fine Damon stood before me. I thought he was gorgeous from afar. Close up, he was tantalizing. Tall, lean, cropped strawberry-blond hair contrasting nicely with tanned skin and dark blue eyes.

"I'm, uh, really much faster than I showed today." I jabbed a finger at my sister-in-law. "You can't tell yet, but she's pregnant and I was being nice and going slow for her."

Raquel rolled her eyes. "Slowed down for me," she muttered. "I could kick your trash nine months pregnant." Tilting her chin, she marched over to another group of runners like an insulted debutante.

17

I glanced into amused blue orbs and had to admit, "She could." I hastened to explain, "I didn't train very well for this race, but I'll be ready for the marathon. I'm a personal trainer and exercise scientist so I obviously know what I'm doing. I plan on qualifying for Boston."

Qualifying for Boston? What kind of crap was I spouting? I didn't enjoy running. I'd only run this 5K to prove to my sister-in-law that I could keep up with her and prove to myself I wasn't the quitter my family imagined. At least the personal trainer and exercise scientist part were true.

Damon grinned. "Why don't we tackle St. George first?"

I reddened. He obviously saw through my bluff.

"Give me your phone number," Damon said.

Phone number? Oh, yeah. Forget this marathon talk and get right into setting up a date. Now it was my turn to grin.

"I'll let you know when we're doing training runs," he said.

Grin disappeared.

"We usually do about seven and half minute miles on our long runs," Damon continued. "Is that a problem for you?"

"I, uh," I stuttered, laboring to regulate my facial expression. Seven and a half minute miles? I'd done that pace on the treadmill, once, for about twenty seconds. "Seven and a half minute miles? Shouldn't be a problem. That's a reasonable pace." *On a road bike.*

"Great. So what's your number?"

I rattled it off, couldn't hurt to let him call. Maybe I could talk him into dinner instead of training runs for the Marines.

"Perfect, I'll talk to you soon." He gave me one more jaw-dropping smile and turned away.

My heart did that weird fluttering thing again. "Um, wait. Don't you want to write my number down?"

Damon glanced back at me. "Oh, believe me. I won't forget the number of a girl I won't be able to keep up with."

Raquel reappeared from flittering around like this was social hour. "Dang," she whistled long and low, watching Damon disappear. "You are in trouble."

I looked down at the clipboard clenched between my fingers. Was I really committing myself to a marathon? Maybe it wouldn't be as bad as I envisioned. Maybe I could learn to enjoy running. I could always back out if it was too miserable. "Yeah and lucky for me, I know who can help."

She smiled. "In exchange for lots of babysitting. Tate *and* the new baby."

"Perfect." That was a condition I could live with.

Raquel rubbed her stomach. "You know what? I think this marathon is going to be a great thing. You're such a fabulous exercise scientist, maybe this will help you get back into your field. I'm proud of you, Cassie."

I still considered running from Race Lady, even with the mayor looking on, and changing my name so she couldn't force me to run this marathon, but Raquel's belief in me altered the way I viewed this race. Raquel knew exactly what to say to rope me into something I didn't want to do. She believed in me. It was worse than the nail in the coffin. She'd thrown the last bouquet of daisies on the embossed lid, shoveled in the dirt, and laid sod over my grave.

I fought it but my eyes leaked a bit. "Thanks, El."

Raquel put an arm around my shoulder. "I think your mom and dad would be proud of you too."

The words slammed into my chest like some medieval torture, spiky clubs with poison on their tips. Why would Raquel bring up my dead parents? I couldn't think about them without breaking down. They and Raquel were the only ones who believed I was some sort of superstar. Unfortunately for me, they were all wrong.

I tried to pull from her embrace. Raquel hugged me tighter. "It's okay to be sad about them, Cassie. It's been almost two years and I've never seen you cry."

That's because I cried alone. I finally managed to create some distance between us, but Raquel kept her hands on my shoulders and forced me to hold eye contact. She studied me for so long I was afraid her eyes would cross.

I glared right back. "I just about cried when you told me you were proud of me. But bringing up my parents who deserted their children and grandson so they could save the world? Call me an insensitive jerk, but I don't waste energy crying about that kind of bunk."

Raquel didn't answer, but she didn't look away either.

How did she always know when I was lying? "I'm going to walk so my legs aren't sore." I broke from her unnerving stare and unwanted touch.

I tossed the clipboard on a park bench, stalked to the fence bordering the park, and easily scaled it. Crossing the road, I came to the rickety bridge. I rushed over it, slowing my steps when I hit the trail. I headed east on the trail until I was certain no one from the park could see me. I used to love coming here with my dad when I was little, chucking rocks from our favorite spot along the bank. Dad would laugh when I splashed him.

Stop it. I came over here to escape thoughts of my parents. I buried my longing for those who loved me the most, and picked through the underbrush down the short slope to the riverbank. My foot struck something soft. I lurched forward. Grabbing a tree branch, I prevented my second nasty spill of the day.

Pushing some limbs aside to see what I'd tripped over, the oxygen whooshed from my lungs. There was a man lying face down amongst the rotting leaves and dirt.

My heart pounded faster than during my sprint earlier this morning. "Y-you okay?"

I knelt down. It was impossible to check his pulse in this position. I climbed above him and pushed. He rolled with the incline, flopping onto his back and exposing the horror of what he'd suffered during his last moments on earth.

I stared at a man with no face. In a rush all the memories of my dad being attacked with a knife and then two years later the agony of seeing my parents bloody and dead in photos provided by the FBI came back full force. I couldn't move. I couldn't run. The only part of my body that functioned was my vocal chords. I screamed and screamed and screamed.

Strong arms surrounded me. I looked at tattooed flesh and screamed louder still.

"Shh, shh. It's me."

I glanced up at his face. Dr. Tattoo. My screams quieted as he continued to hold me. After a few minutes, I gained enough control to block the screams that still needed to see daylight. My rescuer pushed my forehead into his chest with one hand and wrapped the other arm underneath my legs. He easily lifted me from the ground. I closed my eyes, but the man's faceless body was imprinted in my mind.

"You're okay," Dr. Tattoo said. "I've got you now. You'll be okay."

I leaned into his broad chest, clinging to him to stop the trembling. I didn't scream anymore. I didn't tell him how wrong he was. Nothing about today or any other part of my life was okay.

He glanced down at the carnage. "No need to check for a pulse."

My stomach churned. I gulped at the acid building in my throat. Dr. Tattoo carried me up the steep embankment and set me on my feet, but kept his arm around me. I was grateful for the support as my legs wobbled. He pulled a cell phone from his pocket and dialed 9-1-1. I tried not to listen to his description of the body.

He finished and studied me. "Are you all right?"

Swallowing, I whispered. "No, not all right." At least I could talk without breaking down. "I saw him and thought of my dad." I shuddered. "I thought I'd put all of that behind me." I glanced up at him, realizing he had no clue what I was talking about, but he nodded encouragingly so I kept going, "Four years ago my dad was attacked by a man named Panetti." Crazy how that night elicited as many nightmares as the images of my parent's dead bodies.

Dr. Tattoo's eyes darkened to a dangerous glint, it was almost like he hated Panetti as much as I did.

"Do you know Panetti? He was a doctor at Logan Regional before he betrayed my dad."

He nodded. "I've heard the name."

"I can't forget him jabbing a knife into my dad. I think he was the one that ordered my parent's executions also." I pulled away and shook my head. "I'm sorry. I don't even know you and I'm going on and on."

He gave me a quick smile. "When you've been through something like this," he gestured to the body, "You become friends quick."

I bit my lip, trying to hold in the tears. Friends. A friend who was there for me when I fell apart. I liked him. "Thanks."

Sirens blared through the comforting sound of the river splashing over rocks. Dr. Tattoo offered me a smile and a hand, directing me towards the bridge. I had no desire to tell my story to the police but at least I had a friend by my side.

Admitting the Truth

I sifted through an enormous salad with my fork. The metal tines clicked against bright orange stoneware. I'd already devoured everything palatable in the bowl. The only food left was the lettuce and I was sick of green.

I sat with my best friend, Tasha, at our favorite restaurant. Café Sabor was a converted train station—vibrant colors against beautiful restored wood, boisterous waiters, and the best Mexican food in Cache Valley.

Of course Tasha and I didn't allow ourselves to eat the wonderful specialties oozing with cheese. No, we ordered chicken salads, dressing on the side, and tried to contain the drool from the sights and smells of real food so we could justify Cold Stone for dessert.

I set my fork down. Tasha had consumed enough calories to take the edge off. It was time to reveal my news.

"You won't believe this," I threw out the disclaimer first to ease the shock, "but . . ." Pause several seconds to get Tasha excited and work up my nerve, "I'm running the St. George Marathon. Woo-hoo for me, huh?" I pumped my hands up and down above my shoulders. "Woo-hoo, woo-hoo."

Tasha's fork halted mid-launch.

I stopped cheering, lowered my hands, and clutched the cloth napkin in my lap. "I won the entry at the 5K this morning," Hopefully Nana hadn't told her about the rest of my morning. I swallowed hard, sweat rising on my brow. "I'm so excited," I rushed on with my story. "I've never won anything like this before. Well, you know, I've never won anything like anything before."

Tasha's brow squiggled. Her lips flat-lined. I knew what she was thinking—a marathon entry didn't really count as "winning" something, or maybe that's what I was trying to convince myself *not* to think.

"Seriously?" Her blue eyes filled with doubt. "You actually *won* The Health Days Race?" She grinned. "And you didn't throw up on any hot men?"

I shrunk lower in my seat. "No, I didn't win *the* race. I put my name in a drawing and voila." I splayed my hands. "I'm a win-*ner*."

"I see." Tasha returned to separating salad with her fork.

"St. George is a qualifier for the Boston Marathon," I explained, "and just doing something big like this has inspired me to start a new business . . ."

My voice trailed off as my best friend stared at me like I'd grown chest hair. Tasha tilted her head to the side, blonde hair a gauzy curtain over her shapely upper arm. She poked at a chunk of chicken in her salad, set her fork down, took a long drink of water and then said, "*What* new business?"

"Training women in small groups so I can give personal attention but charge less per person." Faced with Tasha's discerning stare, my excitement fizzled a bit. "I read about it in Prevention magazine."

Tasha rolled her eyes. "Your Prevention Bible?"

"Hey," I picked up a fragment of tortilla chip and sucked on the salty goodness of grease, "I read the real Bible too."

"More than Prevention Magazine?" She took a bite of her salad, the actual green part, and waited for an answer I wasn't going to give. Swallowing, she shook her head. "I didn't think so."

"Anyway," I said, "this is going to be fabulous. I've just got to find the right spot and get the word out." I'd gotten the idea this afternoon when I was doing anything I could to distract myself from thinking about a man with no face. The excitement of getting back into personal training almost blocked the bad memories. Almost. "I'll be able to use my degree again."

24

"Which degree are you speaking of?" She snapped her fingers. "Oh, I know. The exercise science degree that you worked four years for, just had to complete, but after one failed business attempt, never use to make money? That degree?"

"Yes, that one." I forced a smile, trying to stay positive and ignore the uppercuts. "It's going to be brilliant. I'm trying to decide if I should design a website or flyers first."

"Whoa, whoa." Tasha held up her hand. "I understand the desire to break free of the receptionist job."

"Loan *processor*." Why couldn't she ever get that right?

Tasha rolled her eyes. "Whatever you want to call yourself. A job that you hate."

"I'm great at my job and I make loads of money."

"Your boss is a pig and you aren't happy." She arched a perfectly plucked and dyed brow, waiting for me to contradict her, which I couldn't do. "While I hate to admit it . . . this is a great idea. You're a fabulous exercise scientist, an extremely fit person, and the best personal trainer I've ever used for *free*," the lovely eyebrow almost reached her hairline, "if you can really convince yourself to charge people this would be the perfect job for you."

"Thanks." Finally, Tasha was giving me a little credit.

"But what does any of this have to do with running a marathon?"

"Running the race this morning just inspired me and I know I can do this new business and run a marathon."

Tasha rolled her eyes. "You've never run over three miles in your life, especially since your high school debacle."

"Yes, I have."

"When?"

"I ran 3.1 this morning." I stuck out my tongue. "So ha."

"3.1? That is impressive." She pushed her plate away and threw her napkin on top of it. "I smell a man in all of this. A sweaty man."

A smile crept across my face before I could lasso it.

"Oh-ho. I'm right." Tasha's answering smile wiped the mirth right out of my soul. "That's why you're doing this. There's a man involved. Don't you love the smell of workout sweat? Fresh and salty. Yum."

I swirled the orange straw through my ice water, though I hadn't committed to the marathon for any man, Damon offering to train with me had helped influence the decision. "Well, there was this one *sweaty* guy at the race this morning." I pushed away the vision of Dr. Tattoo. I couldn't think about him. If I focused on Damon I could discount my attraction to Dr. Tattoo. I really wanted to see him again but thinking of him reminded me of what he saved me from and it was all I could do to not start screaming again.

Tasha moved her chair closer to mine. "I love it. Spill details."

I twisted my lips closed.

"Now," she commanded.

I opened up to defend Damon. "It really was a good kind of sweat."

Tasha grinned, grabbing my hand. "What did he look like? Tell me now before I wrinkle from the wait."

I obeyed, more out of excitement over Damon, than a desire to comply. "He was perfect. Tall, fit, strawberry-blond hair."

She laughed, loud. "Did you really just describe a man with strawberry-blond hair? What kind of a *man* has strawberry-blond hair?" She shook her head. "You always loved the redheads."

"It wasn't red. It was dark-blond with reddish highlights."

Tasha leaned away as if I had the flu. "Great, now you've found some kind of wuss who highlights his hair."

"Natural highlights, you punk. He's leap-years from wussy." I smiled. "He said he'd call me so we could train together."

Tasha grinned. "It all makes sense now. All that crap about qualifying for Boston." She glanced around the

26

restaurant, scoping out the men seated at the table next to us. They both gaped at her blonde beautifulness. Big surprise there.

"I should've known better," Tasha said. "You're running this marathon for a man."

I tossed my head, Tasha claiming I couldn't run just made me want to prove I could. "Am not. I'm running this marathon to change my life. I've finally found my calling, my destiny." I'd lost her to her cell phone. I threw my hands in the air. "Can you at least look at me?"

My phone beeped. I glanced down and rolled my eyes. Tasha thought it was funny to annoy me by texting when we were sitting right next to each other. "Nasty men staring at you." Her head nudged toward the south.

I snuck a quick peek over my shoulder. I shouldn't have. The disgusting men looked familiar, but I couldn't quite place where I'd seen them.

I wrapped my arms around my abdomen. My fear from this morning was pushing my imagination into hyper-drive. They probably weren't even interested in me. "Gross," I whispered to Tasha. "Why do you point out men like that?"

"You always say I'm shallow and only care about looks." She dashed me a chemically-whitened grin. "I'm proving you wrong."

"You're a weirdo. What was I saying?"

Tasha opened and closed her hand several times, imitating a flapping mouth. "You've found your destiny." Her gaze strayed to the good-looking men again.

I stabbed my fork into a tomato, thrust it into my mouth, and enjoyed the zing of juices. "If you can't focus on me, at least you listen well," I muttered around my bite.

Tasha laughed and stared at me with wide, unblinking eyes. "This better?"

"Yes." I bent across the table, dousing my loose-fitting shirt with a salsa spill. "Dangit, Tash. This isn't a joke. This marathon is going to be a good thing for me. I'm finally excited to do something with my life and you laugh, degrade me, act like it's all for a man." I leaned back in my seat to sulk, grabbed my cloth napkin, and rubbed at the spot on my chest.

"Okay, you've found your destiny and it's *not* for a man." She broke a chip in half and popped it in her mouth. "Give me another good reason why you'd run a marathon?"

I pushed my salad around with my fork. "I want to do something my parents could be proud of."

"Oh." Tasha took a deep breath and fiddled with her own fork.

I shifted in the hard wooden seat and looked around for the waitress, speeding my eyes past the spot where those gross men hovered. One of the men Tasha had been ogling at the next table snagged my eye and tried to hold it. I tossed him an embarrassed smile before turning back to my friend.

"I've been working that angle for fifteen minutes," Tasha said, shifting her eyes towards the men. "You and the dark one would make a perfect couple. You know, the kind of couples who look like brother and sister. Why'd you turn away?"

My eyes flitted to the olive-skinned man. He was several notches above cute, but unlike Tasha, I didn't need to drool over every man who glanced my direction. Damon and Dr. Tattoo were enough to think about right now. "I'm not picking up a guy at Sabor."

"Why not?" She turned and gave the man and his friend each an invitation with a glance.

The waitress came with our bill, saving me from an answer. I threw some cash on the ticket and grabbed my purse.

Tasha laid a hand on my arm, restraining me. "Cassie, are you okay, you know, after . . ."

I stared at her. My rayon shirt felt like it was squeezing me. I pulled at my collar. "After what?" This morning's grisly discovery was imprinted inside my eyelids. But how did she know? How did she always know?

"Nana called me." She carefully folded her napkin. "She wanted me to make sure you were okay," She cleared her throat, still studying her napkin, "About the body."

I swallowed hard to keep my salad where it should be. Sweat rose on my back and neck. Would the image of that deformed corpse ever dim?

"You should get some counseling," Tasha said. "There's this guy I used to date who specializes in trauma. He's a fabulous psychiatrist." She grinned. "But unfortunately for him, a lousy kisser."

"If you've already tried him out, I'd better not sign up for his services," I managed to say in a semi-light tone. Clutching my purse, I stood and rushed for the door. I burst into the summer night air and ran into a solid wall of flesh.

Large hands steadied me. "You okay, young lady?"

I looked up at the Nasty Muscle Man who had been studying me at the restaurant and suddenly it clicked. He was the scary guy who I'd tripped on at the race this morning. My heart thumped faster. I jerked from his grip. "Yes, um, excuse me."

Tasha exited the restaurant, gave the hulking man an imperious glare, and grabbed my arm. "Come on, Cassie." She marched me away. "Let's get you home."

I shuddered and glanced over my shoulder. The large man hadn't moved. He stared at me. He wasn't smiling.

The Preparation

I crept down the stairs, cringing at each and every step. There was no way to avoid the groans of this old house. Hopefully I hadn't awakened Nana. She hated early mornings.

Hurrying across the chipped linoleum with running shoes in hand, I touched the back door before I smelled her. Banana bread with a heavy shot of vanilla. I wondered how many loaves Nana must've baked in her life to actually smell like banana bread. Not that I'd complain. Love banana bread. Love the smell of my Nana.

"Cassidy Christensen, what on earth are you doing sneaking out of my house at this hour of the morning?"

Can't say I love her screeching voice quite as much as her smell.

After my dad was attacked by Panetti, I hired professional cleaners to get the blood off my living room walls, sold my house, and moved in with my dad's mother until I could find a new home. Nana, my brother, and my parents were so thrilled with the arrangement I had a hard time moving out. Then my parents died and Nana was diagnosed with adult-onset diabetes. I couldn't leave her alone.

With my share of the life insurance money I could have bought us a mansion and enjoyed positive cash flow for a long, long time. I refused to touch the money created by my loss, especially when I still missed my mom and dad so much. I socked it into a safe investment fund and lived with Nana. Someday I'd find a worthwhile cause for the money, right now I was grateful I didn't have to be alone. Well, sometimes I was grateful.

Flipping on the light switch, I paused by the back door. Rain pounded outside the window, did I really want to run in that? No, but I had no choice if I wanted to prove to everyone that I could run this marathon. "What are you doing awake?"

"Answer the question."

I sighed. A fight in the pre-dawn hours with Nana was never good, but did she have to treat me like I was sixteen? "I told you, I'm starting my marathon training today." Yesterday, I'd done a little online research and printed out the most advanced training schedule *Runner's World* offered. Then I took a Valium and focused on preparing for my sixteen-week stint of glory. Glory? At least the Valium worked.

"Hardly see you as it is," she muttered, "now you're going to be gone all the time." She peered at me from one of her cushioned kitchen chairs, hovering over a cup of cocoa, as if I was going to arm-wrestle her for it.

Her dark gaze seared into me, daring me to say something about the cocoa. I should've snatched it and poured it down the sink. Being fifty pounds overweight and adoring sweets weren't a good combination for someone with diabetes and high blood pressure.

Her childlike defiance softened my frustration. I hurried around the chair to give her a peck on the cheek. Nana's skin was soft and warm beneath my lips. I savored her sweetbread scent before pulling away. "I'll be ready for breakfast a little after eight," I said.

She almost looked loving when I kissed her, but then she patted the back of her head, smooshing the dark grey fluff. "Darnit, I need to go see Maria. My hair is as flat as your chest."

I arched my eyebrows but didn't reply. She'd moved onto my chest. Maybe now was a good time to sneak out the back door. I made it one step in that direction.

Are you actually going to eat anything I cook for breakfast?"

I froze. "Um, what are you cooking?"

31

Nana straightened, puffing out her well-endowed front, a mother hen ready for a fight. "Bacon, eggs, pancakes, anything you want, girlie. *If* you'll eat it."

"Well, I'm in training, you know. I need to limit my fat intake." So should you, I thought.

"In a training bra," she grunted.

I ignored the jab. "But we can sit at the table together. I'll eat my egg whites and banana and you can eat . . . your stuff." I really needed to give her the riot act about what she ate instead of the other way around. "Doesn't that sound nice?"

"It'd be nice if I could put some real food into that body." Nana's arm darted out. She grabbed the skin on my waist and twisted. "No man wants to dance with a girl with skinny legs."

"Maybe not in your day," I muttered, bending down to slip my shoes on.

"Speak up, girlie, you talking to the floor?"

I bit my tongue one more time. Why could I mouth off to everybody but Nana? The worry of Nana having a heart attack always kept me from picking too many fights. "Gotta go, Nana. See you in a bit."

"Be careful out there, it's raining and too dark to run." Nana scowled. "Do you really think you should run alone in a town where people are savagely murdered?"

I clung to my shoelaces. Why did she have to say it like that? The murder last weekend was an isolated incident. Our town was safe. I carefully looped my laces, avoiding Nana's all-seeing glare. Just because I'd been the one to find the body didn't mean I needed to turn into a scaredy-girl who stayed in bed all day. Though bed sounded tempting, if the horrific nightmares would stop the faceless man, my parent's bodies, and Panetti all rotated through my dreams.

The phone rang. Nana flinched and grabbed the cordless. She turned from me and sheltered her mouth and the receiver with her hand. "About time you called. I hate getting up this early. Yes, Cassidy is fine." Nana rushed from the room with the cordless phone.

I couldn't hear anything else she said. It seemed she expected that call, but who would be asking about me at five-thirty in the morning? Nana's sister maybe?

The mysterious phone call gave me a chance to get out without a fight and I took it. I finished tying my laces, plunked a baseball cap over my mass of hair, and slipped out the back door.

Forcing myself past my Nissan Altima, I walked for a few minutes to warm-up before lifting my legs into a jog. It was dark, wet, and cold on the desolate street. Maybe that was why my legs didn't want to move and each step hurt worse than the last. I made it four blocks before changing my plan. I'd walk the rest of the way to the gym, lift on lower body, and get really warm. Then surely I'd be ready to run home. Maybe I'd even take the long route.

An hour later, I admitted defeat. I didn't take the long route. I half-walked, half-jogged the mile home from the gym as rain pinged against my face and my legs throbbed. *26.2 miles?* I needed another Valium.

A few blocks from home, I saw *him*. Damon. Running through the very intersection I was approaching. His long legs chewed up the distance.

He passed under the streetlight. I stopped and squinted through the moisture. It was definitely Damon. All I got was a luscious profile. It was enough. He wore a navy blue shirt and gray shorts. I could imagine how that shirt matched his eyes. I could see the sinewy muscles in his biceps as his arms pumped. Ooh, baby. I wanted to race after him and demand he call me. After all, it had been two very long days since we met.

My legs were too weary to take up pursuit. Within seconds, I could only see a shadow and then that was stolen from my sight by a two-story house. I forced my legs into motion again, dragging myself towards home.

A smaller figure raced after Damon. I squinted. The runner strode under the streetlight. It was . . . oh, no. Hot Redhead in hot pursuit. The woman who'd tried to buy my marathon entry chased the man we both salivated over. Her entire body was focused on the route Damon had taken. She wouldn't have noticed me if I was Daniel Craig. Hot Redhead disappeared from my view.

Pounding footsteps echoed from the road behind me. I jumped and swiveled to see who was coming. Maybe Damon had circled around and I would get to see him. Hidden in the darkness between street lamps, all I could tell was the figure was almost as tall as Damon but thicker. The man was catching up to me, fast.

I wished the clouds and sheet of water would part so I could feel more secure. That eerie sensation of being alone on a semi-dark street with a man pursuing didn't sit well, especially after my Saturday morning fright. My skin prickled. There was something creepy about those footsteps and that shape. I took off at a serious run. I was only a block and a half from home. Surely the man meant me no harm, but I wasn't taking any chances.

I ran the next block faster than my finishing sprint at the race last weekend. The footsteps behind me grew louder and quicker. I risked a glance. The streetlight revealed a man in a hooded sweatshirt. He looked eerily familiar. I swear his dark gaze concentrated on me. He was less than half a block behind me now. Whether he was trying to catch me to show how cool he was or whether he meant me harm, I didn't know. I didn't wait around to ask.

I inhaled sharply and flew onto the neighbor's lawn. Speeding across their grass, I convinced myself if the man got too close I could run onto the neighbor's porch and they would help me. *Ha.* They were all a-snooze in their beds.

I had to make it home. I would run in the house, barricade myself inside Nana's warm kitchen, and sic her on the man. It was harsh punishment but it would serve him right. I glanced at my pursuer. He was still on the street but dang he was fast. Within a few seconds, he could dart onto the grass and catch me.

I pumped my arms to increase leg speed. I dodged a pine tree, spitting gravel and mud into the air as I churned through our closest neighbor's driveway. Just twenty more feet and I would be safe. I didn't dare look and see where the man was, but he was closing in on me. My pounding heart verified what my ears suspected.

Bounding across the lawn, I hurled myself up the steps leading into the kitchen and swung open the screen door.

"Wait," the man yelled.

Cold sweat trickled into my sports bra. I was almost there. Please let me squeeze through that door before he—

"Cassidy," the man called.

I whirled, peering through the gloom. My stalker knew my name. I couldn't decide if I was relieved or more creeped-out. I yanked the screen door against my chest, clinging to it for supposed protection and gasping for air. "Who are you?"

He took a few more steps across the grass and pushed back the hood of his sweatshirt. The porch light illuminated his face. My heart beat quickened, but in a good way.

"Dr. Tattoo?"

His eyebrows arched. "Nice to see you again too."

I released the door handle and descended a step, obligated to gawk at him for a few more minutes. This man had rescued me on Saturday. Surely he wouldn't hurt me now. "You scared the bejeebees out of me."

"Forgive me." He bowed like I was some princess from whom he begged pardon. "You were fast. I could hardly catch my breath to yell at you."

"How'd you know my name?" I asked, the unease in my abdomen warring with my attraction to him. We hadn't done formal introductions as he doctored me at the race or afterward when he held my hand until the police separated us for questioning.

His dark eyes warmed to creamy chocolate. "I heard the announcement that you won the St. George Marathon. Congratulations."

I crept down one more stair. How much of a threat could he be with eyes that amazing? "Yeah, great prize."

He laughed. "I wouldn't have minded winning it."

"You want to train with Damon, too?"

"Damon?" He searched my eyes until I had to look away.

"Nobody." I shivered, battling between the chill of the rainwater and the heat from his gaze.

"You're cold," his voice softened to a caress. "You'd better head inside."

I wished I looked cold enough that he'd wrap me in his arms the way he did on Saturday. I shoved my hands under my armpits and instead of running away as he suggested, I flirted. "Are you still intent on never seeing me again?"

His cheek crinkled. "Now that I know where you live I'm sure I can arrange more coincidental meetings."

I shoved my fears to the back burner, where they should remain, and gave him my most brilliant smile. "Any kind of meeting sounds good to me."

He shooed me with his hands. "Go get warm."

Reluctantly, I started back up the stairs.

"Cassidy."

I spun around. Was he going to bring up the dead guy? Please don't let him ruin this. Seeing him again hadn't stirred those frightening thoughts and I didn't want it to.

"My name isn't Dr. Tattoo."

I waited, unable to hide a tremor of pleasure at the thought of hearing his name.

"It's Jesse."

Jesse. Like the Old West outlaw, Jesse James. The name fit him perfectly. I couldn't imagine Jesse James being scarier or more appealing. "It's very nice to meet you, Jesse."

Jesse inclined his head, gave me one more breathtaking smile, and turned towards the street. I flew up the stairs, banged through the back door, and raced to the window that gave me a view of the street. Huffing for oxygen, I watched my pursuer. Jesse ran past our house looking straight ahead.

What was *that*? I deflated onto a chair. "Why didn't he look back?" I muttered.

"One day of running and already you're acting like a nut job," Nana said from behind me.

Sadly, I agreed with her.

A hard rap on the door jolted me from my Clive Cussler novel. Could I never get a moment to relax? I sauntered to the front door, opening it to a pair of policemen. Their eyes scanned my living room. They hovered over me as if I was in danger.

My stomach clenched at the awful memories their familiar faces triggered but I gestured them into the living room, nodding, "Detective Shine. Detective Fine."

Detective Fine grinned. "You do know that my name is Osborne and his is Johnston."

"I've heard that before but Shine and Fine are much easier to remember." I sucked my gum into my cheek.

"Well, I think the name you've given me fits just *fine*," Detective Fine stretched out the last word, actually brushing his hand through his golden locks.

I didn't roll my eyes, though I had every right to. At least Nana wasn't here to not-so-quietly intone I should pursue Detective Fine.

"Speak for yourself," Detective Shine said, rubbing his bald pate. "Why can't I be Detective Fine?"

He really wasn't bad looking, but seriously. I pointed to his tall, blond, and perfect partner. "Do you really have to ask?"

Detective Shine shrugged in defeat. "Next time I come I'll bring somebody fat and old."

"Looking forward to that." I sat in the overstuffed chair, pointing towards the couch and really hoping there wasn't a "next time." These two seemed to think I was their responsibility since they were always there for my tragic moments. "My parents have been dead two years now. No men with knives showing up lately. Do you guys really have to keep visiting?"

Detective Fine frowned, settling into the cushions. He clung to a small notebook.

"We heard about your discovery Saturday," Detective Shine said, sitting next to his partner.

I shrank into the plush chair and rubbed at my forehead to stop the headache he'd just initiated. As if my nightmares weren't enough reminder. Last night I was chased through my slumber by the man with no face and that Panetti psycho. The only bonus was Jesse had rescued me. I forced my mind back to the present. "The police asked me questions on Saturday. Do we have to rehash this?"

Detective Fine leaned forward. "Cassidy, with all you've been through, have you ever met with a good psychiatrist?"

So they weren't here to question me about the body. They were here to "help." My fingers dug into the bridge of my nose, but didn't relieve the pressure building inside my head. "I have a friend who's setting me up with one." I realized how that sounded and reddened. "I mean, setting me up an appointment. I'll be fine." I stood. "If there isn't anything else?"

Neither of them budged. I sank back down. "Okay. What?"

"Just a few more questions about Saturday and we'll let you go."

I nodded. They had badges and guns. What choice did I have?

Shine leaned towards me. "Do you remember anything strange about Saturday morning?"

"You mean besides finding a dead body with no face?"

"And no fingers," Fine muttered.

My throat tightened. I coughed once. "Excuse me?"

"The man's fingers had been removed. Add that to no facial features, no teeth, no match of his DNA to anyone in our system, and no missing persons reported . . ." Detective Fine's voice trailed off as he was rewarded with a glare from his partner that would've frozen a barbecue grill.

The room turned so cold I had to pull one of Nana's afghans from the rack near her chair. Wrapping my legs underneath my body, I piled the afghan over me. It didn't help much. "Why would somebody do such a thing?" I asked.

The detectives exchanged a look. Detective Shine shrugged. "Who knows? Cassidy, did you notice anyone strange at the race?"

"You think one of the runners killed him?"

"Maybe. Approximate time of death was only an hour before the race started."

I shuddered from my grown-out roots to my chipped toenails. Neither of the detectives said anymore. I sat there and thought about the race. Anything unusual? Jesse and Damon both sought me out. That was unusual. But my police protectors wouldn't be interested in either of them like I was. Then I remembered two other men.

"There were two Nasties," I murmured.

Fine and Shine exchanged a look.

I elaborated without their prompting. "You know ugly dudes who stare. The big one got too close and tripped me." I burrowed deeper into the afghan. "I saw them at Café Sabor later that night. Just the way they looked at me." I shivered again.

Shine made some notes then focused on me. With much detail, I started describing Nasty Muscle Man. Near the end of my monologue, the back door popped open.

"Hello," Nana called out. "Are those good-looking detectives here to see us again?"

"I'll text you the rest," I muttered, Nana did not need additional stress.

Detective Shine handed me a business card. "I understand."

Relief washed over me. Maybe I should rename him or maybe I could explain to him that Shine was for Knight in Shining Armor, not his shiny head.

Nana floated into the room. "To what do we owe this pleasure?"

Detective Fine stood and received the standard hug. "Just coming by to check on our favorite girls."

I marveled at their understanding of my need to protect Nana. Even though I dreaded seeing this pair of detectives, they really were wonderful men.

Nana blushed. "Well, you must be hungry. Cassidy, why didn't you feed the detectives?"

"Waiting for you to come be the Happy Hostess," I muttered.

She frowned at me but lost her glower when she refocused on the detectives. "Well, you'd better come in this kitchen and let me take care of you."

Shine and Fine dutifully followed. I stayed behind to catch my breath. No face, no fingers, and no missing body reported. Had the Nasties killed that man? I prayed it was just coincidence that I'd run into those two twice, but feared I hadn't seen the last of them.

Searching for Support

Raquel studied my training schedule with a wrinkled brow. "You have to start this *when?*"

I paced the length of her living room, needing my sister-in-law's support, but somewhat prepared for her to second Nana's opinion—I was a nut job. I gnawed at a hangnail. Raquel usually believed in me, but this marathon idea was insane. At least that's what everyone kept telling me. I squared my shoulders and pried my finger from my mouth. Nana and Tasha not supporting me just gave me more incentive to succeed. Impressing Raquel, and even though I didn't want to admit it, my dead parents had been the initial motivation, but now I was determined to prove to everyone I wouldn't quit.

"The race is on October 4th," I said, "so I'll have to start the first of June."

Her head jerked up. "The marathon is on October 4th?"

"Uh-huh."

"I'm due the 15th." Raquel gripped the sides of her chair. "What if I come early again? You were the only reason I got through Tate's delivery. You promised me you'd be there." Her words per minute revved. "You know Jared passes out at the sight of blood. My mom lives too far away. You can't miss the hospital. You can't." She was getting hysterical. Pregnancy hormones.

"No way will I miss it." I swallowed. "I'm not going to miss the delivery of the second little person who's going to love me more than anybody else in the world."

Raquel chuckled. Her pinched face relaxed. "You think Tate loves you best?"

"Of course. I'm the coolest aunt ever."

Tate bounded into the room. "Auntie." The four-year old launched himself at me. "What treats did you bring me?"

"To prove my point." I twirled my nephew until he was dizzy. "Nothing too great, buddy." I set him on the carpet and fished a Blow Pop out of my purse.

His face brightened. "A sucker!" He ripped the candy from my hand, planted a kiss on my leg, and tore off for his room again.

Raquel glared. "You need to stop giving him treats."

"But that's why I'm the favorite. The next little guy will love me almost as much as Tater does."

"If you spoil him as much." She refocused on the training schedule. After several long minutes she set the papers on the coffee table, leaned back against the cushions, and rested her hands on the slight bulge of her abdomen. "Um, Cassie, I think this schedule is too intense."

"What do you mean?" I plopped onto the thick beige carpet in her living room and folded my legs around each other.

"This schedule will probably kill you," she clarified. "If you survive, I can't imagine the injuries you'll suffer."

"I don't care." I grabbed onto my ankles and rocked slowly back and forth. I've dealt with pain before. "I researched training schedules online. This one had great testimonials. It's supposed to be *the* training schedule to qualify for Boston."

"I'm sure whoever claims that is right. If you don't injure something and put yourself out of the race." She whistled. "This schedule has you running five to six days a week. Repeats, tempo runs, insane long runs." Her eyebrows arched. "You have three long runs that are twenty miles or higher."

I gulped and squeaked out, "Twenty?" I wanted to prove I wouldn't quit, but did I want to prove it that bad?

Raquel looked down at me, her brown sugar eyes brimming with sympathy.

I cleared my throat. "Twenty milers will be fun." I bounced enthusiastically like a child waiting for a trip to the park. What I had gotten myself into? "I'll have lots of time to . . . think through stuff."

"Uh-huh. You can solve the world's problems." Raquel's lips compressed. "Speaking of problems, I heard your detectives showed up again. Was it about the body?"

I nodded tightly. "Thanks for bringing it up. I almost went half an hour without that horrifying image in my head."

Raquel's gaze softened, but she didn't back down. "Who do they think killed him?"

I shrugged and studied the granite fireplace. "They don't even know who *he* is."

Raquel was quiet long enough, I was forced to look and see what delayed her response. Finally, she clasped her hands together and muttered, "I wonder if it's an identity crime."

I swayed back and forth, trying to assuage my fears like a mother would do for a child. Sadly, I had no mother and Raquel was not helping like she usually did. "Identity crime?"

"Yeah." She rubbed her hands together, looking almost excited. Out of character for her usual sweetheart mode. "I saw it on CSI. This guy killed another guy and hid his identity so he could steal the dude's life. It was psychotic."

I bobbed my head along with my body's rotations. "Sounds psychotic. So, I had a good run this morning."

Raquel arched a brow. "How did your pace this morning compare to Saturday's race?"

"Actual running pace is a bit fuzzy, but I did cross the distance from home to the gym and back and I really sprinted the last block." I smiled, remembering my conversation with Jesse this morning.

"A mile each way?" She leaned into the plush cushions. "Don't let your memories of high school running mess you up. You're going to enjoy running once you wrap your mind around it. It's just a mental block, you know?"

I did know, but I didn't need another reminder of my high school humiliation. At my debut track meet I spewed on the shoes of the boy who our yearbook featured as best athlete, best body, and best face. Why couldn't anyone forget? "Hey, I started at zero. This is progress."

Raquel nodded, elevating her eyebrows. "Outstanding progress."

"Those first two miles are the hardest. They're like a warm-up, right?"

Raquel twisted her face down and to the side. "Um, sure."

"So, that's the mistake I made. I just need to push out more miles. Running to and from the gym is stupid. I never really get warm because I stop and start. Tomorrow I'm starting my real training program. I'm going to do six miles, six days a week." I gave her a significant look, trying to convince both of us that I could really run six miles. "If I do that for four weeks, I should be more than ready to start *this*." I poked at the paper in her hands.

Raquel stared. After several moments of dumbfounded silence, she rose from her chair, walked to her bookshelf, and retrieved three books on running and a stack of *Runner's World* magazines. She crossed the distance between us and dumped the pile in my arms. "Here. You're going to need these."

I didn't remind her I'd learned most of this in college; guess I was due for a refresher course. "Thanks." I turned to leave. My brother would be home from work soon and I didn't need the grief he would give me about my latest passion, my choice of men, or the fact that everyone knew Detective Fine and Shine were coming around again. *Thank you, Nana.* "Tater, come give your auntie a hug goodbye."

Tate raced from his room, threw his arms around me, and knocked several magazines from my hands. "Do you have to leave?"

"Yeah. Your dad will be home soon and *they'll* want family time." I nodded towards Raquel.

"Family time?" Tate giggled. "Nuh-uh. You're scared of my daddy."

I spit out a huffy breath. "Excuse me?"

"When Daddy says your boyfriends are losers, your face gets all red." He patted my arm. "I think you're the prettiest girl ever, Auntie. Why do you like losers?"

I ruffled his hair, enduring Raquel's laughter. "Thank you. I get made fun of without Jared actually being in the house. Walk me to the front door," I commanded.

Tate gave his mom a thumbs-up, picked up my fallen magazines, and followed me. "Will you bring me more treats next time?" he asked.

"Sure thing. What happened to your sucker?"

"I hid it under my bed. I have to lick it slow 'cause Momma won't buy me treats."

I gasped. "No treats?"

He sighed, brown eyes filled with anguish. "I know. If my momma didn't take me to the park and stuff, I'd move to Nana's with you. Nana's always got candy."

I chuckled. "Your mom's a lot nicer than Nana."

I swung the front door open and leaped into the air. "Pelican poop," I yelled, spilling several magazines onto the floor.

A brawny man whose shoulders connected directly to his head stood on the threshold, hand poised to knock. His bushy eyebrows rose.

I placed a hand over my heart. "You scared me." *Muscle Man.* The creep from the race. He more than scared me. Why was he at Raquel's house? I shuddered and pushed Tate behind me, setting my books on the entryway table so my hands would be free.

"Excuse me, ma'am," he said. "I didn't mean to startle you." The look in his pale blue eyes said he couldn't have cared less if I was terrified. "I'm the new Schwann's man. Wanted to introduce myself and give you some samples of our frozen food."

His story wasn't any more sincere than his apology. A twelve-passenger maroon van with darkened windows sat at the curb. "The Schwann man has a yellow refrigerator kind of

45

truck." I patted my nephew on the shoulder with a trembling palm. "Tater, go get your mom." I wanted him away from this man.

"What's going on?" Raquel appeared in the foyer. She picked Tate up. He cuddled into her shoulder. Could he sense I was uncomfortable or was he getting his own bad vibes from the Nasty Muscle Man on our doorstep?

I heard a soft click. My eyes flipped to the van. Muscle Man's thin partner was snapping pictures of us from the rear fender.

My gaze spun back to the man towering a few feet from my nephew and sister-in-law. He plastered on a smile, but it was only lip-deep. What were these two up to? Trying to take secretive pictures of us, of Tate. My stomach dive-bombed.

I put myself between Muscle Man and my family. "We wouldn't care for any samples today."

His fake smile flushed away. Flexing polish sausage fingers, he took a half-step towards me.

I shrunk back, holding my arms out to shield Raquel and Tate. "Don't you take one more step," I commanded, fear giving each word its own octave.

The idiot moved. I slammed the door. The handle turned against my fingers. I pushed against the door with all my weight. Raquel joined me. After several attempts, I jammed the deadbolt into place. My heart thundered in my eardrums.

"Should I call the police?" Raquel asked.

I stared through the peephole at the body-builder gone wrong. Muscle Man glowered at the door as if he could zap me with his bulging eyeballs. I clung to the deadbolt, certain that lowlifes like him had ways to open locks. The door handle rattled again.

"Yes, call the police," I yelled loud enough that Muscle Man could hear through the door.

Raquel scurried away with Tate clinging to her.

The guy lingered for a moment, then gestured to his friend and descended the steps.

"Yes, two men," Raquel said in a rush of breath, returning to the foyer. "Are they still out there?"

"No, they're leaving."

"Can you see the license plate?"

I squinted through the peephole and definitely could not read the license plate. The van pulled away. I should run out there and get that plate number. I froze, clinging to the door, too terrified to expose myself to Muscle Man again.

"No," I squeaked.

"They left," Raquel said. "Maroon van." She kept talking. I didn't move. Finally Raquel said goodbye.

"Detective Shine and Fine on their way to save us again?" I asked.

"Probably," she said. "Who was that guy?"

I kept staring out the peephole, reassuring myself they were gone. "Nasty Muscle Man."

"From the race? What did he want?"

I swallowed, thinking of our last encounter at Café Sabor. What *did* Muscle Man want? "Me."

Al slammed the passenger side door of the van, staring gloomily at the sprawling rock and stucco home. Nathan's daughter rubbed him the wrong way. She looked just like her mother, long legs, dark hair, and those pouty lips, but was feistier than her father. Al could still picture both her parents with infrared dots on their chests. When would the call come to terminate the daughter? Maybe he could just throw her into this job as a freebie, after he got what he needed from her. The thought made him smile.

Al shook his head. Cassidy Christensen. Acting like she could protect her nephew and sister-in-law from him. Just like her dad trying to protect all those slaves.

47

Terry started the van, gunning out of the subdivision. "You think they really called the cops?"

"Let's not wait around to find out," Al snarled. "Did you get some good ones? Me in them? Something that will show him we mean business?"

"Perfect." Terry's head bobbed twice. "Even got the kid in some. If these don't scare Doc Christensen out of hiding I don't know what will."

Al nodded, shaking off the odd mixture of desire and anger Cassidy Christensen produced in him. He needed to concentrate on their objective—one dead body shipped to the finish line first. He couldn't believe Ramirez was baiting them against other operatives. When they'd gotten the tip about Cassidy being at that race he'd thought it was an exclusive. But now there was someone new in the game, a young guy Ramirez thought was the greatest thing since the AK-47. The only good news was the kid had another assignment. They had some time, but Al couldn't afford the distraction of a beautiful woman. He thought of Cassidy's firm body. With or without a financial incentive, he'd be coming back for her.

He looked at Terry. "Let's go earn our money."

"Ramirez won't be the only one paying up," Terry said. "I heard Panetti will throw in something extra when Doc's finally dead. He really hates him."

Al shrugged. "Doc reminds Panetti of what he used to be before he sold out."

Terry arched an eyebrow. "Have we sold out?"

"Nah. You have to care about something to sell out and you only care about the money."

Terry grinned. "Two million dollars is a lot to care about."

"Just keep running, just keep running, run, run, run, run, run." The words bounced around in my brain, over and over again as I trudged mile after mile or maybe foot after foot was more appropriate. It was the fourth day of my six-mile-a-day plan and I'd yet to make it six miles running. My legs had never hurt like this. Weighted squats? Walking lunges? Box jumps? Child's play. This running stuff made my leg workouts look like a stroll through the shopping mall.

I heard steady breathing coming from the rear. My heart thumped a bit faster. I did not like being out alone on these dark streets. The police had found no trace of Muscle Man or his partner, but what if they were watching me? What if whoever murdered my faceless nightmare was out there somewhere? I tried to increase my pace, but I had nothing. My poor legs had been pushed to their limit and no amount of adrenaline was going to quicken my stride.

"Would you rather have me raped and left for dead on the side of the road?" I muttered to my feeble muscles.

I straightened my shoulders and slowed my breathing. The runner was going to catch me any minute, I might as well look confident. "I'm tough. No dude is messing with me." I wrapped my hand around a small bottle of pepper spray I'd hidden in my key pocket.

The footfalls grew louder and louder. I tried for positive thoughts. Maybe it was Damon or Jesse. My heart thumped even more erratically at that possibility. I'd be thrilled to see either one of them. I glanced out of the corner of my eye as the runner pulled level with me. Way too short and definitely female. I released my pepper spray in relief. The woman looked over and smiled.

Oh, no. Hot Redhead. I think I would've preferred my concocted rapist.

"Hey." Her face lit up like I was a free download for her iPod. She pulled her left earbud out. "You're the girl who won the marathon."

"Yep."

49

"Oh, I'm so jealous," she gushed. Hot Redhead slowed her pace to match mine. "I entered the lottery for St. George and didn't get in."

I arched an eyebrow. She must've forgotten that I was already privy to her desperation to run with Damon.

She sighed. "I'm going to have to figure out some other way to enter. I wish they would've let us transfer the entry at The Health Days Race."

How did Hot Redhead chat like this while she ran? I gasped for more oxygen and pushed out the word, "Yep."

"Would you like me to train with you?" she asked.

No, I'd like you to run along, pretty girl, and let me die here by myself. Of course I didn't have the oxygen to vocalize that. "Nope."

Her eyes narrowed. "You're planning training runs with Damon, aren't you?"

"Yep." It was only a partial lie, he *had* promised to call.

Hot Redhead's face balled up. She was going to cry. "You aren't running with him yet," she said.

I stared at her. How did she know that? I shrugged my shoulders. "Soon."

"Well." She flipped her long ponytail over her shoulder. "Good luck with your *training*."

She jogged off and I felt a spasm of conscience. I'd lied to her. I hated liars. And then the poor girl had gotten all upset. She must really want that Damon guy. Not that I blamed her. I watched her backside recede into the coming dawn. I should catch up to her and say she could train with me. I tried to run faster. Nope. That wasn't happening. Maybe I could call out to her. I opened my mouth and creaked out, "Hey, girl." It was a pathetic wheeze. I sucked in all my air and yelled, "Hot Redhead."

She whirled around. Even in the pre-dawn light I could see flashes shooting from her eyes. Hot Redhead flew back towards me. "What did you call me?"

I stopped running. "Um, well, it's just a silly name I made up. You should take it as a compliment, really. Because you are . . ."

She came within inches of my face. I walked backwards, hit a pothole, and stuttered to remain upright. "What did you call me?"

I gulped, I'd pushed the wrong button. "H-hot Redhead."

Tossing her ponytail over her shoulder, she covered the distance I'd made between us. "*Hot* Redhead?"

I nodded, wondering why I was intimidated by a woman half my size. "You should like it."

Her eyes narrowed. "We'll see. But," she poked me in the chest, "if I decide I don't like it, you'd better watch your back when you're out running in the dark."

Hot Redhead whirled and sped off into the morning.

"See if I give you a compliment again," I yelled, after she was too far away to hear me.

Week One

It turned out the whole preparation idea was over-rated. After a few days of agonizing pain combined with fear of Muscle Man, Hot Redhead, or a psycho murderer confronting me on the pre-dawn lit road, I realized I didn't need that stress until the actual start of marathon training. I also admitted to myself, after three weeks of carrying my cell phone into the bathroom and to bed with me at night, that Damon wasn't going to call. I hadn't heard or seen from Jesse in almost as long. I could wait and humiliate myself in June.

Unfortunately, June came and I had to commit. I wanted to believe my parents and Raquel were proud of me and prove to Nana, Tasha, and Jared that I wasn't a quitter, besides I'd told too many people about the marathon to back out gracefully now. I laced up my running shoes, for serious this time, left Nana shaking her head and baking banana bread in our cozy kitchen, and headed to the gym with Tasha for some interval training.

"Can you explain to me why I am here at five-thirty in the morning?" Tasha asked, punching buttons on the treadmill. "Instead of spooning with my body pillow?"

"It's not that early." My treadmill slung into action, I speed-walked to keep up. "And you're going to get the 'best friend of the year' award."

"More like, 'most glutton for punishment,'" Tasha grunted as her treadmill belt started rotating. "Tell me what the 'best friend of the year' is supposed to be doing in this stuffy cardio room."

"I just need you to keep track of how many times I sprint and call me names if I don't push myself hard enough. You know, your normal bosom buddy obligations." I jogged to get warm. I'd allow myself five minutes to warm up then the pace was going to 11.0, 5:27 minutes per mile, the fastest I'd ever run.

Tasha broke into a jog, upping the pace to 6.0. I looked at my 6.6 pace and smiled. I loved beating Tasha.

"So I get to call you slow-poke and lazy when?"

"When you're actually running faster than me."

Tasha scowled, checked her pace and my treadmill display, then sped up to 6.8. "Turtle."

I rolled my eyes, but hit the speed button until it was at 7.0.

Tasha chuckled and increased her pace to 7.2. "Snail."

"Stop it, you idiot. I'm not warm yet." My knees groaned in protest as I jumped to 7.4. I wanted to slow down, not speed up.

Tasha laughed harder. "I thought I was the one who got to call names. Come on, loser, if we're going to sprint, let's sprint." She jammed her finger on the up button, her speed indicator climbed to 12.0.

I pointed. "You're going to kill yourself."

She was still able to keep up, but it takes a treadmill a second or two to respond to changes in speed. The belt would increase its rotations soon and I didn't think Tasha could keep up to . . .

Tasha flew off the back of the treadmill, hit the brick wall, and slammed to her knees.

"Tasha!" I flipped sideways, my left foot caught between the belt and the edge of the treadmill. I went down. The belt ripped at my exposed skin, then slingshot me on top of my downed friend.

"Cassie," she yelled, pushing herself out from under me.

We sat there stunned for half a second. My leg burned. "Thanks for breaking my fall," I said.

"Thanks for coming after me," she muttered. Tasha tossed her head and lifted her shirt, revealing a massive red spot on her back. "Guess twelve is too high for intervals?"

"Guess so." I pressed my fingers softly against her contusion, feeling the sting of my own cuts. "How bad is it?"

Tasha pointed at the crowd staring at us like we were insane. "Not near as bad as our audience." She stuck out her tongue at the cardio room occupants. "We are *fine*, thank you, people."

I laughed, but then my eyes connected with the intense, blue gaze of one of our gawkers. "Damon?" I whispered.

"Who?" Tasha followed my stare. "Wow," she said.

Struggling to my feet, I helped Tasha up. "Let's run outside today." I hoped I could run at all with this treadmill-rash on my leg.

We brushed by the crowd. I studied the industrial flooring, but couldn't help myself. Glancing up, I caught Damon's eye before quickly looking away. His gaze was full of concern, making my humiliation complete.

"Are we stopping to talk to Mr. Strawberry-Blond?" Tasha asked from between her teeth. Damon took a few steps our direction.

"No." I tilted my head proudly and limped toward the door.

Tasha clung to my arm. "Your loss," she muttered.

We left with Damon watching us and two empty treadmill belts continuing their rotation.

Terry studied the pretty brunette and blonde through the scope of his camera. "The pictures weren't enough for the doc?"

Al exhaled slowly, focusing his binoculars. Neither of them appreciated returning to northern Utah, especially with the threats that someone else was going to reach the payday before them. "From what I hear, Doc Christensen made a few phone calls, but he didn't fly off to rescue the girl. The good news is . . . " Al stared at his partner. "I know where he went to get service for his cell phone."

Terry's eyes widened. "So if we can get him to that same spot again?"

"Exactly." Al watched the Doc's young daughter pump her legs and arms in an all-out sprint. After a minute she slowed to a walk. Her friend caught up with her and they both appeared to be laughing.

Several times they'd watched Cassidy Christensen run, but she wasn't very good at it. Al smiled to himself. She'd be easy to catch when they were ready. "We have to up the stakes a bit. I'm thinking if she goes on early morning runs every day of the week—"

Terry picked up the thread, "We can borrow her for a minute, scare her enough to get some good video and voice coverage—"

"And make sure Daddy understands what we're willing to do to her." Al pulled a long blade from his pocket and lovingly stroked it. "I hope he doesn't make us pay up on any threats."

Terry set the camera on the middle console and pressed his long fingers together. "Why you gotta do that?" He gestured towards Cassidy and her friend. "She's beautiful. Don't ruin her face. Cut her somewhere else."

Al rolled his thick neck then massaged his forehead for a few minutes before he managed to say, "I don't care where we cut her, just so long as it scares Nathan Christensen out of the rat hole he's hiding in and into our trap. I'm not losing two million dollars to that punk Ramirez has let loose."

"Agreed." Terry turned and watched the women who were running at full speed again. A smile curled his thin lips. "There are other things we can threaten."

Al grunted, focusing on Cassidy's long, brown hair bouncing off her back. He wasn't sure he wanted to share her with Terry. "We'll do what we have to."

Week Two

Headlights approached me from behind. Squeaky brakes announced the vehicle was slowing. I glanced over my shoulder, still not entirely comfortable on the road by myself, especially in the dark. It would be so nice if I could find a more committed training partner than Tasha, who only showed up half the time and complained until I wished she hadn't come at all. I fingered the pepper spray in my shorts pocket. Just another mile and I'd be safe at home.

The van crept next to me. I increased my pace, searching for a nearby house with lights on. If whoever was in that van tried to bug me, I needed an escape route.

My stomach clenched. Sweat I didn't earn appeared on my forehead. Every house I passed was still in slumber.

The brakes yelped, splintering the pre-dawn stillness. The rear door flung open. I leapt into the air before forcing my feet to go the right direction, away from that van. A burly man bounded from the passenger side. I screamed when I recognized the Nasty Muscle Man from Health Days, Café Sabor, and Raquel's front porch. Forcing my legs into action I flew into an all-out sprint. I hadn't crossed five feet before a strong arm wrapped around my waist.

"Help!"

Muscle Man's other hand clamped over my mouth. His hand stunk like pencil lead. He swung me off my feet, pinning me against his barrel chest. I squirmed and flailed, acid eating at my insides, heels pummeling Muscle Man's shins. I yanked my pepper spray out and pointed it towards his face. He knocked it from my hand. I watched in despair as it disappeared into the weeds. Now how was I going to protect myself?

"Relax, Cassidy," he hissed into my ear.

I didn't know it was possible to feel any more fear, but his casual use of my name made it a possibility. Who was this guy? How did he know my name? And the most important question: What was he planning to do to me?

Hauling me back to the van, he threw me inside the rear door. I bounced off a small table jammed against the far wall of the hollowed-out van's interior.

"Hey, watch the cameras," Greasy Beanpole said from the front seat.

My back and arm stung. Tears swam in my eyes. I leapt back to my feet, ready to fight my way free.

Muscle Man clambered in after me, slamming the van door shut. I punched and kicked at him, some of my jabs actually causing him to grunt. He raised his hand to smack me. I ducked. Muscle Man pulled me upright and slammed his fist into my stomach.

I gasped, trying to catch a full breath. Muscle Man grabbed and spun me, his sweaty chest pressing against my back. Pinning my arms, he said into my ear, "Wouldn't want to leave a mark where someone could see it."

Stomach throbbing, I thrashed against him. The man's arms were as thick as his brain. I'd never escape him. My heart slammed against my chest at regular intervals. At least there was no doubt it was still beating.

"Relax!" He held me tighter, his breath searing my neck. "We're going to drive out west of town where no one can hear you screaming."

I snapped my head back, trying to slam it into him while icy sweat coursed down my back. Muscle Man dodged the blow and tightened his grip until my arms throbbed.

"Calm down so I don't have to hurt you," he said.

My abdomen still ached from his first punch. I couldn't draw a full breath. I looked to the driver's seat, praying my other captor would be sympathetic. Greasy Beanpole slicked back his hair and winked at me. I shivered. This was not how I wanted to lose my virginity. These men were going to beat and rape me. Would they kill me after? My body trembled under the man's arms. Inches away from hysterical, I couldn't organize my frenzied thoughts. What could I do to protect myself?

"Just like you didn't have to hurt that man I found in the canyon," I said, fighting for a bravado I didn't possess.

Muscle Man flipped me to face him. "What man?" he demanded.

"The murdered man." I strained against his iron clasp. "The man with no face or fingers."

His head slowly rotated to Greasy Beanpole.

Greasy Beanpole's shoulders lifted and lowered. "Wasn't me." He turned around and shifted the van into gear.

Muscle Man sighed, relaxing his grip a bit but not enough for me to make any progress towards freedom. "We haven't killed anyone locally," he told me, as if it would make me feel better.

I took a few deep breaths. This guy sucked at reassurance. But if they hadn't killed that man, who had? "What do you want from me?" I squeaked out. "How do you know my name?"

The van slowly rolled down the road, Muscle Man held me steady. "We just need a bit of help," he said, ignoring my second question.

Bile rose in my throat. I'd never heard sex crimes described as helping someone. "What if I'm not willing to *help* you?" I asked.

"We're going to turn on that video camera." Muscle Man flung me around so I faced the rear of the van. A camera and a chair were set up for filming.

I forced a laugh that sounded more like a stifled cry. "I don't do footage for porn videos, but thanks for the compliment." I was shaking so violently at this point, Muscle Man was holding me up for support as much as restraint.

Why was this happening? I couldn't die. I'd accomplished nothing. I suddenly felt a rush of empathy mixed with the sorrow I always carried for my parents. Had they been scared to die? At least they'd died for a worthwhile cause. I was going to die because I'd run outside and pepper spray was no protection.

"Cassidy. Calm down and listen to me. All I need you to do is tell your father that we have kidnapped you and that we're going to hurt you if he doesn't follow our instructions."

"My *father?*" My body slackened in disbelief. An incredulous laugh rolled from my chest. "Hate to break it to you Muscle Man, but I don't have a father." My voice flattened. "Scum like you killed him two years ago."

"I *did* kill him two years ago," he growled.

"You!" I elbowed him in the gut. It didn't faze the monster. "You killed my parents!"

Muscle Man fought to restrain me. "One of my more lucrative jobs."

Anger boiled out of me. I kicked and thrashed. "How *could* you?"

"It was an easy job, believe me." He wrapped his huge arms around my upper body. I bit his arm. He backhanded me and kept talking like we were chatting in the park, "But somehow they resurrected him. He's making a mess for us in Mexico, freeing slaves and killing our men."

Resurrected him? I stopped fighting and spat out the disgusting taste of Muscle Man's skin and my own blood. My cheek ached and I couldn't catch a full breath. Was this guy for real? My brain wheezed, unable to keep up with the lies he was spouting. Even if my father were alive he'd be helping children with his medical expertise. He'd never kill anyone. "My father is . . . alive?"

Muscle Man flipped me to face him. "We know you haven't had contact with your father. That's why we're going to let you go. As long as you promise to be a good girl and not say anything to your police buddies or your grandmother, I promise to not

keep you hostage. Even though you'd be fun to have around."
He grinned, deepening the ridges in his face. "Hostages are such
a pain in the butt."

I shook my head, but it didn't clear the gray matter. My
poor heart wouldn't slow down no matter what they promised,
but at the moment I was almost as mad as I was scared. "Let me
get this straight. All I have to do is read some script for your
home video, claim I have a father, act like a scared little wussy,"
which was no act, "and you'll let me go?"

He nodded. "That's it."

My hands quivered, I had to clench them to pretend I was
in control. "I'm not an idiot, Muscle Man. If you let me go,"
my voice trembled at the possibility, "you've lost your leverage."

His loud chuckle rumbled through the van, bouncing off
the walls and ricocheting back at me. He took his time looking
up and down my frame, his thick tongue bounced over
chapped lips. He rubbed scarred fingers over my cheek. "Don't
talk me into keeping you."

"I-I'm not." I truly was an idiot. My head swam and the
nausea was getting harder and harder to swallow down. The
only thing I wanted was to be miles away from this man who
claimed to have killed my parents.

"Unfortunately, my boss doesn't want me to keep you
long term." His smile stretched from his capped teeth to his
shiny baldhead. "All I need to do is get the Doc out of hiding.
The second he calls your grandma to check on you." He
snapped his fingers. "I've got him."

Calls your grandma to check on you? The early-morning
phone call a few weeks ago. Could it possibly have been my
father? The thought was insane, but I still couldn't dismiss it.

The van stopped. My heart clanked against my rib cage.
What were they going to do to me now? Greasy Beanpole
climbed over the console and started working the camera.

Muscle Man escorted me to the seat, his fingers lingering
on my lower back. I arched away from his touch. "I'm going to
put a blindfold on you and hold a gun to your head, but I
promise I won't hurt you."

60

My digestive system dropped to my running shoes. "That sounds so encouraging."

Muscle Man pressed me into the seat and started wrapping rope around my midsection. I knew there was no hope of escape. Still I struggled.

"Good," he whispered into my ear. "Fight me. We're videoing this. It looks perfect."

After I was securely tied, he covered my eyes with a filthy rag. I tried to fight him, spitting and thrashing. Ineffective, but all I had at the moment.

"Okay," he was at my ear again, his un-brushed breath scratching my skin. "Just respond to all my questions like you're terrified."

"You're nuts," I yelled, centuries past terrified. The cold steel of a gun jammed into my temple. I stopped resisting. I stopped screaming. I stopped breathing. Tears leaked out, sticking the disgusting blindfold to my cheeks. Any fleeting thoughts of resistance disappeared as the pressure from the gun increased.

"Haven't we been good to you, Cassidy?" The man dragged the gun down my cheek and along my jaw line. I flinched away from the steel pressure. I was going to puke. I think I would've rather passed out though.

I gulped and managed to spit out, "Too good."

Muscle Man chuckled. "She's a beauty, Doc. Looks like your wife. Acts like you. Now, if you want this little princess to live a long, happy life I suggest you take a flight to Mexico City. We have a lot to discuss. You don't come, Cassidy joins Mom, after I have some fun with her that is. Say bye to Daddy, Cassidy."

"Bye," I muttered. My entire body shook. I tried to control it with sarcasm, "Thanks for placing me in such a pleasant situation, Dad."

Muscle Man laughed harder. The pistol left my cheek. I took long breaths in and out so I didn't hyperventilate. The blindfold was ripped off me. The ropes untied. Muscle Man wrapped an arm around my waist and escorted me out of the vehicle. Greasy Beanpole watched me with a leering grin.

They both followed me onto the dark road. Fields of hay and corn stretched east and west. I wiped at my eyes, trying to hide the proof of how scared I was.

"You did great, Cassidy," Muscle Man said. "Hope your father is half as cooperative as you. But then if he's not . . ." His eyes roved my frame. "I'll get to fulfill some fun threats."

My stomach rolled.

Muscle Man and Greasy Beanpole headed for the van. Greasy Beanpole jogged around to the driver's seat. Muscle Man climbed into the passenger seat. He left the door open and stared down at me. I knew I should run. I couldn't take a step.

"Why?" I whispered up at him.

"Why what?"

"Why are you doing this? My mom and dad died two years ago."

Muscle Man grinned. "Keep believing that, Cassidy." He tilted his bald mug to the side. "Also believe," he lifted the dull black pistol and stroked its shaft, "that I'll be back," he winked, "if you talk to the police, the FBI, your grandmother, or anyone else. Are we understood?"

"Y-yes," I managed to sputter.

"Perfect." Muscle Man saluted me and slammed his door.

The van spun away, leaving me with more questions than I ever wanted to deal with. I'd seen the pictures of my mom and dad's bodies. Even though I still believed Panetti had ordered their executions, Muscle Man had just claimed that he was the one who killed them. Being face to face with their murderer ripped off the thin scab that had begun to cover the gaping wound my parents had left. A lone tear escaped. I missed them.

Shaking off the sadness and anger, I tried to figure out what had just happened. Muscle Man and Greasy Beanpole were obviously confused, maybe it wasn't even my parents they claimed to have killed. But why didn't they kidnap or rape me?

Why did they video me and try to make me believe my dad was alive? Something was seriously messed up here.

I watched the taillights disappear and still couldn't react. Finally, I forced myself to do the only thing I could. I swallowed my insides back into place and started jogging east.

When I saw another runner coming my direction I didn't know if I should hide behind the towering cornfield to the south or run into his arms. He got closer and I opted for the latter.

"Jesse!"

He glanced my way and crossed the distance between us with a smile on his face. "Cassidy. I was hoping I'd run into you out on the road again." Stopping in front of me, he gestured to the surrounding fields. "You're far from home."

"Not by choice," I muttered.

Jesse cocked his head to the side, studying my disheveled face and hair. "Are you all right?"

I shivered, wrapping my arms around my stomach. The pain from that punch wasn't going away anytime soon. "Some men scared me."

His olive skin darkened. His eyes darted down the road and into the cornstalks as if my attackers were hiding in there. "Where are they?"

I shook my head. "They left."

Jesse took a step closer. His arms opened. I didn't know if it was an invitation. I made it one. Falling against his hard chest, I resisted the urge to bawl.

"They hurt you," he said, his voice tight with anger.

"No, I'm okay," I lied.

"Do you want to tell me about it?" he whispered against my hair.

"No," I moaned. How could I explain that I'd put us both at risk? As tough as Jesse seemed, he couldn't protect me from Muscle Man.

Jesse stroked my hair. Covered with his warm body and arms, I almost forgot my fears. After several wonderful moments, he pulled away and directed me toward the rising sun. "Let's get you home."

I sighed and started jogging again.

"We need to call the police," he said.

"No!" My answer was too forceful, Jesse's brows rose in question. "No," I repeated more softly. "They didn't do anything to me so there's nothing to report." Jesse looked ready to argue. "You just caught me at a bad moment. I've been a mess since finding the body." I couldn't hide the tremor zipping through me. I upped my pace to give vent to the nervous energy.

Jesse nodded, his eyes filled with compassion. "Anyone would be." He paused then said, "I don't like to think about any guy but me bothering you while you're out running." He gave me a smile that made me forget everything but his face.

I concentrated on placing one foot in front of the other so I didn't fling myself into his arms again. "They won't be back," I said, trying to convince myself more than Jesse.

"They better not," he muttered.

We ran in silence for a few minutes. Jesse kept looking at me, as if to check how I was doing.

"Why are blonde jokes so short?" he asked.

What? I stared at him for several seconds before giving in, "I don't know, why?"

"So brunettes can remember them."

I laughed. It was nice. Jesse kept telling me silly jokes the entire distance to my house. It was my second rescue by the tattooed doctor. I hoped if I needed more rescuing, Jesse would be there.

I didn't have an appetite or any desire to run the next day as I stewed about what to do. Should I call the police? They couldn't even find the Health Days murderer, how would they find some guy in Mexico who looked like my dad? Should I tell Nana or Jared? Jared would become even more overprotective of me, I didn't need him hovering. Nana wasn't an option. I couldn't bring myself to cause her stress with her blood pressure already an issue and my constant worry of her having a heart attack. Plus, something about the look in Muscle Man's eyes decimated my desire to confide in anybody. I would bear this burden on my own. Maybe he'd leave me alone like he promised.

I couldn't allow myself to think about how scared I'd been or the remote possibility that my parents were alive and being hunted at this moment by Muscle Man. That thought was so sickening it almost overwhelmed me.

"Seven miles. I'm supposed to run seven miles tomorrow morning," I explained to Tasha and Nana at dinner Tuesday night.

I cringed thinking about being alone on the road, in the dark, with the possibility of those two freaks grabbing me again. "How on earth am I supposed to run seven miles, lift weights, and still make it to work on time?" My Nazi boss would dock my bonuses if I were a minute late.

Tasha and Nana arched their eyebrows at the same time. "Maybe you should've thought of that before you started this insane program," Nana said.

Tasha took advantage of Nana focusing on me to hide half of her meatloaf in her napkin. I wished I could execute sneaky food-disposal techniques like my friend.

I pushed the peas around my plate before scooping up another bite. "I know it seems nuts, but it's going to be a great thing for me, Nana." I turned to Tasha just as she dive-bombed a chunk of mashed potatoes into her milk and winked at me. Luckily for her, Nana didn't notice.

Tasha politely nibbled at a slice of homemade bread, looking innocent of any meat and potato subterfuge. Nana noticed Tasha's almost clean plate. "Do you want some more, sweetheart?" She was armed and ready with a huge bowl of mashed potatoes in one hand and a dish of meat loaf in the other.

Tasha held up her delicate fingers. "No, I couldn't. It was wonderful, as always."

Nana grinned.

"But you didn't finish your milk," I said, hiding my own grin.

Tasha scowled at me.

"You need your calcium," Nana said, gesturing with her hand. "Drink up." She watched as Tasha lifted her glass and took a tentative sip.

Nana shook her head. "A bit more, sweetheart. We don't want brittle bones."

Tasha took another quick gulp. I watched a glop of mashed potatoes slide from the bottom of the glass into her mouth. She gagged. I pressed my lips together, my body shaking from withheld laughter. Tasha set the glass down, smacking her coral lips, as if she enjoyed potato-enriched milk, and eyeing Nana to see if she'd passed.

Nana nodded her approval. "Now that's what I like. A woman who actually knows how to eat." She glanced significantly at my plate covered with the mashed potatoes I'd been building sculptures out of and a hunk of untouched meatloaf. In my defense, I'd made short work of my peas and bread.

"Nana, you know I hate meatloaf."

"You need protein for running," Tasha said.

"Yes, eat a few bites," Nana commanded.

It was my turn to scowl. I cut a tiny bite, shoved it in my mouth, and swallowed without chewing. A quick drink of milk and I could almost feel normal again.

"I thought you *loved* mashed potatoes," Tasha said, not content with forcing me to choke down meat loaf. "I thought all of this running was going to make it so you could eat anything you love."

"Hey, good point." I scooped up a bite of potatoes and plopped them in my mouth. Whipped potatoes, loaded with butter. I thought I was too upset from this morning to enjoy food, but Nana's potatoes proved me wrong. I closed my eyes to savor the taste. I opened them to see Nana beaming at me. That hadn't happened in a while. I took another bite. "Do I look skinnier?" I asked Tasha.

She leaned around the table and gazed at my thighs. "Most definitely. Looks like it's time to go shopping."

I grinned. Eating Nana's calorie bombs and skinny enough for new clothes? This running crap was definitely worth it.

"You are and always will be too skinny," Nana said, flinging her hand at me. "Why, in my day men wanted a woman with some shape." Using her hands, she demonstrated the curves a woman should have. "You have no fat on you. No fat means no chest."

I glanced down. "I think we can blame the chest on mom's genes."

Nana smiled. "Oh, I can agree with that. I've always been well-endowed."

"Has Damon called?" Tasha asked, saving me from commenting on my grandmother's chest.

I shifted in my seat. "Not yet. I'm sure he's still trying to schedule the training runs." After watching Tasha and I fall off our treadmills last week, he may never call.

"I thought he might call for more than training runs."

I let myself eat one more bite of potatoes. "I'm not running this marathon to get the attention of a man, so it really doesn't matter."

Tasha stood, lifting her plate from the table to the sink. "I've seen this Damon guy, remember? *I'd* run a marathon if it meant training with him."

I helped clear the dishes, mulling it over in my mind. Maybe I'd started training to impress Damon but he hadn't called and I was still running. Jesse didn't seem to care whether

I did the marathon or not, but I had seen him out on the road a couple of times so maybe in the back of my mind there was that possibility of furthering a relationship with him.

"So, if you aren't doing this marathon for Damon?" Tasha's booming voice cut into my thoughts.

"I'm doing it to better myself," I said. *And to spite the two of you.*

Nana shoved meatloaf into a plastic container and turned to me with an arched brow. "Cassidy, are you feeling all right?"

I gulped and bent to pull the garbage from underneath the sink. "Fine." Was she talking about my bettering myself or had she noticed something else? I'd tried not to stew about Muscle Man and Greasy Beanpole during dinner. I wished I could tell Nana, but I couldn't worry her. I glanced up to see her still studying me.

"Did something happen at work today?" Nana asked.

"No. Works still boring and my boss is a jerk, but we closed a huge loan today and I'll be getting a fat check next week."

Nana arched an eyebrow, she didn't care about money any more than my parents had. "Well," she said, "'bettering yourself' is one thing, but you had better not be running this marathon to lose weight."

"That's just a side bonus," I said. I looked from Tasha's questioning gaze to Nana's disbelieving stare. "Really. This isn't for a man. This isn't to get skinnier. I'm running a marathon because I want to do it. Because I want to prove I can do it."

Nana and Tasha locked gazes. "Uh-huh," Tasha muttered.

I hated when they did that, acted like I couldn't accomplish anything. I shoved my barely-touched meatloaf into the garbage, ignoring Nana's gasp of outrage. "Plus, I didn't tell you but I think I've found a gym that wants to partner with me on my small personal training groups."

"That's good," Tasha said. "I wish you'd focus on that and forget about this marathon."

"But the marathon is part of that." The part where I believe in myself and accomplish my goals. "Remember

Rocky?" I asked, wishing for their support though I probably wouldn't get it. "Remember how cool it was to see him conquer himself? Push himself so hard you thought he was going to break?"

"Uh-huh," Tasha said again, still sharing some sort of silent conversation with Nana.

I jabbed a finger to my chest. "I'm Rocky."

I beamed at how well I'd put that. I was Rocky. I was going to triumph over myself and gain the confidence to start working as an exercise scientist again.

"Uh-huh," Tasha murmured for the third time.

"Use real words," I snapped irritably. "Why can't I be Rocky?"

"You can be anything you want." Tasha turned to retrieve more dishes.

Nana rolled her eyes and started scrubbing at baked-on meat loaf.

"Nana?" I paused for a few seconds, hoping she'd glance at me.

"Yes, you can be Rocky."

"No." I shifted from one foot to the other, a plate clutched between my fingers. "I have another question." I waited for her to look up.

"Spit it out."

I gulped, obviously I wouldn't have her full attention and this question needed it. But I couldn't hold it in any longer. "Are my mom and dad still alive?"

The casserole dish slipped from Nana's fingertips, clanking into the glass cups in the sink. Soapy water spewed onto the tile backsplash and Nana's cotton shirt. Nana spun from the mess. For half a second shock and disbelief poured from her eyes. But then her face softened into the wrinkles I liked, the ones that hid her scowl and showed she was concerned about her granddaughter. "Why would you ask that, sweetheart?"

I shrugged and looked down at the chipped linoleum. Warmth from Nana embarrassed me, she usually only called Tasha and Tate sweetheart. "Just missing them, I guess."

Nana's soft arms surrounded me. I set the plate on the counter, leaned against her wet shirt, and sighed. Water poured into the plugged sink, a few more seconds and we'd really have a mess, but I couldn't leave Nana's embrace to prevent it.

Tasha looked like she'd rather be anywhere but in Nana's kitchen watching her best friend's display of sadness. She reached behind us and shut off the tap then turned to study the pictures of Jared and Tate on the fridge.

"I understand," Nana said. "I miss them too." Nana rocked me for a few seconds.

"Would it be crazy to tell you that I'm kind of doing this marathon for them? Raquel told me she thought they'd be proud of me for accomplishing something big. For not quitting." I sniffled and continued, "I really like the sound of that."

Nana kissed my forehead. "I think that's the best reason I've heard yet."

She released me and hustled back to dinner cleanup. It wasn't until I climbed into bed that I realized she'd never answered my question. Maybe my parents were alive and Muscle Man and Greasy Beanpole were going to kill my mom and dad all over again. I trembled in my bed. My attempts at sleeping were a complete waste of pillow time.

Week Three

"If you go slower on the eccentric contraction, you'll increase your strength without increasing size."

"Ha," I sneered as I turned to face the person trying to instruct me on how to lift weights, obviously the weirdo didn't know I was the fitness trainer of the year.

The mocking words died in my throat as I came face to face with, "Damon?" I clung to the set of dumbbells in my hands.

He grinned. "Hi there."

For over a month now I'd been thinking about this man. Usually my fantasies increased a man's attractiveness by about thirty-two percent, and the actual re-encounter was a disappointment. Not so with Damon. He was so much better looking in real life than I could mentally sketch.

"Hi," I whispered, then turned and re-shelved the fifteen-pound dumbbells rather than let the words, *Why haven't you called*, spring from my mouth.

I forced myself to pivot back to face him, pressing my ponytail a few times to create some lift in my mop of dark hair. I wished I were one of those girls who had beautiful wisps of hair curling around their face. I really wished I were one of those girls who wore makeup to the gym . . . or at least brushed my teeth and put on deodorant.

"How's your marathon training going?" Damon asked, leaning against the weight rack.

"Well, let's see. I've made it through one week and I wish my legs would fall off and never come visit. And you?"

He chuckled. "It can't be that bad."

"Oh, but it is. I've fallen off a treadmill."

"Yeah, I saw that one. You okay?"

I nodded and changed the subject. "I went to a sports massage therapist for some relief. She worked on me for an hour then told me, 'You'd better ease up on the running for a few weeks until your body adjusts or you may do permanent damage.'" I couldn't believe I was admitting this to him, but the smile on his perfect face kept my tongue rattling along. I pushed a hand through the air. "What's a little damage? So I take a few extra ice baths."

"Ice baths already?" His eyes widened. "How far are you running?"

I bit my lip. "I was supposed to do ten on Saturday." I ducked my head. "I made it eight."

Damon was almost successful at hiding a smile. "And you took an ice bath?"

"Hey," I defended myself. "My legs were swollen like a pregnant woman with toxicity."

He glanced down at my lower limbs. "Hmm. Haven't checked out many pregnant women, but your legs look good to me."

I did a little victory dance, complete with fingers jabbing ceiling-ward and my head bobbing. "Oh, yeah. My legs look good."

A half-laugh emitted from his perfect lips. He glanced around the weight room as if checking to see if anyone else had witnessed my display.

Embarrassed, I looked at the weight rack. "I'd better get back to my workout. I still have to run home somehow."

Folding his muscled arms across his chest, he tilted his head to the side. "You want to go on a training run this weekend?"

I pumped my eyebrows, recovering from my embarrassment. "Just the two of us?"

He cleared his throat and blinked. "Well, there are a few others who will be tagging along."

I pivoted and grabbed a pair of twenties from the rack. "Sounds great." Oh, I am a dork. Twice in one minute I'd proven just how big of one. "Where should I meet you?"

He sidestepped between me and the weight rack so I had to face him again, had to concentrate on that devastating smile and feel my stomach flutter. "I'll call you and set up the run and then maybe I could check if you," his gaze swept my body, "and your good-looking legs, have room in your schedule for dinner."

The redness in my cheeks had nothing to do with the twenty-pound weights I was trying to curl. "Just the two of us?" I asked again.

His navy blue eyes twinkled like the sky at midnight bursting with stars. "Definitely just the two of us."

I tilted my head to the side and hid my smile. "You give me a holler, I'll see if I can fit you in."

His grin widened. He turned and strolled towards the Smith machine.

"Damon?" I called to his back, panicking slightly. "Do you remember my phone number?"

Damon glanced over his shoulder. "Of course."

"Then why haven't you called me?"

He laughed, loud. "I've been traveling for work. Plus, I've been working up the courage." He winked and turned away.

I watched him pile the Smith machine with forty-five pound plates in dumbfounded silence. *Him*, courage to call *me?* I glanced at my red-hued, make-up free features in the mirror. Dark hair and eyes, slightly upturned nose, rosebud lips that definitely needed lipstick to be noticed. Why would a man like that need courage to call a girl like me?

Focusing on my next set of hammer curls, I shook my head in embarrassment. He was teasing me. Of course. What else could he have said when I put him on the spot like that?

I went through the rest of my biceps and triceps exercises fully aware that Damon was lifting on lower body mere feet away. He didn't say anything else to me, but every time I glanced his way he'd catch my eye and either smile or wink.

73

I knew one thing guaranteed. I was going on a run with him and then to dinner. Marathon training definitely had its perks.

I arrived at the designated spot several minutes early. Two lanky men stood in the church parking lot, each had one ankle propped on the fender of a red pickup truck, leaning into a hamstring stretch. I stood there, shifting my weight from one foot to another and trying to look unassuming. Should I introduce myself? Wait for Damon to show up? Act like I belong and stretch un-warmed muscles?

I paced to keep warm in the early morning chill and searched the street for Damon. I smiled in response to the questioning glances of the men and wondered what in the world I was doing at six a.m. on a Saturday pretending I had a dream of keeping up with seasoned runners. Damon hadn't even told me how far we were going. How big of a fool would I be before this morning was over?

I hadn't run outside since Muscle Man and Greasy Beanpole accosted me. Training on a treadmill just wasn't the same. What if I stunk so bad, literally and figuratively, that Damon cancelled our dinner date tonight?

A silver convertible of some fancy make and model slid into the parking lot. The silver symbol on the front meant Chrysler, I think. I do know it was a beautiful car and the man who climbed out of the driver's seat put the vehicle to shame.

Damon's face split into a grin when he saw me. "Cassie." He strode across the parking lot, taking my hands in his. "You look great."

I glanced down at my T-shirt and baggy shorts. Again, I wished I'd put makeup on, but I had a strict no make-up during exercise rule. It clogged the pores and looked horrific when you started sweating. "You mean my legs look great, because my face will look a lot better tonight when I fix up a bit."

His smile widened. "You look great right now. Lucky for me, you don't need to fix up." Damon held onto my hand and turned both of us to face his friends. "Joe, Trevor, this is Cassie."

I reached out to shake each of their hands.

"Nice to meet you," Trevor said.

"So, you're running St. George?" Joe asked.

I pumped my eyebrows, rolling onto the balls of my feet. "If I can't fake a significant injury before then."

Damon chortled. "Told you she was funny." He inclined his head towards me. "You ready?"

I exhaled. "Not getting any faster standing here."

Damon smiled, released my hands, and we took off on a jog through the parking lot.

I stayed close to Damon's side, listening without comment to their easy banter. The pace wasn't bad and the scenery was terrific—Damon included. Maybe I could handle these early morning runs sabotaging my one opportunity to sleep in.

"Is this your first marathon, Cassie?" Joe asked.

"Yes."

"But you've been doing shorter races," he stated as if everyone was a regular member of the racing circuit.

"No." I swallowed then admitted in one breath, "The first race I ever ran was Health Days."

Damon stared at me. "Are you serious?"

"Um-hmm. I'd never run over three miles until a few weeks ago."

They all shared a significant glance. I didn't try to interpret what it meant. "Have you been running together long?" I asked to change the subject.

"Trevor and I did cross-country in high school," Joe said. "We met Damon at Health Days."

75

I glanced at Damon. I'd assumed he was from the valley and these were lifelong friends. We obviously had a lot of acquainting to accomplish. I felt giddy thinking about it.

We weaved through a subdivision and up a winding road towards Green Canyon. Oh, no, hills. Big hills. So far I'd only made a moderate fool of myself. I could hold my own with the flat running and the pace they were setting, but I was not prepared for inclines.

By the time we reached the parking lot at the base of Green Canyon I couldn't breathe or talk. It was all I could do to keep putting one foot in front of the other. I looked over at Damon. Could he tell how out of running-shape I was? How could I be such a champ at lifting weights, spin class, and every other form of exercise I chose to do, yet running devastated me?

Damon exchanged a glance with his friends and seconds later Joe and Trevor loped away from us without another word.

I increased my pace. It hurt.

Damon's fingers brushed my arm. "It's okay, Cassie. We'll just let them go ahead a bit and catch us on the downside."

I glared at him. "You think," gasp for air, "that I can't keep up."

He studied the tree branches waving above our heads. "No, it's not that." The jerk wasn't even breathing hard. "But this is a pretty intense trail run and . . ." His words dangled as I narrowed my eyes.

"I just want a chance to be alone with you," Damon said, spreading his hands in innocence as he ran effortlessly. He gave me one of his award-winning grins and almost got me.

"Bull crap." I stayed strong, rising above the effects of his smile. "I'm not," two long breaths, "letting you miss out."

I dug deep and followed Joe's freakishly long legs up the uneven trail. Birds chirped in the leafy canopy above us. I dodged over rocks and logs and kept as close to Joe as I could, without going into anaerobic shock.

Damon's breath itched at my neck. He stepped so close he clipped my heel. "Cassie, you don't have to do this."

"I *am* doing this," I shot back.

"Cassie, this is a fourteen-mile run, half of it straight uphill."

Holy schmack, you people are insane, I wanted to scream, but knew I couldn't afford the oxygen loss. I kept my mouth closed. Figuratively anyway. In reality it was hanging open as I gasped for air. Fourteen miles! Who brought a beginning runner on a fourteen-mile uphill run? But this wasn't Damon's fault. He had no way of knowing how pathetic I was. Why hadn't he seen through my lies about him not being able to keep up with me?

Damon sighed behind me. "Whenever you're ready to turn around, let me know."

I shook my head and concentrated on running. Time and trees blurred as I focused on keeping my legs rotating and staying within sight of Joe's striated calves. The "Eye of the Tiger" kept playing through my head. Not the entire song, I wasn't lucid enough to recall more than the chorus.

I was Rocky. I could do this. The chorus kept coming over and over again. Annoying, but better than the phrase the song was drowning out, *I'm not going to make it. I'm not going to make it.*

I tripped on a root that flung itself out of the ground at me. Slamming onto the rocky trail, I had a brief respite from motion. I caught my breath. The ache in my side eased. My head cleared. *Oxygen is a wonderful thing.*

Damon was instantly by my side. He grabbed my elbow and helped me stand. Joe and Trevor either didn't notice I'd fallen or didn't care, they kept up their excruciating pace.

I shook Damon off with a muttered, "Thanks," and did the last thing on earth that I ever wanted to do, forced my legs into action.

"Cassie," Damon said. "You just fell. Why don't you take a break? I really don't care if we take it slow."

"I care."

"Are you sure you're all right?"

"Marvelous."

"You didn't injure anything?"

"Shut-up," I said. *Or I'm going to injure you*, I would've added if it didn't hurt so much to talk.

Damon didn't say anything else, but he stayed within inches of my backside, obviously preparing himself for my next crash.

I wanted to curl up in fetal position and have someone place chocolate on my tongue. I ran instead. My calves screamed in agony. I couldn't catch a full breath. My stomach churned, preparing itself to spew. My head felt like it was going to explode from the lack of oxygen.

I hate running.

How could I have forgotten how miserable running was? Through all the agony my poor body and mind endured, I kept plodding along. Actually, it felt like racing not plodding. I wondered what kind of a fool I was to think I could keep up with Damon and his friends. A part of me was extremely grateful   for Damon's kindness. Another part wanted to scream at him that he should've told me we were running fourteen miles uphill. He was probably just being nice because of the load of guilt he shouldered.

I glanced away from Joe's rotating legs and checked my surroundings. Still lots of trees, rocks, and canyon walls closing in on us, but nothing signaling that we were nearing the end of the trail. I prayed, *Please let me make it to the top without puking or passing out and I'll read The Bible more than I read Prevention Magazine.* I figured a little bribery wouldn't hurt my prayer.

I kept going, one foot in front of the other, the ache remained in my legs but also lodged in my knees, hips, and gut. The only good thing about this run was for the first time in almost two weeks I didn't have the energy to worry about anything but putting one foot in front of the other.

The worst thing about this run was Damon saw me at the sorriest I've been in a long time. How awful did I look? Damon didn't say anything. The man stayed close behind me in a silent show of support. I decided if I lived through this I could really like the guy. I might have to apologize for telling him to shut-up.

"Bout a half-mile more to the turn around," Joe called over his shoulder.

Half a mile. I could do that. I could make it. I didn't know how I was going to crawl back to my car, but that was a worry for another minute. Right now I had to focus on getting my legs to the apex of this blasted hill. Maybe my torturers would actually pause and let me catch a full breath before they kicked my buns again. I did *not* like Damon's friends.

It was the longest half-mile in recorded history. I thought I would see the finish line around the next bend in the trail, behind the next overgrown tree, over the next rock-covered rise. Half an *hour* must have passed before we cruised off the trail and onto a rutted road framed with poplar trees. A rusty gate stood a hundred yards away.

"Sprint to the gate," Trevor called out.

Sprint to the . . .what? Were they masochists? Trevor and Joe took off like the Batmobile. Damon stayed by my side. One glance at his concerned face and my pride kicked in triple time. I lifted my legs, pumped my arms, and flew over potholes and hard-packed dirt. I swear the gate grew farther away. I had to occupy my mind with something other than how much this hurt. I started counting down from thirty. Surely it couldn't take any longer than thirty counts to reach an end to my misery.

30, 29, 28, I promised to never do this to myself again, 26, 25, 24, I tasted bile and prayed harder, *Please, don't let me throw up.*

21, 20, 19, these men were idiots, 16, 15, 14, black spots appeared in my vision, 10, 9, 8, the gate was there, a few more steps, 5, 4, 3, I grabbed the gate, sagged to the ground, and everything went black.

"Cassie, Cassie!" Damon's voice echoed around the edges of conscious thought. He scooped me off the ground and cradled me in his arms. This man was not only fine but tough. I was not a lightweight.

"Cassie."

I opened my eyes and stared into perfection. "I made the gate," I said.

A short bark escaped his lips. "Yes, you made the gate."

I leaned into his sinewy shoulder. "My prayers have been answered. Bury me here, please."

He laughed again. "You okay?"

"Sure. Never been better." I'd made it to the gate. My breathing was almost back to normal. My prayer had been partially answered—I made it to the top of the hill, I didn't throw up, but I had passed out. Maybe I would just have to increase my Bible reading but not surpass Prevention.

Then it registered: I was in the midst of a full-body hug from Damon. Okay, okay. I'd read my Bible more.

After a few delicious seconds, I dredged up some pride. "You'd better set me down. I know I'm not light."

"You're fine," he said, but he set me on my feet. Luckily for me, he kept one arm around my waist.

"Ready to run back home?" I asked, forcing a bright smile. Now that full consciousness had returned, my throbbing legs reminded me of the abuse they'd endured.

Damon looked at me like I was insane.

"Where are the guys?" I looked around at the path we'd taken through the trees and a wider road winding down the canyon, noticing for the first time that we were alone.

"The 'guys' are sprinting back down the road to get the truck and rush you to the hospital. None of us have cell phones on or there would be an ambulance on its way."

"Oh, no," I groaned. "I'm fine. How embarrassing is this?"

Damon lifted a stray hair and tucked it behind my ear. "It's not embarrassing at all."

"For you." I harrumphed and spun away from him. My legs crumpled and I made friends with the dirt road. Damon lifted me up and into his side again. I brushed at the brown clinging to my hands and legs.

"I bet you can't wait to take me to dinner tonight," I mumbled. "Or rather carry me to dinner."

"If you aren't in the hospital, I'll be thrilled to carry you to dinner tonight."

"Ha-ha. Please stop making me laugh. I am *not* going to the hospital. If there's a road why did we run up that uneven trail?"

Damon chuckled. "The trail is more interesting."

I rolled my eyes and determinedly put one foot in front of the other. Damon kept one arm securely around my waist, supporting more of my weight than I was. We walked at a decent pace, but it still took us an hour to cross a few miles. When I saw Joe's truck barreling up the pot-holed road I almost collapsed with relief. He and Trevor must've sprinted down that road. I can't imagine anyone running seven miles and then driving back over them that quickly.

I barely managed to convince them not to take me to the hospital. They were all humiliatingly nice about the incident. Trevor kept telling me how tough I was.

Suffering a load of embarrassment was worth it though. Damon drove me home, Trevor followed in my car. Nana was out shopping, so Damon was able to "assist" me all the way up to my bedroom. The hug he gave me when he said goodbye made me think tonight was going to be a lot of fun.

The First Date

"So this boy almost killed you and now you're letting him take you to dinner." Nana knitted, her needles automatically counting out the pattern without any conscious thought. Years of practice.

I looked at my most recent afghan, pewter blue and off-white. Where would I put this one? She'd been making me afghans since the day I graduated high school and she deemed I was ready to, "marry and start my own household." To date I had twelve afghans but no house to put them in and no desire to explain to Nana that I didn't really enjoy afghans, they didn't keep me warm and they were kind of ugly.

I leaned back from peering through the curtained side light next to the front door. Still no sign of Damon. He'd said seven. It was now six-fifty-nine and forty-three seconds. Yes, I counted the seconds. I planned on getting a kiss tonight.

"It's not like that, Nana," I said.

"Oh, and what is it like?" Nana sat in the padded rocker placed strategically in the front room to view any guests who came to the door and all the traffic on our not-so-busy street.

"I tried to kill myself," I muttered, "in front of his friends mind you, and he's still willing to take me to dinner. Maybe I *should* worry about him."

"Speak up, girl, I hate it when you mumble."

I glared at my grandmother. "You be nice to him. He's a really great guy."

Nana grumbled something incoherent and pulled the yarn tight. "I'll decide if he's a great guy or not."

Ignoring her, I sniffed my elbow. Was my perfume too strong? Too floral? Maybe I should wash it off and restart. Straightening my flowing skirt, I hoped my stomach looked flat in this fitted shirt. I bit at my lip then cursed myself. Had I just taken off my meticulously applied lipstick?

A knock on the door surprised me. I spun around. Damon peeked through the sidelight and waved. How had he gotten to the door undetected? I'd only turned my back for a moment. Had he seen me sniffing myself?

I ripped open the front door and started to hyperventilate. I'd never seen him in anything but workout clothes.

He wore jeans and a button-down shirt. His hair looked darker with a bit of gel in it. His blue eyes twinkled at me. His perfect mouth split in a smile. What on earth was this man doing on my doorstep? I grinned, mentally patting myself on the back. *I must've done a lot of things right in heaven.*

"Cassie," he said, covering my hand with his. "You look amazing."

"I, uh," I sputtered, *was thinking the same thing about you.* "I know it," I managed.

His grin widened. "Are you ready to go?"

I nodded dumbly. From behind us a voice screeched, "Cassidy Christensen, you are not leaving this house until I meet this young man of yours."

Oh, Nana. How *could* I have forgotten my guardian?

Damon's surprise only showed in his eyes. "You look so great, I didn't even notice anyone else was here," he murmured in my ear.

I giggled like a teenager. His spicy cologne made me feel faint. I better not pass out on him again.

With a gentle sweep of his hand, Damon simultaneously turned me to face my grandmother and made me tingle all over.

"This is my grandma," I said.

Damon gave her his grin and strode forward. Nana dropped her needles and yarn into her lap, not seeming to notice that several stitches unraveled. She offered her hand with the grace of a queen.

Damon bent low over the calloused fingers. "I'm Damon Cartwright," he said. "It's a pleasure to meet you."

"You can call me, Nana," she said, apparently awestruck by his gaze.

"Nana!" This degree of warmth had never happened on a first encounter. "You barely know him."

"I like what I know," she said.

Damon laughed. "Well, thank you, ma'am."

"Now," Nana withdrew her fingers and regained some sense of propriety. "Tell me where you're taking my granddaughter."

Damon glanced back at me with a wink. "Anywhere she wants."

"Just because you're handsomer than Rock Hudson doesn't mean you can be cute with me, young man."

I groaned. When would I ever convince Nana that not only was Rock Hudson dead, he swung from the other side and wouldn't have looked at her if he were alive?

Nana pointed her knitting needle at Damon. "You must have some idea where I can start the search if she turns up missing again."

"Again." I blew out a long breath, my heart rate increasing. Maybe Nana and Jared didn't need to go insane every time my cell phone died and they couldn't reach me.

"Again?" Damon arched an eyebrow at me.

"Damon promised me dinner," I said to Nana.

"I was hoping she liked Mexican, maybe Café Sabor."

I sighed, relieved he'd picked up on the hint that he didn't want to hear the stories.

Nana nodded her approval. "I think she'll be more than happy with Café Sabor." She offered her hand again. Damon gave it one more squeeze before sauntering to my side and holding the door open for me.

"Café Sabor is my favorite restaurant," I informed him.

"Really? That's why I like you so much." Damon winked.

"One of the many reasons," I reminded him.

"Make sure she actually eats," Nana admonished us from behind. "She's anorexic you know."

My cheeks flushed. I was several dress sizes above anorexic, but try convincing Nana of that. "Thank you, Nana. Thank you very much." I clutched Damon's hand and hurried him out the front door before she could reveal anything else that would hurt my chances of getting a kiss tonight.

Damon settled me into the car and jumped into the driver's seat. He didn't start the vehicle, but smiled gently at me. "Why do you live with your grandmother instead of your parents?"

"Nana and I kind of watch over each other," I swallowed and looked away, "because my parents are dead."

"I'm sorry," he said.

I brushed that away with a wave of my hand.

"How are you feeling?"

I was so grateful he changed the subject that I grinned. "Wonderful."

He wrapped his fingers around mine and squeezed. "Not sore from this morning?"

"This morning?" I was drawing a blank. All I could feel was the pressure of his hand on mine.

"We went on a run. You passed out."

"Oh." I exhaled slowly. "Thanks. I'd almost blocked the painful memory and here you are bringing it up again."

Damon chuckled, rubbing his thumb along the back of my hand. "Sorry for your distress."

"You'd better be, it was your fault."

"Did you call your doctor like I told you to?"

I shifted uncomfortably on the leather seat.

"Seriously, Cassie." He rolled his head to the side. "Why didn't you call?"

"I'm fine."

"I'm worried about you." He squeezed my hand. "You're going to be on a lot of outside runs. What if you'd been out there by yourself and this had happened?"

I arched an eyebrow. "I'd stand back up and hobble home."

Damon shook his head. "You are so competitive. You probably race through town like a maniac afraid another runner might catch you."

I thought of Jesse chasing me through town and for some reason felt guilty for being with Damon. I thought of Muscle Man chasing me and for some reason felt mad that neither Jesse nor Damon could protect me from him. I winced and turned to stare out the front windshield. "Dinner sounds good now."

"We'll go when you promise me that you'll call your doctor on Monday."

Why did everybody think they had to tell me what to do? I exhaled slowly, pivoting in the soft leather seat and giving in. A fight on the first date wasn't a great idea. "Okay, okay. First thing Monday morning old Doc Thurston gets a treat."

Damon entwined our hands and brushed those perfect lips across my knuckles. "Doc Thurston is a lucky man," he murmured.

I held in a sigh of pleasure, suddenly glad I'd backed down. "So are you."

He chuckled. "So am I."

We made it to the restaurant, through a dinner filled with interesting conversation and meaningful glances, and almost through the entire night without mishap. Damon paid the bill and we were standing to leave when it happened. Hot Redhead walked past our table. She paused in awestruck wonder as Damon rewarded her with an undeserved smile.

"Hello," she whispered breathlessly. "I don't know if you remember me. I met you at The Health Days Race. Elizabeth Randolph."

Damon nodded. "Of course I remember you, Elizabeth. It's nice to see you."

She giggled and stared at him from beneath obviously fake eyelashes, or maybe she just had a better eyelash curler than me.

I rolled my eyes, focusing on a toddler chucking tortilla chips at his mom. I didn't need to watch Elizabeth drool over my date. The effect this man had on women was incredible.

Damon lifted his hand and settled it on the small of my back. "Enjoy your dinner," he said.

Elizabeth's gaze fluttered from Damon to me. Her eyebrows arched. "Oh."

"Yes, hello," I said. "Good to see you."

I turned to walk away. The petite redhead grabbed my arm and whirled me back to face her. I've got to give it to her, she was pretty tough for a skinny chick.

"How dare you?"

"How dare I *what?*" I added the raised eyebrow for emphasis, but I knew exactly what she was thinking and in my defense, I felt like a jerk. I'd made fun of her for trying to get Damon to date her by running the St. George Marathon and here I was succeeding in the venture.

Elizabeth glanced at Damon who watched us with interest. She moved closer to my side, opposite of Damon and whispered in my ear, "You told me you weren't interested in him."

I turned my head and whispered back, "Hate to break it to you sister, but he came after me." I grinned and shrugged my shoulders. "What's a girl to do?"

Her hot glare burned me as she said into my ear, "You're going to be doing a lot of running in the dark streets of Smithfield. I'll find you."

"Get in line," I muttered.

Backing away, she gave Damon one more dazzling smile. "See you later," she said in a voice dripping with hope. She didn't even bother with a glare in my direction before whirling and strutting away from us.

I glanced at Damon. "Whew. That is one angry woman."

"What did she say to you?" he asked.

I forced a smile. "You're a very desirable commodity. I came between you and the wrong stalker this time."

"Cassie?" He tilted his head to the side, studying me. "You're joking, right?"

I lifted my shoulders. "I hope so."

The drive home was quiet. Damon tried to get out of me what happened with Elizabeth, but I didn't know how to explain without looking like a bigger fool. I couldn't get over that interaction. Something was off about the chick.

By the time we got to my doorstep, I realized I'd ruined the mood thinking about Hot Redhead instead of my date. Damon escorted me up the steps and leaned in expectantly. I gave him a quick hug, burying my face in his shoulder.

"Thanks for dinner," I said, way too upbeat. I pulled away and grabbed for the doorknob. "And thanks for rescuing me from the dirt this morning."

"I thought you blocked that out," he said.

"You reinstated the memory," I reminded him.

He moved closer. The look in his eyes melted me. "I'd like to see you again."

"Running or eating?" I asked, clinging to the doorknob for support.

"Both. But maybe not such an intense run next time." He leaned in again. Oh, this guy was an expert.

"Sounds good. I wouldn't want to put you to shame two weeks in a row." He was so close. I melted into the wonderful scent of his cologne. He looked and smelled good enough I almost forgot about Elizabeth's threats.

Damon shook his head with a laugh. "We wouldn't want that."

I opened the door and pantomimed a phone. "Call me," I said. "Maybe I'd cancel a date or two for you."

"I would appreciate that."

I slipped through the door then glanced back at his face. He watched me with an almost sad expression. I closed the door, waited until I heard his footsteps recede, and pounded my head against the grainy wood a few times. "Stupid, stupid, stupid."

He wanted to kiss me. I knew it. But I wanted our first kiss to be perfect, and after the awkward confrontation with Elizabeth, I just hadn't been in the right frame of mind. I trudged up to bed, praying he would call again.

Week Four

I'm a tough chick. I have nothing to fear. I repeated these words to myself as I ran early Monday morning. I couldn't let Hot Redhead, Muscle Man, Greasy Beanpole, and whoever murdered that poor faceless man, confine me to treadmill running. Outside runs were better for my training, more enjoyable, and there was the possibility of running into Jesse again. Even though Damon pressed upon my mind in a most delicious way, I couldn't seem to rid my daydreams of Jesse.

I still felt sore from Saturday's run when I thumped out of bed, but the training schedule said an eight-mile run. I'd be proud to hit six.

I was halfway through my six miles when I heard steady footsteps approaching from behind. I risked a glance, praying for Jesse, Damon, or somebody I didn't know. A tiny figure was all I could make out. It was still too dark for clarity but the shape of the runner filled me with relief. I didn't like Hot Redhead, but she was nothing compared to the fear I had of Muscle Man. If Hot Redhead attacked I could sit on her and possibly win the battle.

I increased my pace a bit. Keeping my distance was still a better plan than fighting a feisty woman. Mere feet from Sixth South and the approaching footsteps got louder. Half a block down Sixth South and the footsteps thundered. My heart raced. I tried to go faster. I could see the Rec Center now. A hundred more yards and I would be safe amongst my fellow muscle heads.

"Cassidy," she called out.

Dangit. It was definitely her. I kicked my legs into an all-out sprint. Her pace matched mine. Her sweet breath brushed my cheek. The hairs on my neck stood up. Come on, who has good-smelling breath in the morning?

I flew through the Rec Center's parking lot with Hot Redhead by my side. The front doors beaconed safety. I knew my friend Bryce would be sitting at the front desk. Well, friend is pushing it, but he did offer a cheery hello every morning. Maybe he would keep her out.

I grabbed the front door, yanked it open, and inhaled the comforting smell of sweaty bodies.

"Cassidy, stop!" Elizabeth's tiny hand grabbed my arm.

I yanked my limb away and hurried into the gym's foyer.

"Morning," Bryce muttered with a chin lift.

"How's it going?" I swiped my card through the scanner, not looking at the woman who followed me like a symbiotic life form.

The scanner beeped, "Welcome." I hurried to the double doors and burst through. Elizabeth stuck to my shadow. I whirled around, sick of this, ready to fight. "You can't follow me through these doors." I gestured to the invisible line between the doors. "This is my safe zone. You didn't check in. Bryce," I pointed at Hot Redhead like a preschool tattle-tale, "she can't be in here. She didn't check in."

Bryce stood. "Do you have a membership here?"

Elizabeth planted her hands on her hips. "I just want to talk to Cassidy."

He eased back into his chair and nodded. "Just as long as you don't use the facility without paying."

"Oh, I'd never think of it." Elizabeth smiled sweetly at him. "I just want to talk to my friend."

Bryce obviously couldn't resist returning the smile; he ducked behind his computer with red cheeks.

I backed away. I hated girls who used their looks to their advantage. "I'm not your friend."

She rolled her eyes. "I'm not going to hurt you, Cassidy."

"How do I know that?" I clung to the door, pulling it slightly in front of myself.

Hot Redhead pointed at me. "Look at yourself. You've got me by six inches and forty pounds."

"Hey!" I protested. Then I got curious. "Forty pounds? How much do you weigh?"

She flung her hand at me. "Never mind. I just wanted to say that you don't want to date Damon."

Aha. Trying to steal the man, again. "Why wouldn't I?"

"You're just not his type."

"Hold up. The guy recognizes quality," I clucked my tongue and tilted my chin down and to the side. "Ain't my fault that Damon thinks I'm hotter than Hot Redhead."

Elizabeth's delicate forehead squiggled. "You called me that earlier."

"Yeah. Do you like it?"

Elizabeth fluffed her ponytail and coughed, but not before I saw her smile. She liked it. "Maybe." Her eyes narrowed. "Wait a minute. Where do you get off claiming Damon thinks you're hotter than me?"

"Hey." I shrugged. "The dinner invites tell all."

She rolled her eyes. "He's just playing with you. Why would he want someone who can't run and has more muscle than boobs?"

"Uh!" I looked down, realizing she was right. I stared pointedly at her full chest. "How much did your fakies cost you?"

She turned away. "I was trying to be nice, but I can see that won't work."

Making fun of my concave chest was nice? I took a long breath and tried my best. "Thank you, Hot Redhead, for helping me realize that I could kick your trash. I didn't intend to steal your spot as Damon's training beauty. I'll try to *really* enjoy him for you. Maybe I can even give you a call after our first kiss. What's your cell number?"

Elizabeth gasped. "That's your idea of an apology?"

"Yep. See you on the road." I turned away, but called back over my shoulder. "Oh, and my regrets that you didn't get into The St. George Marathon."

I smiled in response to her scowl and strolled away. I should've felt guilty. Hot Redhead had chased me into the Rec. Center to "try" and work it out. But she didn't try very hard. *More muscle than boobs.* Who says something like that? Well, I'd probably say it if I had a chest to back it up.

What did I care? Damon was taking me out to dinner, not Elizabeth. I just wondered why she was so obsessed with him.

Perusing the overstocked aisles of Smithfield Implement, I wondered if Tate was too young for a pocketknife. They had some beauties. I felt eyes on my backside. Spinning around, I saw no one. I poked my head into the main aisle and almost collided with an elderly man. He gazed up at me. "You okay, sweetheart?"

I smiled, placing a hand on my heart. "Yes, thank you."

He gave me a grin before puttering off to the tools. I looked around one more time before walking down the aisle to look at the bike tubes. I'd almost convinced myself nobody had been watching me when I got that eerie feeling again. I slowly checked over my shoulder when I heard his deep voice, "You're dating that redhead."

I whirled to find Jesse within touching distance. I sighed with relief that it was him and not Muscle Man, taking a moment to admire what his body did to a black T-shirt and nicely-fitting jeans. Looking up I saw that a frown marred his exquisite face. I rubbed at the lines in his forehead.

Jesse grinned. Ooh, I liked that smile. "Do I look that upset?"

"Yes." I licked my bottom lip, pulling my fingers back to my side of the line, though they longed to touch him more. "I don't like seeing you upset."

93

"I feel the same." The warmth of his smile faded. "I don't like seeing you with that guy either."

I blinked several times. "Why do you care who I date?"

He folded brawny arms across his wide chest. I studied the dragon encompassing his left forearm and took long breaths to remind myself this was not the man for me. "You're a beautiful girl, Cassidy. Please don't get mixed up with someone who's not worthy of you."

My eyes narrowed at the compliment diffused by a warning. "And who would be worthy of me?" I took a step closer and poked him in the chest. "You?"

His face drooped. "No, not me." He did a quarter-turn. "Please just trust me and stay away from him," he whispered, looking back at me with tortured brown eyes.

Why not him? My gut ached. Why did I want a man who obviously wasn't interested? But I couldn't give up on Jesse that easily. I pushed a bit harder. "Why would I stay away from him when you've given me no good reason?" *Please tell me you want me for yourself.* I hoped my eyes conveyed the message I didn't dare verbalize.

Jesse twirled a curl of my hair between his fingers. Gently, he brushed it back from my face. His fingers caressed my cheek. "I can't give you a reason, but I wish you'd trust me."

His arms were covered with tattoos. His sculpted face had a decidedly rough edge to it. The only thing that looked trustworthy about this man? His eyes. "That's all you've got?"

Jesse sighed. He dropped his hand. I leaned towards him, wishing for another touch. "Please be careful," he said, before walking away.

I studied his broad back until he disappeared around the aisle, wondering what he had against Damon. Damon was new to the area and traveled for work. He claimed not many people even knew him. Was Jesse just being jealous or was there truly something about Damon that deserved the warning? The jealousy card made me angry. Jesse had opportunities to ask me out, but always walked away. I shivered, trying to decide what unsettled me more—his touch or his warning.

Damon glanced up from his menu. "How'd your run go this morning?"

"Fine." I didn't elaborate on my nine-minute per mile pace or tell him I'd spent the entire twelve miles checking the horizon for Muscle Man. By the time I finished the run my head pounded so hard I had to take a nap and Excedrin to combat it. Focusing on Chili's menu, I debated whether to order fajitas or quesadillas.

I looked up. Damon stared at me. Had he been watching me the entire time? Something about that stare was unnerving. Jesse's warning flashed in my head before I could shoo it away.

"Bet you missed running with me," he said.

I smiled. "No, I miss Joe and Trevor."

"They're loads of fun, but I'd rather be with you." His grin turned down. "Why won't you run with me? I just like being with you."

I pumped my eyebrows. "I've heard that one before."

"I'm not concerned about pace on distance runs."

I toyed with the straw in my water glass then took a short drink. "You would be if you saw what my pace really is." Damon wasn't dangerous; he was more concerned about running and being with me than anything else. Jesse must just be jealous. A thrill shot through me. Could I make Jesse jealous enough to touch me again?

Damon reached across the table and covered my hand with his. "As competitive as you are, I think you'd keep up."

I exhaled slowly. "Have you ever thought that maybe, just maybe, I'm not a masochist?"

Releasing my hand, Damon straightened. "What does that mean?"

95

"Maybe I don't want to kill myself trying to keep up with you and worrying about slowing you down."

His mouth formed an O. "I thought you were going to qualify for Boston."

I searched for the appropriate response that wouldn't ruin my free dinner.

"He actually exists."

I heard the voice behind me, but didn't want to believe it could really be him. Pivoting slowly, I confirmed it. "Hey, Jared." My brother looked so much like my dad: dark-blond hair, hazel eyes, fair skin, and lanky build. I'd loved my dad so much the similarities almost convinced me to forgive Jared for being such a punk. I gave my sister-in-law a smile. "You look pretty, El."

Raquel beamed back at me, twirling a beautiful wrap between her fingers, her stomach outlined by a fitted, black shirt. "It's the pregnancy glow."

Damon stood and smiled at Raquel. "There is nothing more attractive than a woman expecting a baby."

She blushed and grinned. "Well, thank you."

Jared grunted. "Oh, great, a kiss-up."

Tilting her head towards my brother, Raquel said, "Damon, this is my husband, Jared."

Jared shook Damon's hand begrudgingly. "Nice to meet you." He released his hand and glared at me. "You're dating a smooth talker."

I rolled my eyes. "Don't be such a jerk-wad, big brother."

Damon clapped Jared on the shoulder. "You've got a beautiful wife and sister. That should be a compliment to you."

Jared grinned. "Seriously. I must be doing something right."

"Join us?" Damon gestured towards the two empty seats.

Raquel glanced at me, communicating with eyes and eyebrows. I nodded my head that it was okay, though I dreaded what my brother might reveal. *Farewell to another goodnight kiss.*

Jared pulled out a chair for Raquel. "Thanks. I'd love the chance to get to know the man that Cassie can't stop talking about."

I whirled to confront Raquel. "I haven't said one word to *Jared* about Damon."

She elevated her shoulders. "You tell me everything at your own risk. You know I can't keep anything from him."

Jared pulled her to him and kissed her quickly. "That's right. My wife loves me too much to not share the juicy Cassie gossip."

Leaning back in my chair, I folded my arms across my chest and sent my flowing sweater off one shoulder. I straightened it and said, "You two must have awfully boring conversations because there rarely is any 'Cassie gossip.'"

Jared clucked his tongue. "Keep telling yourself that." He swiped my menu. "I might as well look at this since I know you're getting a salad."

I wrenched the menu from his hands. "For your information, I am planning to order the quesadillas."

Jared gasped like a woman and put his fingers to his lips. "Don't do it, sis. All that cheese. It'll never come off your waistline."

I shoved the menu back at him. "Shut up and figure out what you want before the waitress comes. I'm hungry."

Jared winked at Raquel and studied his menu. Damon offered his menu to Raquel, leaned close to me, and whispered, "I suddenly understand where the sarcasm comes from."

My lower lip protruded. "I don't act like him." I pointed at my oblivious brother, discussing the Chili's menu with his wife.

Damon's lips brushed my ear, making it extremely hard to take the offense I deserved. "You *are* much more attractive."

"What does that mean?"

"Putting aside your superior beauty, you can definitely tell you're siblings."

I pulled back, grateful to see the waitress approaching. This dinner was not turning out anything like I'd hoped.

Jared did everything in his power to embarrass me in front of Damon. I don't know why I was surprised; he'd been perfecting his scare-away-Cassie's-dates tactics since high school. I thought when the food arrived he would stop, but it seemed he was just warming up. "The whole family is so glad Cassie turned out. I mean, you should've seen her at twelve. Nana almost disowned her."

"Jared," I warned. "I'll tell Nana you were the one who set her shed on fire."

"She had braces, a headgear, glasses, and then my mom permed her hair." He whistled, ignoring my warning and swirling his hands around his head to demonstrate how big my hair had been. "Scary. At least she looked good as a witch on Halloween."

Damon covered my hand with his. "Well, it all worked out well." He winked and I felt a bit better.

"Then there was the time she climbed on top of the school dressed in a bunny suit and—"

"Jared," I yelled, drawing stares from everyone seated close to us. "Well, at least I didn't blow up the post office box with a dry ice bomb."

Damon's eyebrows shot up. He stared at me. "Dry ice bomb? And what were you going to do in the bunny suit?"

I squirmed, my flesh matching the inside of a watermelon.

Jared just laughed. "That was a good bomb, wasn't it?"

"Do you want me to shut him up?" Raquel asked me.

"El, I know he loves you." I rolled my eyes at my brother. "But I don't think anybody can shut him up."

Jared stared at Raquel with that fawnlike admiration I've always envied. Just once, I'd like a man to look at me like that. "Was I being rude to Cassie?"

The way Jared asked just reaffirmed what my brother was trying to accomplish; he didn't want to hurt me, he just wanted to scare away Damon. I just wish I understood why he acted like this. I was 25 years old. Overprotective was getting old.

"Yes, my love. Shut up and eat."

He grinned, kissed her, and dove into his steak fajitas. I sighed with relief and tried to enjoy my quesadillas.

We were almost through eating when Jared dropped the worst bombshell of the night. "So, Damon, what do you think of Cassie's idea?"

Damon set his fork down and eyed my brother. "What idea is that?"

"Getting back into personal training." Jared smiled at me. "Tell him about it, sis."

I ducked my head, pushing around a piece of lettuce with the tip of my fork. "I, um, want to start using my degree again." I took a deep breath and tilted my chin. The warm look in Damon's eyes encouraged me. "I've worked out a lease agreement with a local gym to train clients in small groups so I can charge them less and still give individual attention. I'll combine cardiovascular and strength training for an intense, effective workout. So many women are afraid of lifting weights, I think it could be amazing."

The way Damon studied me was better than the way Jared looked at Raquel. It was like Ghirardelli's compared to Hershey's.

"What do you think?" I whispered.

Damon nodded. "I think you're amazing. It's brilliant. So many women could benefit from strength training but you're right about them begin afraid or maybe wanting to lift but not having enough knowledge or the money to hire a personal trainer." He grinned. "I love it, Cassie. Let me know how I can help."

I grinned back at him. He loved my idea. Any uneasiness Jesse's warning had created was pushed aside, I could easily let myself fall for Damon. "You already have," I said.

Al squinted against the bright sunlight. "Where are they supposed to be?"

Terry pointed. "There's some caves down there where they were waiting for the transfer."

They scrambled down the dirt path and bustled into the quiet cave. Al resented being sent on a reconnaissance mission when they should be finding a way to get the video to Nathan Christensen. His contact, who had delivered the original pictures of Cassidy, had disappeared. If Al couldn't get the video into Nathan's hands, his plan to kill the man would fail. Whoever else was competing on this job would get to Nathan or Nathan's family first. Two million dollars, gone. But no one said no to Ramirez when asked to run an "errand."

What in the world was going on? This place should be oozing with Ramirez's men and slaves ready to be transported. Why hadn't they reported in this morning?

The light from outside barely penetrated the opening. Al stumbled over a box and came face to face with a Spanish worker. Al shook the man. "Wake up. What's going on here?"

The man didn't respond. It was then Al felt the stickiness on his hands. He peered through the gloom at a deep cut in the man's throat and the blood staining his shirt.

"Aagh!" Al jumped away. "He's dead." He snatched the flashlight from the man's belt and switched on the light. The dim beam cut across the cave. Supplies. Piles of severed ropes. Dead men. Not a slave in sight. He glanced back at Terry. "See if any of them are alive."

Terry nodded and started poking at the man closest to him. A groaning rasp tore Al to the right. He grabbed a worker struggling for breath through the slice in his throat. "What happened?" Al demanded.

"They . . . got us," the man rasped out.

"Who?"

"The big," he gurgled and spit blood before continuing, "black one and . . . the Doc."

Al dropped the flashlight, lifted the man into his arms, and picked his way out of the cave. Terry caught up as they reached sunshine and left the reek of death in the darkness.

"Doc," Al muttered.

Terry slammed his fist into his palm. "We've got to get him."

Al could only nod. The man had to be stopped.

Week Five

Damon stood next to me at the starting line. He cocked his head to the side and glanced down. "Just pace yourself. Don't go out there and kill yourself at the first. Stay with a group you're comfortable with until you're ready to up your pace a bit. This isn't about winning, it's about forcing yourself to run at a faster pace than you normally would and getting used to the excitement of racing."

"Okay, oh glorious Race Coach."

Damon smirked at me. "Okay, my little smart-aleck."

Ooh. He'd referred to me as *his*. Happy morning to Cassidy.

Raquel finally convinced me that running a few local races this summer would help prepare me for the marathon. Because of my first and only race experience, I was a bit leery. But I'm willing to try anything that will help me make it through this marathon. At least she let me out of my promise to run in Princess Leia braids.

A tall, exotic-looking woman appeared a few runners away. She caught my gaze then turned to her friend. "*That's* the girl who tried to sell the entry into St. George."

I sucked in a quick breath. *Her* again. Race Organizer Lady. I ducked behind Damon. Several seconds passed without Race Lady coming to scream at me. I peeked around Damon's chest. She gave me a glare then started marching in place and chatting with her friend. At least she didn't have a megaphone strapped onto her running shorts.

Damon peered down at me. "You okay?"

I flung my head from side to side and shook my shoulders. "Just stretching. Getting warm, you know?"

He laughed. "Uh-huh."

"So I take it you're not staying by my side during this race?" Not that I really wanted him to. I had no desire to prove to him once again how pathetic I was. I kept praying I could cross the distance without passing out. We didn't need a replay of the canyon run two weeks ago.

Damon pulled one of his legs behind him for a quad stretch, looking over the smattering of racers. "Um, I wasn't planning on it. Do you want me to stay by you?"

"Absolutely not. I don't think you could keep up with me."

He grinned and switched legs. "That's what I like about you."

"The only thing?" I asked, licking my lips so they would glisten.

"Oh, no, there's a long, long list." He leaned closer. How did he smell so good this early in the morning?

"Hello, Damon," a syrupy voice came from his right.

Damon straightened and turned. I silently cursed whoever had interrupted us.

"Hi, Elizabeth. How are you?" he asked.

Hot Redhead. I cursed not only her, but her ancestors and her descendants. I hope none of her descendants are shared with Damon. My stomach turned. That was a sickening thought.

"Fabulous," she said. "I'm so excited about this race. Are you all ready to go?"

"We're ready," he said, giving me a smile and a quick squeeze of the hand. "Looks like a great morning for a race."

We're. I loved that Damon gave my nemesis plenty of reasons to be jealous.

"Any race is great if you're in it," Elizabeth said.

Hot Redhead hadn't looked my direction, apparently we aren't on speaking terms. Not that I missed out on any stimulating conversation.

I stuck out my tongue and shimmied my head. "Blah, blah, blah," I muttered.

Damon tossed me a grin. I felt a tap on my elbow. Who was going to interrupt us now? Rolling my eyes, I turned to face . . .

"Jesse?" I tried to straighten my eyeballs and gave him my loveliest smile.

"Good morning, Cassidy."

"How's you?" I tripped over my own tongue. *How's you?*

"I'm fine. Thank you for asking." He glanced over my shoulder, his smile faltering as he met Damon's gaze.

His formal speech contradicted with the image that screamed, "Don't bring this one home to Dad." Luckily for me I didn't have a dad to worry about. But there was Nana. And the fact that I was dating Damon, who was currently crowding into my space. Why couldn't Elizabeth distract him when I needed her to? I couldn't drag my eyes from Jesse's tanned face.

A race organizer lady-different one from last race and minus the megaphone, thank heavens-moved to the front of the group of runners and started yelling. I forced myself to ignore Damon and Jesse, tuned out the race lady and pumped myself up. Singing my Rocky theme song, I knew I was ready for this race. Well, at least I was more ready than I had been for the Health Days Race. My stomach kart-wheeled and I felt the sudden urge to go to the bathroom.

Concentrate, Cassie. I glanced over at Hot Redhead. She looked directly at me and tilted her head towards Damon. *He's mine*, she mouthed.

I rolled my eyes. The woman not only had the rear-end of a teenager but the mentality. I shouldn't get pulled into her little games, but . . . "Keep dreaming," I said aloud.

Damon looked down at me. "Dreaming about what?"

"You." I winked obnoxiously.

Damon grinned.

Elizabeth rolled her eyes.

Jesse's mouth tightened.

I reddened.

A shot rang out. Runners surged around me. I looked on in surprise as Damon, Elizabeth, and Jesse sailed away in a flurry of legs and pumping arms. Forcing my feet into action, I took up a desperate pursuit. I didn't need to play games, but I still wasn't going to allow Hot Redhead solitary access to my man.

The first couple of miles went by in a blur as I played catch up. I forgot everything Damon had told me about finding a comfortable pace and waiting until my muscles were warm to increase my leg turnover. All I could think about was defending him from the psycho chick running by his side.

Dodging through clumps of runners, who also seemed intent on keeping up with Damon and Elizabeth, I hardly noticed when we passed the three-mile mark. I gave it everything I had and heard somebody call out "Mile Four," as I pulled parallel with Damon. I could see Jesse's striated calves a hundred yards ahead of me. Did he really have a cluster of tattoos down there as well? Everything about the man confused me.

"Hey," I gasped to get Damon's attention.

Damon's head jerked towards me. "Cassie? You okay?"

I held up an okay symbol rather than waste the oxygen to reply.

"Maybe you should slow down. I don't think you've trained to sustain this pace."

"I'm good," I muttered. How did he know what I'd trained? So he'd seen me run and it wasn't a great performance, but I proved I could conquer mind over body. How many people can claim they've pushed so hard they've passed out? Those were bragging rights.

Hot Redhead glowered at me, but there was nothing, short of tripping me, that she could do to displace me from Damon's side. We flew on, my legs churning up the distance like champs. Well-maintained houses with chipped wood in their flowerbeds streamed past us. I'd never been so proud of myself. We passed mile marker five. I let out a breath of relief. One more mile. I could handle one more mile.

But that mile started to handle me. My head spun as I forced my legs to keep rotating and hold even with Damon and Elizabeth. I have no clue how Elizabeth ran so effortlessly. She had half the stride length of Damon and she not only kept up, she also made cute comments and laughed at everything he said. If I didn't dislike her so much I would have been impressed.

Damon worried over me. He asked me how I was doing so many times that I almost told him to shut up again, but I was grateful to be by his side so I kept my mouth closed. I sensed he wasn't giving this race his all but I didn't care. I was staying with him and Elizabeth and that was all that mattered.

I suddenly felt extremely uncomfortable in the nether regions. I ran harder and prayed the urge would go away. We had half a mile left and I pumped my arms and lifted my legs in full sprinter's mode. Elizabeth glanced over at me and upped her pace. Damon and I kept time with her quick strides.

The dizziness was stronger now and the urge to lose my bladder close to unbearable. I focused on one thing. Beating Elizabeth.

I saw the finish line looming ahead. I dug deep. My poor legs groaned through the pain and responded to my brain's commands to go faster. Raquel was right. I did have horse legs. I guess all that strength training must be good for something. I kept moving, but the lactic acid accumulated at sonic speed. My muscles burned like they would never be oxygenated again.

Twenty yards to the finish line and suddenly I felt wetness running down my legs.

Holy schnikies! I kept running, but the shock of urinating on myself stole my thunder. Damon sprinted ahead, Elizabeth right behind him. I crossed the finish line trailing both of them.

I should've been proud of my time: forty-two minutes for a 10K. I never would've believed that was possible a month ago.

But all I could think about was the fact that I had disgusting wetness pooling in my shoes. I had peed on myself. How gross was that?

I slowed to a walk, pondering my options. I could stick with Damon and Elizabeth and risk them smelling my misfortune. Or I could run and hide. Then I saw the perfect alternative—an irrigation ditch.

Damon circled around and came back to me. Elizabeth trailed him. He squeezed my shoulder. "You did great, Cassie. Man, you are tough. I didn't think you were ready for that kind of speed."

I shifted uncomfortably, watching him inhale and imagining that he could smell my stink and would soon run away. "Thanks," I said. "Um, excuse me for a minute, I'm really hot."

Damon and Elizabeth's faces registered confusion. Sure, we'd worked up a sweat, but it was still an early summer morning in Northern Utah. The temperature couldn't have been above sixty-five.

I walked away from them, bent down to untie and slip off my shoes and socks, and plunged into the irrigation ditch. The cold water rinsed me off. I've never felt so relieved.

A tanned hand extended from the grassy bank. "Cassidy?" Jesse questioned.

I grasped his hand and let him pull me out of the water. "Thanks!" I beamed, loving the way his deep-brown hair curled around his temples.

"Are you okay?" he asked.

"I am now." I winked, loving each chance I had to be near this man. "Great race."

"Thanks." He grinned at me. "You did well."

I looked up to see Damon and Elizabeth at the edge of the ditch, staring at me like I was insane. "Cassie?" Damon said. "You okay?"

I smiled at Jesse, clung to his hand, and waddled up the bank. Damon's focus on our clasped fingers forced me to release my grip on Jesse. Dangit.

I punched Elizabeth in the shoulder. "Good race."

"Ouch." She shifted away from me. "What was that for?"

"It's what friends do when they kick it hard together. You're an amazing runner. Great job."

She looked at me like I was insane. Good heavens, I'd given the woman a compliment. "Would you prefer I slapped your butt?" I asked.

Jesse's cheek twitched as he hid a grin.

Elizabeth glanced at Damon. "Did you see what she did?"

Damon shook his head. "I'm staying out of this one."

"She punched me." Elizabeth rubbed her shoulder. "Thinks she's going to slap my butt," she muttered in disgust.

I stuffed my socks into my shoes. Water dripped down my legs. My feet were accumulating dust. I didn't care. The semi-clean water had cleaned me off enough so I didn't stink. I could deal with the rest later.

"Hey, Cassie," Damon said, acting like Jesse didn't exist. "Walk with me. We'd better get some food in you before you dive into any more dirty water."

I had a hard time prying my eyes from Jesse. "I'll see you later," I murmured, almost wishing he'd demand I go with him instead of Damon.

Jesse nodded once and stalked off into the crowd. I debated going after him, but I still had some pride. Damon obviously wanted me around. Jesse was still an unknown. "Lead the way. Do you want me to smack you too?"

Damon's eyes flickered after Jesse before he turned to me with a smile. "Maybe later." He winked at Elizabeth. "Great race, Elizabeth. See you around."

We walked away from Hot Redhead. I glanced back to see if she pouted. Her scowl looked more like intense concentration. She'd probably never lost a man to a lesser specimen than herself and was planning how to remedy the problem. I didn't let it bother me. Actually nothing could bother me right now. I'd rocked in that race—well, minus the peeing down my leg—and I'd gotten the guy. I searched the crowd for Jesse, wondering if I'd succeeded in obtaining the wrong guy.

"I don't want a girl's night out. I want to be with Damon."

"Obviously Damon doesn't want to be with you," Tasha said.

I shoved her. "That is totally untrue. He referred to 'us' several times today. Like we're a serious couple."

Tasha rolled her eyes. "You need a break from Damon."

Raquel appeared by my side, offering her plastic card to the man behind the counter of Cache Valley Fun Park. "Why does she need a break from Damon? They've only gone out a few times."

"Thank you," I said. I flung a hand towards the cash register. "And thank you. You don't need to pay for this . . . thing we're doing."

Raquel smiled. "It's Jared's card."

"Oh, in that case, you'd better pay."

"Cassidy?" A deep voice questioned behind me.

I whirled around and had difficulty breathing. "Jesse." He wore a long-sleeved white T-shirt, a nice contrast to his dark coloring, and jeans that fit him perfectly. Why did this man always look so appetizing to me? "What are you up to tonight?" I tried to act nonchalant, it came across as demanding.

He placed his arm around the shoulder of a tween girl. "This is my niece, Alisha. Tonight's our monthly date."

"Hi." The cute brunette greeted me, then turned to smile worshipfully at her uncle.

"It's nice to meet you, Alisha," I said.

A throat cleared, several times.

"Oh." I gestured vaguely. "These are my friends, Tasha and Raquel." I didn't clarify very well, hoping he wouldn't remember who was who and ask for Tasha's phone number. Jesse shook each of their hands and exchanged pleasantries. I watched closely for signs that he lingered over Tasha's fingers. Satisfied that he didn't, I grinned at him. "We're playing laser tag. Want to join us?"

Jesse looked to his niece.

Alisha wrinkled her nose. "Only *boys* play laser tag."

I flung a hand in the air. "That's exactly what I tried to tell them."

Alisha stared at Tasha and Raquel then shook her head at me. "Sorry they tricked you into laser tag."

Jesse laughed and squeezed her shoulder. "Guess that means no. Hopefully we'll see you later." He gave me one more slow smile before turning with his niece towards the skating rink.

We all watched them walk away. Tasha gave a low whistle. "You have been holding out on me. From dry spell of the century to two fine men after you."

I shook my head. "Jesse isn't after me. He's never even hinted he wants to take me out." I glanced quickly at her. "But that doesn't mean *you* have a green light."

Tasha smacked her lips. "Honey, I've never seen a man less interested in me than that wowzer of a specimen."

I studied her closer, not sure if I trusted her to not compete. "He's a plastic surgeon."

Her perfectly arched brows lifted. "Hmm, maybe I'd better try harder."

My eyes narrowed. *Negative info, negative info.* "His entire upper body is covered with tattoos."

Tasha licked her lips. "I'm drooling here. You know I love a good tat."

"It's not just one. You can't even see his original skin color."

She clucked her tongue. "He's got bad boy, rich honey written all over him. *Loving* the possibilities," She rolled the L with a look that I knew had years of experience convincing men to fall for her.

I clenched a fist, trying to think of something to dissuade her.

Raquel stepped between us. "Enough slobbering over Jesse. It's our turn to play."

The front desk kid escorted us towards a darkened waiting area and started fitting vests on us and dishing out instructions I didn't pay attention to.

"Why are we playing laser tag?" I asked. "Isn't this something little boys do for birthday parties?"

As if to prove my point a gang of boys burst through the dark curtain screaming and pointing.

"I killed you like twenty times."

"Oh, yeah, then why do I have 6800 points and you only have 1900?"

"The stupid corner things got me. I would've won."

"Ah-loser."

The boys put their finger and thumb on their forehead and all started to scream, "Loser, loser."

I tilted my head towards the invigorated young men and lifted my palm toward Tasha. "To prove my point."

"You've never played laser tag?" she asked.

"You seem to keep forgetting I'm an adult."

"A boring adult." Tasha shoved me into the darkened room with white lights that lit up my button down white shirt like a billboard. *Shoot me, shoot me*, my shirt shouted.

"You're going to love it," Raquel yelled behind me, squeezing her trigger repeatedly.

My vest buzzed. I looked down at my gun, it wasn't working anymore. "Hey."

Raquel giggled and raced past me. "Gotcha." She pointed at some target in the corner, pumped another round into the green neon circle, and activated an annoying siren. "Don't let those things get you, remember?" Then she was gone.

No, I didn't remember. I hadn't paid one bit of attention to the instructions. The red light on my gun registered again. I looked around and called, "El? Tash?"

My jacket buzzed and my gun went dead. I gave myself whiplash trying to find one of my backstabbing friends. I whirled around and realized the target had zapped me.

"A thousand negative points," Tasha called out as she sailed past me, shot the target, and went into hiding behind one of the dozens of fluorescent-lit poles.

"Dangit." I ran to hide behind a pole and waited for my gun to regain power. It flashed red and I decided enough was enough. I went berserk. Sprinting between safety posts, my finger pumped so quickly I could hardly see which targets I hit. I screamed and dove and giggled when they hit me. After a few minutes I realized Tasha was right. "This is fun," I yelled.

I saw Raquel dodging in front of me. Firing pell-mell, with no hint of aiming, I heard my gun say, "Good hit."

"Woo-hoo," I yelled. "I got you. I got you!"

I flew off to find Tasha, shooting some things on the wall for extra points.

Tasha ran towards me. I shot her, cackling when my gun confirmed the hit. She didn't run away.

"Raquel's down," she screamed.

"I know. I shot her a second ago."

"No." Tasha grabbed my arm and pulled me with her.

"Hey," I protested. "You can't pull me into some ambush. Be a good loser. I am kicking some serious bum here."

Tasha stared at me, her eyes wide. "Cassie. Raquel's in trouble. She's on the ground. She's hurt."

It finally sunk in. "No." I stopped resisting and ran alongside my friend, ripping off my vest and dropping my gun. "Where is she?"

"Over here."

We rounded a corner and saw Raquel's dark shape. She knelt behind a post, both hands cradling her stomach. I dropped to the ground. "El? What's going on? What happened?"

She looked up at me. "I don't know. I pulled something. I'm cramping and . . ." She grimaced. "I feel like something's coming out."

My insides gelled. "From down there?" I pointed below her rounded stomach.

Raquel nodded.

"Fluid or . . . ?"

"Fluid," she confirmed.

I grabbed her arm. "We've got to get you to a doctor."

She groaned in pain but let me slip off her vest and lift her from the floor. I wrapped my arm around her waist and ushered her out of the darkened playing field. Jesse and his niece were hovering over a video game in their roller skates.

"Jesse," I cried out.

He whipped around, studied Raquel clutching her abdomen then refocused on me. "The baby?"

I nodded.

Jesse flung his roller skates off. "Alisha, go get our shoes and meet me at the front door." He hurried to my side. "What happened?"

I elevated one shoulder. "She's cramping and bleeding."

Jesse swept Raquel into his arms. Tasha and I rushed to keep up with him. We burst through the double doors. I looked down at Jesse's stocking feet. He didn't seem to care he was ruining a pair of socks.

Jesse glanced at me. "Cassidy, reach into my back pocket and get my keys."

I flushed with embarrassment, unable to ignore the surge of excitement as I fished in Jesse's pocket for the keys.

"Having fun there?" Tasha asked.

I glared at her, pulled the keys out, and clicked the unlock button. A tan Denali lit up a few cars away. I should've known he'd have a sweet ride.

Jesse loaded Raquel into the front seat. Tasha and I climbed into the back. I handed over his keys, feeling another thrill as our fingers brushed. Alisha ran to us, climbed in back, and tossed Jesse's shoes over the console.

"Thanks, Lish." He slipped his shoes on without tying them, yanked the vehicle into gear, and floored it out of the parking lot. "Are you having pain?" he asked Raquel.

She nodded, bending forward and clutching at her stomach. "Cramping."

"How far along are you?"

"Twenty-eight weeks."

Jesse dialed into his cell phone and demanded, "I need Celeste." Seconds later, he said, "Celeste, this is Doctor . . ." He glanced at me, cleared his throat, and then gave a forced chuckle. "Yeah. You know who I am. Hey, I'm bringing someone in. She's 28 weeks, hemorrhaging, and cramping. Back door? I owe you. I know, the list is long." He hung up the phone. I wondered who Celeste was.

Within minutes we barreled into the emergency room parking lot. Jesse jerked the SUV to a stop by a door that said, "Authorized Personnel Only." He ran around to unload Raquel. "Will you park my car and meet us inside, Cassidy?"

"Of course." I'd do anything he asked. It only took a minute for Tasha, Alisha, and I to rush into the emergency room waiting area, but the glowering receptionist would not let us see Raquel.

"B-but," I stuttered. "I'm her sister."

The girl tossed her highlighted mane. "Please wait over there, ma'am." She pointed towards a row of uncomfortable-looking chairs. Her maroon nails had dragon stickers on them. "I will let you know when I have some information."

After I called Jared, Tasha and I paced the open area praying for good news. Alisha sat down and thumbed through People Magazine, a bored girl stuck in a hospital waiting room with strangers.

I gnawed at my thumbnail. All I could think about was the baby. Jared and Raquel wanted him so badly. Heck, I hated to have it be all about me, but I wanted the little one too. He had to be okay. He just had to.

Fifteen minutes after we got there, Jared burst through the sliding glass doors.

"Cassie," he yelled.

Twenty people turned to glare. He didn't seem to care. I ran to him. Jared grabbed me, jerking me into a fierce hug. "Is she okay?"

I shrugged helplessly. "I don't know."

He nodded. "Thanks for taking care of her." He squeezed me again. "Where is she?"

I pointed to the double doors. "They won't let you in."

Jared's face hardened. "See if they can stop me."

The doors swung open. Jesse stood framed in them. Jared released me and stormed towards the doors. He rushed past Jesse and into the emergency room as the receptionist's painted-on mouth twisted in panic. "You can't go in there."

Jesse walked to her desk. "It's all right, Donna."

The girl smiled and licked her lips. "If you say so, doctor."

Jesse reassured her for a bit too long. She was grinning like he'd asked her to the Doctor's Masquerade Ball by the time Jesse strode to my side.

"Is the baby okay?" I ignored my jealousy in the face of some-thing more important.

Jesse nodded. "The heartbeat is strong. They're trying to determine what caused the cramping and blood loss. They're testing her now to see if she lost any amniotic fluid."

"B-but Raquel and the baby are okay?" The tremor in my voice echoed throughout the waiting room.

Jesse smiled softly at me. "Raquel and the baby are both doing great."

I sniffed. Jesse opened his arms. I ignored Tasha's raised eyebrow and fell. Clinging to him, I savored his musky scent. "Thank you for rescuing me, again."

Jesse chuckled. "It's becoming a habit."

"Maybe I could pay you back somehow."

He leaned close to me and whispered in my ear, "This is what friends do. Besides, fishing for my keys was payment enough."

I hid my face in his chest to hide my reddened cheeks. Loving the feel of him. Comfort and so much more. This spot was becoming a sanctuary.

Week Six

The next week I went through Jesse withdrawal. Neither he nor Damon appeared on the road. My only excitement—Elizabeth. Her bouncing tread approached me from behind early Monday morning. Hot Redhead sprinted to my side then slowed her pace to match mine. I tried to outrun her, I swear, but she wasn't enough of a threat to increase my adrenaline. Especially when compared to Muscle Man. If I thought it was Muscle Man I would be sprinting and digging the pepper spray out of my sports bra.

"Hi, Cassie," Elizabeth sang out.

My head swiveled to look at her in the murky pre-dawn. "Wow. We're happy this morning. That's a surprise."

Her perfect pout tilted up. "Why shouldn't I be?"

"I don't know." I shrugged. "The race on Saturday was fun, huh?"

I caught a momentary scowl but it was there and gone before I could comment on it.

"I know something about you that's going to make Damon want to keep his distance," Elizabeth said with a smirk.

It was my turn to scowl. "You got nothing on me, chickie."

Hot Redhead pumped her eyebrows. "Oh, I don't?" Every word she spoke was like a song. I hated the lilt of her sweet soprano.

"So what do you think you can blackmail me with?" I chuckled to show how out of whack she was, at the same time searching my brain for some stupid move I'd accomplished lately.

Elizabeth paused to share her fake grin. I waited, wondering what she thought she could say to Damon that would keep him away from me. The thought twisted my gut. Even though I wanted to become more than friends with Jesse, I enjoyed dating Damon. I didn't need her sabotaging it.

Elizabeth didn't leave me in agony for long. "What about the fact that you urinated on yourself Saturday morning?"

I gasped, but covered it quickly. Staring at the dark road flowing under our feet, I said, "What are you spouting about now?"

"I thought you'd gone nuts after the race. I could not figure out why you would jump in that stream, but then it hit me." She waited until I squinted at her before sharing a haughty grin. "Your shorts and legs were wet before you went for the stream. When you bent down to take off your shoes." She held her nose. "You stunk. I thought at first it was sweat, but nobody sweats that much—especially when it couldn't have been over seventy."

"You can't prove anything," I said. What would Damon think? Who would he believe?

"Your face will be all the proof I need."

"So what?" I challenged, anger overcoming my fear. "Damon is impressed with how hard I push. How many runners can claim they've kicked it hard enough to pee on themselves?"

Elizabeth's eyebrows arched. "Why would anyone *want* to claim that?" She raced around me and called over her shoulder, "Have a good run, try not to have an accident."

I shook a fist at her retreating back. Like I peed on myself daily. I felt like the little kid who gets caught wearing her grandma's Depends at a sleepover and no, that never happened to me.

I watched Elizabeth prance down the semi-lit road. I knew she was right. Urinating down your own legs was nothing for any woman to brag about. Hot Redhead quickly disappeared from my view. Dang her.

Nana and Tasha both waited for Damon to appear Saturday night. I sat between them on the couch, uncomfortable, ready to be saved by my date. I hoped he'd still want to date me when Elizabeth revealed my bladder problems. What if she had already? My brain spun with excuses and funny comebacks. I couldn't let Hot Redhead make Damon think I had the urinary control of an infant.

Nana's knitting needles flew with her fingers. She pulled a length of yarn and said, "When are you going to stop this running nonsense?"

I stared from her to Tasha. This was why Nana wasn't sitting in her chair. This was why Tasha wasn't out flirting with some man. This was why they'd sandwiched me. "Who says it's nonsense?" I asked. I gave her an indignant, picked-on look. I could have sworn Nana had given approval. That she knew one of the reasons I was doing this marathon was so my dead parents could have a reason to brag about me to their angel buddies.

Nana shook her head and kept knitting. "I don't want you to get hurt. You've had passions before, but none of them were dangerous to your health."

"Dangerous to my health?" I asked, shifting the ice pack I held against my knee underneath the couch cushions.

Nana pointed at the ice pack with her needle but said nothing.

"Come on, Cass," Tasha piped in. "Damon is interested in you, not the fact that you're running a marathon. You got the guy. It's time to give up the dream."

"I am not doing this for Damon." I jumped to my feet. Rushing to the front window, I pushed the curtain aside and prayed for a low-slung silver car to arrive.

"You're never going to be able to finish this," Nana said. "Just like all those businesses you started. The charities you want to organize. The hobbies you pick up. You never finish anything. Stop now before you waste more time and get seriously injured." She yanked the ice pack from the couch cushions and held it aloft as proof of her argument.

My shoulders rounded. My stomach ached. Was it too much to ask for my loved ones to believe in me? *Wait a minute.* I lifted my head. I'd spent the past week taking care of the one person who never ragged on me, or at least only cussed me with significant cause. "Raquel believes in me."

Tasha snorted. "Raquel believes in the Easter Bunny."

My eyes narrowed. "My parents would be proud of me."

Nana exhaled and closed her eyes. "Raquel is only helping you so you won't injure yourself worse than you already have. Jared thinks the entire thing is nonsense." Setting my future afghan aside, Nana rose and crossed the room. "There are plenty of other things you can do that would make your parents proud, like your new personal training business."

Tasha nodded in agreement then picked at her fingernail polish. She obviously didn't want to be in on this intervention. But nobody said no to Nana. *Except me.* I straightened my shoulders.

"Tasha was right. You obviously started this for Damon." Nana pointed out the front window. Damon strode confidently up our walk. The sight of him was like a stone in my stomach instead of a flutter. What would he think if I gave up? What would Jesse think if I gave up?

"He likes you for you, Cassie," Nana said, patting me on the arm. "You don't have to kill your body to impress him."

I shook off her hand and looked down my nose at her. "I'm *not* doing this for him and I'm *not* giving up."

Nana stared at me, pursing her lips. "We'll see," she muttered.

The doorbell rang. I rushed to it and slipped out before Damon could say hello to my naysayers.

He gave me a quick hug. "You look beautiful. How are the legs?"

I put on a brave smile, cursing Nana for starting my date with a negative feeling. "Twenty more ice packs, a hundred more shots of Ibuprofen, and they should be golden."

Damon chuckled. "Always the truth with you."

Wrapping his long arm around my waist, Damon escorted me to the car. I wondered who I was being honest with. Was I really as tough as I portrayed to Damon or was I a loser who would quit like Nana had prophesied?

Week Seven

Creeping down the slight bank of the river that ran through Smithfield Canyon, I was impressed with myself. I'd finally grown a brave bone. My idea to recreate a scene that gave me almost as many nightmares as Panetti chasing me with a knife was idiotic, but the possibility of the murder never being solved grated on me.

I reached the spot where I'd found the body that fateful race day and just stood there. The police caution tape had been removed weeks ago. As far as I knew, my detective buddies had seen no progress on the case. Why did I think I could help?

My legs started to tremble as the memory of the man invaded my brain. I sank onto my knees to avoid running away. Someone had killed that man and taken his identity. I was sure of it. Maybe if I could remember something about the body, besides his gouged-out head, it would spark some memory and I could give the policemen some kind of clue.

I stared at the spot I'd found him, reliving the awful moment when I had turned the body over. Fighting back a wave of queasiness, I bit the side of my tongue. It was all I could do to not start screaming again. *Look past the face. Look past the face.* I could see long, lean arms poking out of a T-shirt, but that was it. I couldn't tell how tall the man was, what color of hair he had, or anything else about him.

I closed my eyes, wishing I hadn't willingly let the memories come. Now I couldn't shut them out.

Twigs cracked. A bird flitted away. My eyes popped open. I jumped to my feet, ready to sprint for safety.

Jesse held out his hands defensively. "It's okay, Cassidy. It's just me."

His eyes were dark chocolate and oozing concern, but I wasn't in the mood to be rescued. He crossed a couple more feet. I backed away, thumping into a scratchy pine tree.

Jesse stopped, watching me warily for several seconds before asking, "Are you all right?"

I shook my head.

"What are you doing here?" His tender voice and broad shoulders exuded the need to shelter me.

I wrapped my arms around my stomach, wishing I didn't want his protection so badly. Who was he? The good-looking bad boy or the kind-eyed plastic surgeon? "I could ask the same of you."

"I saw you from the road."

My stomach lurched. I swiveled my gaze to the lush vegetation: bushes, weeds, pine and aspen trees. It was impossible to see the road from here. A quiver of fear shot through me. How could a man be so attractive and so unsettling at the same time?

"Are you following me?" I demanded.

Jesse grinned and the attractive factor shot above my unease. "It isn't the first time."

Unsettling and attractive were now battling. Was I just being paranoid? I had plenty of reasons to be. I clutched my hands behind me, the poky pine needles embedded into my palms. "Who are you really?"

He cocked an eyebrow. "Excuse me?"

"You seem like this nice, good-looking, smart guy, but no way are you just showing up every time I need you." I jabbed a finger at him. "You're following me, and," my voice quivered as I produced a lie, "I don't like it."

Jesse's lower lip protruded slightly. He jammed a hand through his dark hair. I felt like such a jerk. I took several steps towards him. A soft breeze brought his musky scent to me. "Okay," I said, "so maybe I like it, but you've got to understand why I'm a bit freaked out."

Those eyes met mine. Everything in me melted.

"I feel like . . ." Jesse crossed the remaining distance between us. The way he held me with his eyes incapacitated me. Reaching out, he brushed those wonderfully calloused fingers down my cheek. "I'm very protective of you, Cassidy."

I gulped, loving his touch, yet still terrified by his words. "Why do you need to be protective of me?"

Jesse's hand dropped. He studied a grove of aspen trees. "I can't tell you."

Shivers radiated throughout my body. Who was he? What did he know that I didn't? Was he in league with Muscle Man and Greasy Beanpole or was he safeguarding me from them? I didn't dare ask. I wasn't sure I wanted to know.

Jesse stroked my arm. "Please don't be afraid. I'll make sure you're okay."

"You promise?" I yearned to believe he could protect me if Muscle Man returned. His brown eyes caressed me. I held my breath, praying for the right words.

Jesse exhaled slowly and said, "I'll do my best."

He was physically and mentally strong, but still Jesse couldn't promise to protect me. The disappointment was bitter, but somehow I knew he was giving me all he could. I was actually grateful he hadn't given me an empty promise. Jesse would do his best and it was all I could hope for right now.

I allowed myself to enjoy his touch and gaze for a moment before sidestepping around him. As much as I wanted to trust him, I still wasn't sure why he wanted to protect me or if he was good or bad. The warm look in his dark eyes was too tempting. The only thing I was sure of—I couldn't trust myself to be alone with him right now. I was milliseconds away from throwing myself against his chest and begging him to stay with me every moment.

I scurried up the incline, but had to look one more time. Jesse watched me. I ran. The only other choice was to leap into his arms.

"Are you sure you're supposed to be riding the bike this far?"

Raquel's legs rotated slowly so she could stay next to me while I ran. She'd volunteered to ride next to me, keeping me company for a few miles of my long run. She pushed back on the handlebars, adjusting on her padded seat. "Sure I'm sure. My doctor said light cardio would be good for me. It's been weeks and we haven't seen any more blood."

"But doesn't the bike hurt . . . down there?"

"Not too bad. Jared put an extra-soft seat on for me and the baby is doing fabulous. Stop worrying."

I smiled, settling into a steady rhythm of steps. "Glad to hear it. Maybe I can stop doing your dishes."

Raquel laughed. "I wish you and Jared could relax that much. So, have you seen Jesse lately? I sure like him."

I swallowed. Unfortunately I liked him more than I should and who knew if he actually liked me or was just "protecting me."

"He's been busy," I muttered.

There was silence for a few minutes before she asked, "How was your date with Damon Saturday?"

"The date was great." I concentrated on the road. "It would've been better if Nana and Tasha hadn't tried to sabotage it before I left."

Raquel's eyes burned into the side of my cheek. I studied the well-kept homes and lawns that eased past us.

"Nana and Tasha are in league again? Last time they got together they talked you out of traveling to South America to volunteer in orphanages."

The bright morning sun crested the roofline of the house we were using for shade. I squinted and groaned. "How did I let them do that? I was all set up and excited to go."

"It was a month after your parents died."

I stared at the road. She would have to bring that up.

Raquel sighed. "What are they giving you a hard time about now?"

The blacktop swam underneath me. "Nana claims that you and Jared don't think I'll finish the marathon either."

"What? Why would we say that?"

"I don't know. Well, I could see Jared saying it, but I thought you said you were proud of me. That my parents would be proud of me."

"Yes, I did, and yes, they would. Hell-freeze, Nana," Raquel mumbled something else, probably a swear word I wouldn't approve of. "Your grandma always has to manipulate everything for herself. Is she upset because your knee is hurting or can she seriously not stand for you to succeed?"

"Something like that." I kicked at some loose stones on the road as I shuffled by. In her own twisted way Nana had my best interests at heart. "Come on, El. Tell me the truth. Does Jared really believe in me?"

The uncomfortable silence gave me all the answer I needed. I sniffed, increasing my leg speed. This was supposed to be a slow, long-distance run but I needed some space.

Raquel caught me in seconds with her bike. "You know what a Papa Bear Jared is. How much he worries about you. He'll be really proud of you when you cross that finish line." She arched over her handlebars to peer at my face. "Are you tearing up on me?"

I turned away. "The leaves on that poplar tree are huge."

Raquel snorted. "Honey. It's okay to be mad at your family. Nana, Jared, Tasha. I know, Tasha's been your best friend since you used to wear Depends to sleepovers."

I cringed, why did Tasha have to share that with everybody?

"But all of them act like jerks once in a while," Raquel continued. "I know they're all trying to take care of you, protect you from yourself, but you're a tough lady, Cassie. You can handle things on your own. You could've handled South America and you can definitely handle this marathon."

I mulled over her little pep talk. "You think they're trying to protect me because of Mom and Dad dying?"

Raquel shrugged and nodded at the same time. "Sure. It's not like you've screwed up your whole life. It's just been since your parents' deaths that you . . ." Her voice trailed off. Her high cheekbones turned crimson.

"Since I stopped believing in myself," I muttered. "Which makes a bit of sense if you think about it because with Mom and Dad gone, who do I have besides you? Jared, Nana, and Tasha don't give me much reason to believe in myself."

Raquel sighed. "They think they're helping. I know Jared just worries about you and doesn't know how to show it."

I ignored that because I knew it was true and we both knew there was nothing we could do to change it. "Do you think Mom and Dad are really dead?"

Raquel's head whipped around so fast she smacked herself with her ponytail. "What?"

"Never mind." I brushed my hand through the air and increased my pace. I had to be careful what I said. What if Raquel got the truth out of me? She claimed I was tough, but really I was just terrified. If she knew about Muscle Man's threats she'd tell Jared and make me call Detective Fine and Shine. I refused to tell them. They couldn't find the faceless man's murderer and they definitely couldn't protect me if Muscle Man came back. I shivered in the morning air.

"What kind of a question is that?" Raquel asked.

"How do you think they get those begonias so big?" I pointed to a well-kept yard bursting with flowerbeds and greenery. The pink and red begonias ruled over marigolds and petunias.

"Honey, we all saw the pictures and read the tributes from the villagers who buried them. I'm sorry they're gone, but there's nothing we can do about that."

"I know. It's just . . ." I turned my head again. "Oh, I love the smell of pine trees. When I have my own house I'm planting a whole forest of pine trees in my backyard."

"Are we going to talk about it?"

"Don't you love the, feel of the air on summer mornings? Refreshing yet still warm." At least all this talking was making the miles go fast.

Raquel sighed. "Okay. I get it. I can only talk to you about your family until I hit your uncomfortable button. But you listen to me for a second. Yes, your mom and dad are gone, but you still have people who love you. Nana, Tasha, Jared, Tate, me. Especially me. Obviously, I adore your brother and think he's terrific, but he can be a beast too. He doesn't know how to take care of you *and* enjoy being your brother."

I tilted my head to the side, really listening. I seldom gave Jared enough credit. He was the overbearing big brother who thought he had to be my parent now.

"You don't have to fulfill Nana or Jared's prophecies about you or let them hold you back," Raquel said. "But like I said earlier, they're just trying to protect you."

"From doing something great?" I couldn't help but respond.

"I don't know what they're trying to protect you from, but there is definitely some internal need for Jared to keep you safe. I can't psychoanalyze everybody, just you." She smiled then her face sobered. "Maybe they're trying to give you an excuse to quit."

I scowled at her. My legs churned through the distance and my head ached from withheld tears. How could I get Nana and my brother to stop coddling me and believe I could succeed? "Why would they do that?"

"Well, even you admit you've started some things in the past couple of years that haven't panned out like we all hoped.

Maybe they want you to blame them for quitting the marathon instead of blaming yourself."

I turned and stared at her. "That is nuts."

She grinned. "It's your family we're talking about. Nuts is normal." Her grin disappeared. "But they're wrong this time. You're dedicated. You're going to make it." Her long legs rotated, pushing and pulling on the pedals. She tossed her highlighted ponytail over her shoulder. "You will make your parents proud. I can just see them cheering in heaven."

I swiped at my face before she could see how her words struck me. Pressing my lips together for a few seconds I was finally able to respond, "Thanks, El. I love you like my own blood."

"Back at ya." Raquel's legs flew into triple speed. "Race ya to the next block," she yelled.

I laughed with relief and flew after her.

Damon and I walked to Nana's front porch late Saturday night. Well, he walked and I tried not to waddle. My legs were a waste of muscle and bone. I'd finally agreed to go on another training run with Damon, Trevor, and Joe because it felt safer than running alone. Fifteen miles. Fifteen.

At least the hills had been minimal this time and I'd managed to run the route without passing out or urinating on myself. Tonight Damon had taken me to a movie, for which I was grateful until I had to get up and move again.

Damon smirked at my obviously uncomfortable stride. "I can't believe you're already sore from this morning."

"Don't flatter yourself. It's an accumulation of a week's worth of damage."

He reached for my hand, giving it a squeeze. "Make sure you stretch tonight, or it'll be worse tomorrow."

I groaned, leaning closer to him. "Thanks for the encouragement. How could it possibly be worse?"

"Don't stretch and you'll see."

We stopped under the glaring porch light. "Aren't you a ray of sunshine," I muttered.

Damon smiled innocently. His eyes traveled across my face. The smile slowly disappeared as he focused on my mouth. I knew what was going to happen, but did I want it to happen? All night long I couldn't stop thinking of Jesse. The way it felt when he touched me. His dark eyes. His declaration that he wanted to protect me. Him warning me away from the "redhead".

Damon wrapped his large palms around my back.

I leaned around him and peered through the glass sidelight.

He arched a brow. "Problem?"

I chuckled nervously. "Wanted to make sure Nana wasn't watching."

"Uh-huh," he murmured, his eyes focused on my mouth.

I studied his perfect face inches from my own. "Poor Nana," I said. "You know how she worries about me. I know it's kind of mean to deny her a show, but some things have got to be private, like my first kiss in a year."

Damon's eyes opened. He backed up an entire foot. His hands stayed awkwardly on my back. "A year?"

Did I *really* just say that? "Well, um, maybe it hasn't been that long."

He grinned and shook his head, bringing his hands back to his sides. "That's . . . sad."

My blush deepened. At least he knew I wasn't a player. "Well, it depends on your perspective. It shouldn't be sad for you because you get to be the person to remedy it."

"I do?"

I teetered and had to lean against the house for support. "I, uh, was hoping so."

Damon nodded, brushing a lock of hair off my cheek. I grabbed his hand, refusing to lose this moment. Damon pulled my hand around his shoulder then returned his fingers to gently stroking my cheek. "Then this is definitely good news for me," he said.

I giggled. *How embarrassing.* "Yes, definitely good news for you. Sad news for all those other boys who tried and failed. But look at you. Here you are."

Damon's fingers slid into my hair. With gentle pressure he brought my face within centimeters of his. "Here I am," he whispered.

The closer Damon's lips got the quicker my mouth moved. "Yes, you're definitely the lucky one. But then I'm the luckiest one. Both of us are, I believe. Lucky, lucky, lucky."

"Cassie," Damon said, his breath warming my lips like hot cocoa on a snowy day. He was that close to me. I fought the urge to scream that I wasn't ready to kiss him and laugh with sheer delight.

"What?" I asked.

"Shut up."

I laughed. "I guess I deserve that after telling you to shut up on our first run."

"Now," he said.

"Right now?"

I watched his lips cover the last few centimeters. The instant of contact was better than anything I'd experienced in longer than a year. The spice of his cologne. The warm night surrounding us. His arms caressing my back. His firm lips demanding a response. I pictured his brown eyes, the way his dark hair curled around his ear, and his cheek crinkling when he smiled.

Oh, no! How could I be thinking of Jesse while kissing Damon? I tried to clear the image but couldn't do it. Pulling away, I caught small, quick breaths.

Damon leaned back and stared at me. "You okay?"

I wrapped my arms around my waist. "Fine, thanks."

Damon's eyes darkened to midnight. He jammed a hand through his short hair. "Not the usual response to a first kiss."

My head snapped up. "There was nothing wrong with the kiss." There was something wrong with me.

"I'm sorry, Cassie. I was under the assumption that you were interested in me."

"Interested?" I guffawed. "Of course I'm interested. What lipstick-wearing, romance-reading female wouldn't be interested in you? The kiss was amazing."

Damon's lips split into a grin. "You *did* like it?"

"Of course I liked it." I had liked it. Damon was real. Damon was here. Maybe if we tried again. "Just slow down next time."

"I thought I went pretty slow the first time." His eyes twinkled. "But you're telling me there's going to be a next time?"

I sidled closer to him. "Yeah."

"When is this next time going to happen?"

"I thought within the next half-second would be good."

"The next half-second?"

I grinned at him. "Shut up and kiss me already."

Damon chuckled. "Hey, that's my line."

I grabbed him and pressed my lips to his, praying this time I could concentrate on the right man.

Week Eight

Slipping some clogs onto my feet, I was out the door before I remembered my grandmother. I hurried to the entry of her bedroom and called through the open doorway, "Nana, I'm going to help Raquel for a while."

She banged on the door of her master bath. "I'm in here."

"I guessed that." I leaned into the doorjamb, tapping my short nails against the grainy wood. "Do you need anything while I'm out? I could run to the store after I leave Raquel's."

"No. You always buy too much lettuce and junk. I'll go tomorrow. Would you bring in the mail though? I hate that slobbery Phillips' dog yapping at me every time I get it."

"Okay." Utah's summers may be dry, but I still began to sweat twenty seconds after my forehead hit the sunshine.

I grabbed the mail from the box, inhaling the scent of the neighbor's rose bushes and ignoring their yipping puppy. I shuffled through the mail as I raced back to the coolness of the front porch. Credit card offers. Letter from Nana's sister. Scary. Aunt Ella was almost ornerier than Nana. Electricity bill. A letter for me?

I stopped next to the screen door, examining the white envelope. No return address. Postmarked in Mexico City. My heart leapt a few inches in my chest. Mom and Dad had been killed in Mexico City.

I dropped the rest of the mail onto the porch swing and ripped the envelope open. Inside was a single typed sheet.

Dear Cassidy,

Didn't want you to think I had forgotten about you. Thank you for helping us trap your father. Don't forget the promise you made to me. You will tell no one about our meeting.

If anything goes wrong. If your father has any indication that we are waiting for him, you know who I'm coming after. What fun that will be.

Hoping to see you again,

Muscle Man

P.S. I like the nickname you gave me.

I read the note several times. My fingers trembled so horribly I could barely make out the words on the last reading. Muscle Man. Checking in to renew his threats. I shivered. At least he was in Mexico. Hopefully. I looked at the postmark. Four days ago. He could be here now. Would he really come for me?

My gut clenched. Sweat ran down my chest. I wiped more wetness from my forehead and clutched the letter until it crumpled.

Should I tell Detective Shine and Fine? What could they do besides refer me to the FBI? The last FBI agents we'd dealt with had chalked my parents' deaths up to the unrest in Mexico. They wouldn't believe me if I said I had proof of the man who'd killed my father. They wouldn't do anything to protect the poor man that Muscle Man was hunting. All I'd accomplish by squealing to the police or FBI was Muscle Man fulfilling his threats. My entire body shuddered. I had to be more careful what I said. What if Nana or Raquel suspected something had happened?

"Cassidy?" Nana yelled. "What did you get in the mail? Some love letter from Damon?"

I folded the note and envelope and shoved them in my back pocket. Pushing through the front door, I handed Nana the rest of the mail. "Nothing too exciting," I said.

Nana eyed me suspiciously from her chair. "What about that letter you were gooing over on the front porch?"

"Letter?" *Gooing?* She completely misinterpreted my expression. Dying. Trembling in fear. Definitely not gooing.

"I saw you reading some letter. Who was it from? Why are you so flushed? Go get a drink of water then I want some explainin'."

134

I rushed into the kitchen, guzzled a cool glass of water and splashed some on my face.

"Get in here," Nana called, "and tell me who that letter was from."

I stuttered back to the living room. I was an adult. Nana wasn't getting this letter from me. I wouldn't give Muscle Man any reason to come back.

I faced her squarely, anything less would've caused suspicion. "It was from Thomas Rendenhall. You remember him?"

"That boy you dated who went off to medical school?" She'd resumed clicking needles, another afghan on the assembly line.

"That's right."

"Thomas Rendenhall." Nana harrumphed and clucked her tongue at the same time. "I wasn't a fan. Smart but a bit pompous." She arched an eyebrow. "And not as good-looking as Damon."

"No."

"Or as nice."

"No." But speaking of doctors had me thinking of Jesse instead of Damon. I reddened imagining how Nana would react to him.

Nana's eyes narrowed. "But Thomas may have been smarter. What's Damon do for work?"

I sighed. "I've told you before." When you gave me the "boys just want one thing" lecture before our first date.

Nana's eyes narrowed. "Well tell me again. I'm getting old and senile."

"I wish," I muttered, picking at a loose thread on the afghan hanging on the wooden rocker by the door.

"Speak up, girl, and stop unraveling my work."

My hands snapped to my sides. "Damon is a financial planner. He has clients throughout the country and travels a lot." Even though Nana was grilling me, I started to breathe easier. She was past questioning on the letter and onto lecturing me about mumbling and ruining her afghan.

135

She tilted her head. "Well, that could be good, but not quite as good as a doctor. I love doctors."

I nodded that I knew. Her husband and favorite son had both been renowned surgeons—before Grandpa died of a heart attack and Daddy was murdered. No. I wasn't looking for a doctor. I battled with Jesse's image in my brain. I needed to push him out. No reason to follow family tradition there.

"What did Teddy want? He want you back?"

"Thomas," I corrected then shrugged. "He didn't say. Just trying to keep in touch, I think."

Nana clicked her needle against the wooden armrest of her floral chair. "Well. It's impressive to me that he didn't just Facebook you or something silly like that."

I grinned. "Didn't know you knew what Facebook was."

She swatted with her needle, pulling several stitches out of the afghan. Grunting, she waved me away with the same needle. "Get out of here. You need to go help Raquelly. You coming back for dinner?"

"No. I'll eat with Jared and El."

"Figures," Nana muttered. "You and Raquel can eat your health junk together for all I care."

I hurried from the house, grateful Nana had bought my lie and sick that I was still a part of Muscle Man's memory. The letter in my back pocket burned through my pants to the underlying skin. Was there anything I could do to protect myself?

"I don't look like I've lost a darned pound!"

Damon and I walked out of The Cache Valley Mall towards his car. He needed some new dress shirts for work and I was only too happy to spend time with him. But all the mirrors by the dressing rooms had convinced me that my marathon weight loss was on a plateau. Just five pounds lighter and I'd be content.

Damon cocked his head and let his eyes rove my body. "Why do you want to lose weight?"

"Because I'm too big!"

"I like the way you look." He opened the passenger door and I slid in.

I waited until he settled into his seat before saying, "You like fat women?"

He shrugged. "Guess I do."

"Agh," I grunted. "Way wrong answer."

"What?" Instead of starting the car, he pivoted in his seat to face me.

"You're supposed to convince me of how thin I am. You're supposed to convince me that I don't need to lose a quarter of a pound, let alone a whole one."

A bemused smile crossed his face. He folded his arms over his chest and said, "You know I love this. You explain exactly how it's supposed to be. None of these guessing games, trying to figure out what my woman wants. You lay it all out there for me."

I tingled all over at him calling me *his* woman. Damon was almost too good to be true. He liked my bluntness, what a relief to not have to play stupid dating games. "Well, I'm so glad you like it. Now get to work!"

His eyes twinkled. "Get to work on what?"

"Ugh," I grunted again. "Do I have to always spell it out? You need to convince me how perfect I am." I beckoned him with a hand. "Make it good and gushy now."

Damon laughed. No, laugh isn't strong enough. He cackled. For a full minute. I timed him. That's how annoyed I was. Then he leaned across the console of his car, took me in his arms as best he could, and said, "You're perfect."

I blushed and looked away, forgetting all about my annoyance. "My thighs are too big."

"The most perfect thighs in the world. You should never lose a pound."

"Quarter of a pound," I reminded him.

"You should never lose a quarter of a pound," he said. "Actually, you should gain some weight."

"No, no, no." I leaned back in his embrace. "Now you're pushing it too far. There's a delicate bal—"

His lips cut off my protests. Several minutes later my head was whirling. Damon broke off the kiss and cupped my face with his hand. "Anything else I need to say or do?"

I grinned. "Yeah, kiss me again."

He complied so quickly I forgot about my weight gain.

Yanking weeds out by the fistful, I cringed as another dribble of sweat ran down my back. Normally I did yard work in the morning, but my running schedule messed that up and Nana was getting fed up with the condition of her flowerbeds. "Should make her get out and weed them her own dang self," I muttered.

"Hope I'm not the subject of your angry murmuring," a very masculine voice said from much too close behind me.

I flipped over onto my haunches, staring up into the warmest brown eyes. "Jesse." My sweat production tripled at the smile he bestowed upon me until I remembered that I'd almost put him and my desire to be around him out of my mind the last time I was with Damon. I forced myself to frown. "What do you want?"

Jesse reached out a hand. I couldn't resist placing my hand in his and marveling that I could still tremble from his touch through a dirty glove. He lifted me to my feet then released my hand. Being on his level did nothing to diminish his attractiveness. "I just saw you out in the yard and thought I'd say hi."

I slowly pulled off my garden gloves, tossed them on the ground, and folded my arms in front of me. Defensive stance. That should stop him from smiling at me like that. "I don't like you," I informed him.

His eyes lost their warmth, but the smile stayed in place. His muscled tattoos flexed as he clenched both hands at his sides. "Why not?"

"You show up whenever you want to say 'hi', you claim to be protecting me, yet you never stay around long enough for me to get to know you."

Jesse's brows lifted. His grin reached his gaze again. He tilted his head to the side. "Forgive me?" he asked, wiping a smudge of dirt from my cheek.

I scowled deeper as my cheek hummed from his touch. Just being around him made me want to forgive anything he did wrong for the next twenty years. "I'll forgive you when we start dating."

Jesse slowly shook his head. "Cassidy. I wish I could explain. Each chance I have to see you is great. You make me laugh and you make me . . ." he smiled and winked, but didn't finish his thought. "But I can't be with you right now. If I were able to date you, I would be pounding on your door every night."

Good to know that he actually liked me, but his answer was just confusing. "What kind of a stupid excuse is that?"

He ignored my question and took a step closer. "Are you doing all right? Has anyone bothered you?"

The sun's singeing rays couldn't warm me enough. I shivered, not wanting to dwell on our last conversation, when he'd basically revealed to me that no one could protect me. "N-no."

Jesse studied every inch of my soul. I squirmed and picked at the dirt under my fingernails. It was obvious we were both hiding something. I wished I trusted him enough to ask and tell.

"If you aren't interested in anything happening between us," I whispered, "please leave."

Jesse's warm fingers lifted my chin until I was forced to meet his dark eyes. "I wish things could be different," he said. He took a quick step, bent down, and brushed his lips over mine before I could think to protest. A searing joy shot through my body. My lips felt branded, like I belonged to Jesse and would never be the same if he didn't do that to me continually.

He stepped away, but his eyes held me captive. "I'll see you soon, Cassidy."

I couldn't even formulate a goodbye as he turned and strode away.

"So that's it then," I muttered several minutes later, still standing in the same spot and dreaming of him reappearing. "No promises. No spilling of the guts. Just kisses me and makes me want him then walks away." I fell onto my knees and ferociously attacked the morning glory. I shouldn't have told Jesse I didn't like him. I should've told him the truth. I loathed him.

Discovering the Truth

I danced through Nana's house with a dust rag in one hand and a bottle of Pledge in the other, sweeping dust off surfaces like Cinderella. Nana was at the grocery store and I was under strict instructions to "clean the pigsty without doing a half-A job." Which basically meant I got to turn U2 up loud and spray lots of cleaner-thank heavens for failing eyesight.

"I still haven't found what I'm looking for," I sang along with Bono until I registered the phone ringing through the blaring music. Dashing around each room, I finally spotted the cordless in the kitchen. I grabbed the phone and pushed the talk button. "Hello," I yelled to be heard over the music.

Some words came across the line but I couldn't understand them. I sprinted to the stereo and clicked off the power. "Sorry. The music was too loud. Shall we try that again? Hello. You've reached the Christensen residence. How may I help you this fine day?"

A muffled man's voice demanded, "Who is this?"

Taken aback by the abrupt response to my good humor, I said, "This is Cassidy Christensen. Who the crap is this?"

"C-Cassie," the man stuttered my name with something akin to reverence.

"That's right. I'm Cassie." I lifted some nick-knacks off of a low shelf and swiped my rag across the cherry wood. "With whom am I speaking?"

"Are you all right, Cassie?"

I was so sick of that question. No one could protect me, but everyone wanted to know if I was all right. "Uh-huh. Fabulous. Who *is* this?"

141

"Is your grandmother there?" The man obviously didn't want to reveal himself.

"No, she's at the store." The guy's voice sounded familiar, but I couldn't place it. Then it hit me. "Uncle John?"

"Yes," the voice grew stronger. "This is your Uncle John. How are you, Cassie? Are you truly okay?"

"Not dead yet."

Uncle John inhaled so quickly there was a small snort. I couldn't tell if he laughed or thought I was nuts.

"I've recently taking up running," I informed him. Resting the phone in the crook of my neck I sprayed a side table in the kitchen with Pledge.

"Running? That's wonderful."

Wonderful? The voice sounded like my self-centered uncle, but I'd never heard him call anything wonderful. I attacked the surface with my rag. "Hey, you'd better come see Nana, she's worried about your latest girlfriend choice. Seems the plastic surgery overload raised some concerns about how 'genuine' she is."

"Cassie, are you sure you're okay? No one's tried to hurt you or threaten you?"

My heart slammed into my lungs. I couldn't breathe for a second. Finally, I whispered, "How do you know about that?" I dropped my cleaning supplies onto the table. "Is this really Uncle John?"

"Cassie. I need to know you're safe. What happened? Did the men hurt you?"

How did he know it was men? Did I dare confide in him? What about Muscle Man's threats?

"Please tell me, Cassie. I've been so worried."

Uncle John worried about me? And why did he keep injecting my name into every sentence? I paced the confined kitchen. Finally, I couldn't hold it in any longer. "They made me do some video. They claimed Daddy was still alive and they wanted to trap him or something. Do you know what's going on? Why they would do something like that? It terrified me. I couldn't run outside for weeks. One of the men said they'll come after me again if they don't get this guy they're claiming is my dad."

There was silence on the line.

I gripped the phone until my palm ached. "Uncle John?" My heart beat quick and hard. "Please tell me the truth. Are—" My throat caught. I cleared it and tried again. "Are Mom and Dad still alive?"

"Cassie. Oh, sweetheart."

Suddenly I realized this could not be my uncle. He'd never used a term of endearment with me or anyone else. Come to think of it, he'd never shown much concern for me or anyone else.

My throat scratched. Tears stung at my eyes. I swallowed and ventured, "Dad?"

"Oh, Cassie. I've missed you."

The tears clogged my throat. "It's really you. You're really alive." My heart thumped so hard I feared some arteries would be damaged. "Where's Mom?"

"I need to tell you in person. Don't worry, love. I'm coming to you—"

There was a horrible bang and then his voice cut off. "Dad, Dad!" I yelled. I pressed the phone into my ear. He couldn't really be gone. "Dad," I called over and over again. Only silence answered me.

I clung to the phone, tears streaming down my face.

Had that really been my father? How could I have found my dad and lost him again? I sunk down the kitchen wall to the scarred linoleum. I couldn't stop the wetness pouring from my eyes. Were my parents alive? Could it really be possible? "Daddy," I whispered, cradling the phone against my ear in the hope that he might still be there.

"Cassidy?" Nana's voice came to me through a haze. I pried my eyes open. They were swollen and aching. My cramped fingers slowly released the phone planted against my ear. It was making that annoying screeching sound, "Please hang up and try again, beep, beep, beep."

Nana pulled the phone from me, pushed the end button, and set it on the table. She tugged on my arm. "Cassie? Are you okay? Did you fall?"

I let her drag me to my feet, collapsing against her soft frame. "Oh, Nana."

"Are you hurt?" she demanded.

I shook my head. "No." I took a step back so I could focus on her face as I asked the question. "Nana, what really happened to my parents?"

Nana studied me for a few seconds then turned away and walked to the grocery sacks she must've set on the table while I was comatose.

I followed her, running in front of her so she had to face me. "A month ago two men grabbed me from the street and pulled me into a van. They made me speak into a video camera. They told me they wouldn't hurt me, they were just trying to flush my father out of some remote village in Mexico." It spilled out so easily, a huge burden lifting from my shoulders.

Nana's eyes registered shock but her lips stayed in a pressed line.

"They told me I couldn't tell you or the police and since they haven't come back I had almost forgotten about them until I got a threatening letter the other day. And then while you were at the store the phone rang . . ." I paused, the tears welled up again, choking me.

Nana stepped closer. She gently touched my arm. "Who was on the phone?"

I glanced at her lined face. She knew the truth. I know she did. "I thought it was Uncle John at first, but it wasn't." I took a deep breath and then said it, still unsure if I had imagined it all, "It was my dad."

Nana closed her eyes. Her body swayed. I waited for her to deny my claims. She shook her head and with eyes still pressed shut said, "Why would he call? Why would he risk putting us all in danger?"

I grabbed Nana's arm. When she still didn't open her eyes, I shook her. "Nana! What is going on? My dad's alive? What about Mom?"

Nana's eyes flew open. She stared at me like she wanted to pick me up and rock me to sleep. "I'm sorry, honey. Your mom is gone. The funeral for her was real."

Part of the hope I'd had deflated. I sank into a kitchen chair and buried my face in my arms. I cried for several minutes with Nana patting my back. I'd had such dreams of seeing my mom again. Why had I let myself believe that she may be alive? Dad would've told me. Finally, I raised my eyes. I could barely see through the after-effects of all the sobbing. "But Dad?"

Nana sank into the chair next to me. "He's alive. He's been in hiding to protect all of us, but he's still helping rescue the slaves."

My head shimmied in shock. "Slaves?"

Nana nodded solemnly. "Your dad's been fighting to protect them for years."

"I thought he donated money and medical care to the orphans."

Nana smiled at my naivety.

"How does he protect them?" I asked, not sure if I really wanted to know.

"He frees them." She shook her head sadly. "It's an awful racket. Sometimes the children's own families sell them into slavery or they get tricked into believing they're going to make money for their families. Sometimes the slavers don't waste time with that and just kidnap them outright. Mexico's government is rotten as moldy brussels sprouts, the slavers pay them to look the other way and let the children be exploited. Because your dad was so effective at stopping the slavers, they tried to kill him."

145

"Who killed my mom?"

She couldn't hold my gaze any longer. "Your parents were both shot by a sniper when they left the villages for supplies. Your mom died." She paused to let the words sink in. "Your dad lived. His friend, Sham, was with them and found a way to get their bodies to a safe place. They faked your father's funeral and nursed him back to health. They knew the only way to protect him, and us, was to pretend he was dead."

"You were the only one who knew Dad was alive?"

"Jared and I."

"Oh." So many pieces falling into place: Jared always acting like an overprotective oaf. Nana talking me out of volunteering in South America. But why didn't they tell me? "Couldn't you trust me?"

"It wasn't like that." She shook her head. "The less people who knew the better and who knew how long your dad would survive? Once we found out he'd made it, Jared and I decided we couldn't put you through losing him twice." Nana rolled her neck, pressing her fingers to her forehead and staring through me. "I can't believe they know he's alive. Did he expose himself? How would they figure out it was him?" She sighed and dug her fingers into the sagging skin that formed her eyelids. "There will be a huge price on his head. Panetti and Ramirez want him dead for so many reasons. Oh, Cassie, you should've told me someone was after him. I could've warned him."

Panetti? The name brought dark memories. The guy still visited my nightmares. "How could you warn him? Muscle Man acted like the only way to flush Dad out of hiding was by this video he made. He said that he could kill Dad if he could lure him to a spot where he could call me." My heart sank. The phone cutting off. I gripped the edge of the table for support. "Oh, no. Oh, Nana." I swallowed hard. "Our call was cut short. What if Muscle Man got him? What if he's already dead?"

Nana's soft hands wrapped around my forearms. "Who is Muscle Man?"

146

"The dude who forced me to make that videotape. He told me he just needed to trick Dad into making a phone call and he could capture him. He said that he was assigned to kill Dad the first time and he would stay dead this time. I don't think he was bluffing. The dude was terrifying." I gnawed at my lip. My eyes clouded over again. "Oh, Nana. What if Muscle Man got him and Daddy is truly dead this time?"

Nana's arms came around me. "Don't worry." But her voice sounded very worried. "Sham will protect him. What did your dad tell you to do?"

"I barely realized it was him before the phone cut off, but he told me to stay put. He said he was coming here."

She tossed her head. "No. He mustn't come here. They know he's alive." Her hands trembled on my back. "Anyone could target him here."

"Nana, what are we going to do?"

"You're going to do what your dad told you and stay put. I'm going to use the contacts your dad told me only to use in an emergency." Her lips formed a thin line. "Sham will know what to do."

"Who is Sham?"

Nana's lips came up. "The only man I know who's tougher than your daddy."

Al stared down at the man pinned between him and Terry. It had been too easy. Nathan Christensen was so focused on talking to his daughter he hadn't even noticed their approach. Al knocked him unconscious. He and Terry hoisted the doctor between them and scurried off toward the designated kill spot.

147

It would've been even better if Al could've just put a bullet in Doc's head and left him to rot, but he had to wait. He wouldn't kill him until the first half of the payment was in his bank account. Then Al and Terry would drive the body to Acapulco or they wouldn't get the second installment. Apparently Mr. Ramirez wanted to make sure Nathan Christensen didn't come back from the dead a second time.

Al could see their shack. Only a few more yards to safety. Terry had made sure they were well prepared—getaway van, refrigerated box to transport the remains in, a computer with internet connection to confirm they had the doc and make sure they received the first half of their payment before they gave away their leverage.

Terry banged the door open. The trio shuffled through. Al slammed the door behind them and dropped Nathan in the dirt. Terry grabbed his digital camera, shot several angles of the unconscious man's face and then hurried to the computer to download the pictures. Al fidgeted. They had to be done and gone before Doc's large African friend came back from the marketplace.

"Ready?" he asked. Terry nodded. Al hit send on the pictures and wiped away a trickle of sweat.

An instant messenger popped up on his screen. *Is Nathan dead already?*

Al typed quickly. *Not dead, unconscious. As soon as I have confirmation of the first million in my account I will plug him and deliver what's left to you.*

The words appeared on his screen. *Check your account. The money is already there.*

"Terry," Al's voice pitched up several octaves, excitement coursed through him. "Is it true?"

Terry moved into Al's spot, punched some keys, and after a few seconds nodded. "One million dollars confirmed." He pounded Al on the shoulder, backing away.

148

Al grinned. He turned to type a response to their sponsor.

"One million *dollars*," Terry celebrated by his side, staring at the computer screen over Al's shoulder. "And another mill once they get the body. Tell Mr. Ramirez that we love work—" There was a loud thud.

Al whirled. A black shadow hovered over his chair. He didn't have time to raise his hands before a solid hit to his head let him know he had lost—again.

Humiliation Galore

I glanced at Damon, not ready to exit his vehicle. "Do we really have to go on a run with the whole group this morning? I thought it could just be you and me." I'd actually prefer the large numbers, especially since Muscle Man and Greasy Beanpole could be coming for me and this setup made Nana worry a lot less, but I wasn't in the mood to deal with Hot Redhead when I was so worried about my dad.

Damon covered my hand with his. "What are you afraid of? You're running great. You can keep up with anybody here." He gestured to the half-dozen runners milling about the parking lot at the base of Logan Canyon. What was it with runners and canyons? Did they enjoy running straight uphill?

Damon gave me a quick peck on the lips, released my hand, and jumped out of the car. His door slammed, but I needed a minute. I took a couple of calming breaths, told myself my dad was going to be okay, then forced myself to jerk the handle and swing my door open. The heavy metal thumped into something, followed by some muttered curses.

My eyes widened. I jumped out of the vehicle and grabbed Damon's arm. He was bent over, clutching his abdomen.

"Oh, Damon. I'm sorry. I wasn't paying attention." I stroked his arm consolingly.

He didn't straighten, but glanced up at me, acknowledging my words with a shake of his head and a forced smile.

"Are you all right, Damon?" Hot Redhead asked, coming level with me. "I can't believe Cassidy would do something like that to you. That must *really* hurt."

150

I didn't give her the courtesy of turning around, but kept patting Damon's arm and muttering useless, sympathetic words.

"It was just an accident," Damon said from between clenched teeth. "I'm fine."

The entire group was upon us now.

"Girlfriend just take you out?" Joe asked.

"I think he was begging for it," Trevor said. "I saw him cop a cheap kiss a couple of seconds ago. You were totally justified in slamming the door into him, Cassie."

I shook my head. "Thanks, Trevor. I feel so much better now."

Damon straightened, ignoring his friends. "Let's run."

Slowly everyone turned away and started jogging up the path. Everyone but Hot Redhead. She couldn't miss such an opportune moment. The three of us formed the rear of the pack.

Elizabeth slithered next to Damon. "Are you sure you're okay? That was a hard hit Cassidy put on you."

Damon rubbed at his lower abdomen. "I'll be fine, thanks Elizabeth."

I shook my head. "I am so sorry."

Damon grabbed my hand, pulling me closer to him. "If you say that one more time, I may not forgive you."

"Say it again," Elizabeth muttered.

"Thanks for being so great," I whispered, squeezing his hand before focusing on my stride.

The first of the run was a lot less demanding than I'd feared. Trees, shrubs, and wildflowers lined the trail on one side and The Logan River flowed down the other. It was picturesque and Damon was a champion. The time flew as we chatted and laughed. Even though Elizabeth insisted on staying close by Damon the entire run, we had a good time. My legs were just beginning to tire when we reached the turn-around point.

I flew back down the trail. Elizabeth ran ahead so we got to enjoy uninterrupted talking and companionable silence. The birds chattered to us and the river added its rushing happiness. I just hoped Damon wasn't watching Hot Redhead's perfect backside in those miniscule shorts.

We made it to the parking lot and were milling around stretching and sharing funny running stories when Hot Redhead unleashed her claws.

"So, have any of you ever urinated on yourself during a run?"

One of the girls shrieked, "Ew. Are you serious?"

Several of the group exchanged glances. Damon looked at Elizabeth like she was a weirdo. I liked that, but knowing what was coming had my gut twirling. I pulled my foot behind me for a quad stretch and studied the leaves of a towering cottonwood tree.

"I haven't." Hot Redhead tossed her long hair. "But I know Cassidy urinated down her leg during Hyde Park's 10K and I just wondered if anyone else could claim such an honor. How did it feel, Cassidy?"

I held myself back from tackling her and peeing in her face. See how she'd like that. "You know it was kind of warm, a bit sticky. Just the usual urine." I bent into a hamstring stretch and avoided looking at anyone.

Silence scratched through the park for a second before a loud chuckle broke the most awkward moment of my life. Another laugh joined it milliseconds later. When Damon's throaty laughter complimented the other two, I allowed myself to stand up and face everyone. Joe and Trevor were exchanging looks with Damon and all of them laughed uproariously.

Hot Redhead faked a laugh. "Pretty funny, huh? Cassidy has bladder issues."

I didn't see anything funny about it.

Trevor walked over and clapped me on the back like a football buddy. "Cassie. I have to say you are the rockingest girl I've ever known. What kind of a girl runs so hard she passes out and then races so hard she pees on herself? That is tough." He winked at Damon. "If my buddy ever gets tired of dating you. I'm in line."

Joe nodded. "I'll fight you for position, Trev."

Trevor and Joe walked off to Joe's truck laughing and talking.

Damon smiled at me. "Trevor's right. You're the toughest runner, girl or boy, I've ever met."

I gave him a shy smile. "You don't think I'm disgusting?"

"No. I've heard it happens. Never personally experienced it, but you know . . ."

I smacked his arm. "I know. You're perfect."

The rest of the group dispersed, muttering quick goodbyes. A tall blonde named Jocelyn walked up to us. "It happened to me last year during the Park City Marathon. It's nothing to be embarrassed about."

I gave her a smile. "Thanks. It's not something I usually brag about."

Jocelyn laughed and gave Hot Redhead a scathing look. "I don't believe you brought it up."

All of us turned to Elizabeth. She planted her hands on her hips. "I didn't do it to be mean."

"Uh-huh," I said.

Elizabeth whirled and stomped away. I could hear her muttering to herself all the way to her car.

Damon turned to me. "I'd better get you home. I want to make sure you've showered before our date tonight."

Nathan and Sham ducked into a crowded shack at the market. Wind chimes and colorful wraps floated around them. Nathan grabbed his friend and held tight, partially for support, mostly because of his gratitude. After Sham had rescued Nathan yesterday afternoon he'd hidden him at a friend's house and watched over him throughout the night. This morning Nathan had awoken with a tremendous headache and a determination to get to America.

"Once again you save my life," he said to Sham as they threaded through the overcrowded tables. "Where would I be without you?"

Sham's handsome ebony face split into a grin revealing straight, white teeth. "Dead. Over and over again."

"Thank you, my friend."

Sham directed Nathan towards the back of the shop where a connected run-down building boasted a friend's living quarters.

Nathan grabbed at his head as they started moving again, hoping the headache would settle soon.

Sham glanced at him and ground his teeth. "I should have killed those men," he said.

Nathan shook his head. "There wasn't time. Besides, you know more will come. Always more."

Sham grabbed a brightly-colored scarf off one of the tables and tossed it to Nathan. "Wrap that around your head. We'll get you some clothes and find a spot to hide out until tonight. Then we will go back to the village."

"No," Nathan said. "I'm done hiding. Ramirez and Panetti have discovered I'm alive. They've threatened my daughter. I'm going to America."

Sham stopped next to the shack's door and stared. "America? What's that going to accomplish, besides you dead for good?"

"I have contacts in the FBI. People I trust. They would love to bring Ramirez and Panetti down. It's got to be those two."

Sham pushed the swinging door aside and ushered Nathan to a chair. "You've freed many. It could be another slaver."

Nathan shook his head, gratefully sinking into the wooden seat. "No one else would've made this connection. No one else has the resources to hire killers like those two." He exhaled slowly. "I'll be the bait to bring Ramirez, and hopefully Panetti, down. My life would be well worth it if I could stop them."

"No." Sham's skin stretched taut across his broad cheekbones. He grabbed onto Nathan's forearms and begged him with his gaze. "Please, my friend."

Nathan studied a worktable overflowing with wooden flutes and toy drums. "I have to do this. I can't risk them killing my daughter, son, daughter-in-law, or grandson. Did I tell you? I'm going to be a grandfather again soon."

"Congratulations." Sham's tone was flat. The sparkle had left his eyes. "It seems you are decided. I will come with you to America."

Standing, Nathan wrapped his arms around his large friend. "Someday soon I will take you to America, but not this trip. You protect the children here and I'll protect mine at home."

Sham's bright eyes conveyed his frustration but finally he nodded. "Let's gather what you need. I will pray for you until you return safely."

Nathan forced a grin, squeezing Sham's broad forearm. "I am protected already."

Week Nine

I signed the credit card bill and shoved it into the plastic holder. "Fifteen dollars for a meal at Café Sabor?"

Tasha chuckled. "You've never gotten a real meal before. Costs a bit more than a salad. How was the pasta?"

"Wonderful. You should try it." I glanced discreetly around the restaurant. Nana had gotten word that my dad survived Muscle Man's latest attack and was on his way, which meant Muscle Man was also en route. I couldn't let him catch me unaware.

"Yeah, right," Tasha said. "When I start running marathons maybe."

"Man, I love this carb-loading stuff."

"I'm jealous." Tasha sighed and shoved away her plate of salad. "But I won't be jealous in the morning when I'm sleeping and you're running twenty miles. Speaking of running, I've got to sprint to the bathroom, I'll meet you up front. You still want to go to Cold Stone, right?"

I smiled. "I'm not sure if ice cream works for carb-loading, but might as well try it out."

"Oh, good, I was afraid you'd get all nutrition religious on me and refuse ice cream."

I placed my hand on my heart. "I would never betray my ice cream addiction."

"That's why I love you." Tasha grabbed her purse and scurried off.

I walked through the restaurant and out into the warm summer night. There were small gatherings of people waiting outside for a table to open up. None of them looked like the two I feared, but I had to check. I also constantly searched for my dad. I couldn't wait to see him again.

A young family waited in the balmy summer night air. The mother chased the two-year old while the father swung the baby seat like it was a carnival ride. A group of elderly couples returned my smile. There was a tall, attractive man standing off by himself. My eyes brushed by him and returned quickly. Damon?

What was he doing here without me? I crossed the distance between us. He looked amazing in a dusky button-down shirt and khakis.

"Hey, hey hey," I said. "Fancy meeting you here."

Damon turned to me. His eyes widened. He offered me a smile, but it didn't carry the usual dazzling power. "Cassie. I should've known . . ." His voice trailed off. His smile tried to grow. "You look fabulous, as always."

I did a little twirl. "I guess the running really is working. I bought new clothes to show off." Was I making him uncomfortable or was it just the fact that I'd caught him at Café Sabor without me. "Who are you here with?"

He shifted his weight from one foot to another and looked over my shoulder. "A friend."

"Sweet." He was here with a buddy. Thank heavens. "Maybe your friend and my friend could hook up. We could all go to Cold Sto . . ." Words failed me. Hot Redhead strutted around me and sidled into Damon's side, looking for all the world like she belonged there. I think I needed to be sick.

"Sorry," she said, gazing up at Damon with adoration. "Didn't mean to leave you alone so long."

Damon gave her an uneasy half-chuckle, his gaze still fixed on me. Elizabeth slowly followed his eyes. "Hello."

"I, um," I stuttered, "this is a bit awkward."

Elizabeth smirked at me and looped her arm through Damon's. Her French manicure trailed across his forearm. "Only for you."

Damon's gaze swiveled to her. He seemed surprised that she dared touch him. Or maybe I was dreaming up meanings to make myself feel better. At least Damon had the good sense to step away and gently remove her fingers from his skin. Smart thing too, I was about to utilize the tackles I learned watching college football with my dad.

"Would you excuse us for a minute, Elizabeth?" Damon asked.

Her perfect pout deepened, she reached for his arm again. "If I have to."

Damon extracted himself from her. "I'll meet you inside."

Elizabeth smiled at him. "Don't be long." She slithered away, giving him one more sultry look before sliding through the restaurant doors.

I fought it, but couldn't stop the grimace that distorted my face. "Nice friend."

Damon reached for my elbow. I shook him off and stomped down the sidewalk.

As soon as I was far enough away that none of the spectators could hear my rampage, I let loose. "How could you? I mean. You can date anyone you want, but . . ." I gestured at the wooden door that Elizabeth had disappeared through. "Hot Redhead? The crazy woman? You've seen the way she acts around me. You do realize she has some psychotic obsession with you? Are you completely dense?"

"Cassie." He reached for my arm and put such sensation into the speaking of my name I almost folded.

Jerking away from his warm touch, I snacked on the inside of my lip to keep under control. I wasn't going to cry, that was for wussy chicks, but I couldn't deny the risk of turning into one of them was huge.

"Cassie," he tried again, this time without the touch, "Elizabeth called and asked me to dinner. She's been begging me to help her for weeks. I knew we were going out tomorrow night so I didn't think you'd mind. All Elizabeth wants are some training tips. She's a nice girl."

I just stared at him. He was an idiot. Did I really like this guy? I studied those dark blue eyes and thought about how much I'd enjoyed being around him. His good qualities almost overpowered his stupidity.

"Cassie, it's not like you and I are dating exclusively."

That did it. The tears I had been fighting for the past twenty-three seconds squeaked over my bottom lids and rolled traitorously down my cheeks. Was I really this upset or just prideful? I brushed at the right side angrily. Damon reached up and gently lifted the drop off the left side of my face. "I guess you were under the impression we *are* dating exclusively?"

I rolled my eyes, wrapping my arms around my stomach. "Whatever." For weeks I'd been trying to banish Jesse from my mind and remain faithful to Damon, but did he care? No. He had the nerve to take out Hot Redhead. "I'm on a date myself."

Tasha ran down the sidewalk screaming, "Cassie, are you okay? I overheard this redhead telling the hostess to get a table for two under Damon's name. *No.* You wouldn't . . ." Her voice trailed off as she noticed my stance, my red eyes, and Damon's confused face.

"Here's my date now," I announced. "You ready to go, sweetheart?"

Damon ignored Tasha. He crossed the distance between us, wrapped his arm around me, and whispered harshly in my ear, "I had no idea, Cassie. I thought you were just playing with me. Just having fun. You never said you wanted to be a couple."

"I shouldn't have to say it," I muttered. *I'd kissed this jerk. Multiple times.*

Damon's lips caressed my earlobe. "You should've told me. I couldn't have imagined that someone like you would feel like this for me. If I had known . . ."

He left that hanging there. How could he not have known? And how could he not think he was worthy of me? Definitely a line to get himself out of trouble. I pulled from his grip, two more fat tears creeping onto my skin. Dang, my emotions. "Yeah, well you should've known. But too bad for you," I said. "Now you've driven me to the other side." I grabbed at Tasha's arm but instead of her skinny forearm I connected with broad muscle.

I looked up and sighed, "Jesse."

Jesse wrapped his arm around me, glared at Damon, and said, "Maybe I can save you from that desperate step."

I grinned. "Maybe you could . . . if I liked you."

The olive skin of his cheek crinkled. "Maybe we can remedy that problem as well."

I imagined all the ways he could do that and melted into his side.

"Cassie!" Damon's hand grabbed my wrist, wrenching me back to reality. "You aren't going anywhere with him."

I narrowed my eyes. "You've lost all rights to input in my life."

Damon's face turned a brilliant shade of red. His glower at Jesse terrified me. Jesse ignored him and turned me away. "Can I give you a ride home?"

I looked at Tasha. She pumped her head with an awed smile. "Go," she said.

Jesse led me to his Denali. Amazingly, Damon's betrayal didn't sting with Jesse's arm around my waist.

Jesse and I chatted about running, Raquel's health, and anything else but the awkward confrontation outside Sabor. I loved that he didn't feel the need to pry into my emotional upheaval. He helped me out of the Denali and walked me up the sidewalk. I turned to him before we reached the front porch.

"How did you know to rescue me again?" I asked.

He studied the rose bushes. "I keep pretty close tabs on you, Cassidy."

I waited until he met my eyes. "You're stalking me or something, then you kiss me the other day, and now I'll never be the same again." I tapped my fingers on my arm. "Is it some big surprise I can't let myself like you?" *Because I'm dying to be near you and you don't seem to reciprocate that feeling,* luckily I caught myself from vocalizing the last sentence.

Jesse licked his lips. "I keep hoping that will change." He slowly crossed the inches separating us and lifted his hand to my cheek. My entire body quivered as his rough fingers caressed my flesh. Before I could sort out my jumbled thoughts, he lowered his head and did the branding thing with his lips again. This time it was much worse. He increased the pressure on my lips until my head swam.

I grabbed Jesse's shirt and yanked him closer, reassuring myself that he wouldn't slip away. After several wonderful minutes, he did the unthinkable—pulling away and gently loosening my grip. Holding onto my hands, he whispered, "I shouldn't have done that."

"Why?" I couldn't think of any good reason we weren't doing it this instant.

"I'm here to protect you, Cassidy, not become involved with you."

I blinked several times but the picture was still the same. Jesse writing me off again, but this time he had some sort of reason. "Protect me? Who *are* you?"

Jesse grinned and tenderly kissed me again. "I'm Dr. Tattoo," he whispered against my lips. "I'm the man who's going to make sure they don't hurt you."

They? Was he talking about Muscle Man and Greasy Beanpole or somebody else? I wrapped my arms around his back and held on. "Who?"

He trailed a hand down my face. "You're going to have to trust me."

"I'll trust you when you tell me what's really going on here, kiss me without saying you shouldn't have, and take me on a real date."

Jesse's low chuckle rolled over me. He disengaged my arms, gave me one more mouth-watering kiss, and backed away. "Someday, Cassidy. Someday I won't have to walk away."

With that he winked, pivoted, and jogged to his SUV. I stood there staring after him, wondering who he was and why I was so smitten by him.

I cruised through the first eight miles of my twenty-miler. When I wasn't checking for Muscle Man my mind wandered back to Jesse's kiss last night. I sighed like a love-sick teenager. If only I could see him more, get to know the real Jesse.

But what about Damon? I forced myself to remember Elizabeth clinging to him. His tender whisper made me cringe, *I had no idea, Cassie. I thought you were just playing with me.*

Turning up the volume on my iPod I tried to blast Jesse and Damon from my brain. Running was too conducive to thinking. I was on mile fourteen and feeling pretty good when I realized I hadn't eaten. Slowing to a walk I jerked open my fanny pack and grabbed a Gu. I gagged as vanilla-flavored sludge stuttered down my throat. I swigged a gulp of water and started running again. Minutes later, I saw two bikes heading my direction. I squinted. It couldn't be. A hundred yards away and Tasha screamed, "It's us, baby."

Love leapt from my heart. I threw my hands in the air with pinkies and thumbs extended. "You two rock."

"Couldn't leave you all alone," Raquel said.

They circled around on their bikes and slowed to match my pace.

"How'd you find me?" I wished I could stop running and hug them.

"You told me your route," Raquel said with a grin. She looked awkward on her bike, her huge abdomen protruding close to the handle bars. "Remember?"

"My brain's so fried I can't remember why I'm even out here." Safety and gratitude almost overwhelmed me. My friends were here. I had no reason to worry about Muscle Man or if I would finish the run.

Tasha laughed. "You're doing great. We thought we'd catch you down on The Island." She gestured to Utah State University's football stadium east of us. "You're almost to fourteenth north."

I calculated quickly in my head. "I've only got a little over five miles left."

Raquel nodded. "Your stride looks good. How ya feeling?"

"Great." I didn't tell her I'd forgotten to eat anything until a few minutes ago. Especially after she'd lectured me about keeping the calories coming so I didn't hit the wall.

"You've got a really good pace right now. You're sure you aren't going too fast?" Raquel asked.

I evaluated. My legs rotated faster than they probably should have, but at this pace I could finish twenty-six miles faster than three-thirty-five. My first really long run and I was on track to qualify for Boston. The thought propelled me faster still. "I'm great," I yelled.

"We'll match your pace so don't worry if you need to slow down," Raquel said.

"Whatever," Tasha said. "Keep kicking it, sister." She paused for half a breath. "What happened with *Jesse?*"

I grinned, remembering the feel of his lips. "Good stuff."

"He is . . ." Tasha whistled. "Gorgeous in an extremely manly sort of way. Did he show you anymore tattoos?"

I arched an eyebrow, might as well leave her wondering.

"You saw Jesse again?" Raquel asked. "What about Damon?"

"Damon's out," Tasha informed her.

I nodded my agreement. Damon was definitely out.

Raquel and Tasha peppered me with questions about Jesse and Damon, but all the talking started wearing on my oxygen supply. Good friends that they were, they kept a conversation going that required minimal input from me. I wished I could express to them how much I appreciated it. The miles flew by.

I could see Sky View High when my legs suddenly felt so heavy I could hardly lift them. Out of sheer habit, I kept running. The bright morning sun dimmed. Raquel and Tasha's voices came from a tunnel. I wanted to take a drink of water, but I didn't have the energy to unfasten my water bottle from my fanny pack.

I lagged behind my friends. They kept talking, oblivious to my darkened state. It was all I could do to put one foot in front of the other. My entire being focused on rotating through each step, but the feeling of despair overwhelmed me.

I watched Raquel and Tasha move farther away from me. I wanted to call out. I needed them. I couldn't find the oxygen to beg for help.

A hand on my back jerked me from my confusion.

"It's okay. You can do it, Cassie."

"Damon?" I managed.

"You're hitting a wall. It sucks, but you have to push through it. Come on, sweetie. Keep running. I'll stay with you."

I listened to him coaxing me along, almost forgetting I'd been furious with him last night. Ignoring the part of me that said he had no right to call me sweetie, I focused on the ground and continued my labored gait. One step. The next step. I felt my water bottle next to my mouth.

"Drink this. It'll help."

"What's wrong with her?" Tasha's voice came to me through the haze.

I looked up and saw the biker duo peddling up to us and jumping off their bikes.

"She's hitting the wall," Raquel said.

Damon and I kept running. "She's okay," Damon said. "I'll stay with her."

Tasha and Raquel rode behind us and talked in hushed voices.

Damon talked and talked. I hardly heard what he said, but the one thing I remember is he didn't apologize for last night. Which I really think would've helped. The haze lifted and some strength came back to my legs, though they still felt weak.

Finally, I could see my house. Damon put pressure on my arm. "Let's walk the last little bit. You doing okay?"

Slowing to a walk was heaven. "I may just survive," I said.

Damon chuckled.

I looked askance at him and muttered, "Thanks."

"Anything for you," he said.

He didn't deserve a response.

Tasha and Raquel approached on their bikes. "I just called Nana," Tasha said. "She's got breakfast ready for us."

Damon nodded. "Yes. Get some food in her. That will help." He waved them on. "You two go ahead. I'll bring her in."

"You okay, Cassie?" Raquel asked.

"Yeah. I'm good. Thanks for riding with me."

"Sorry. We were talking. We didn't realize . . ."

I shook my head. "You guys were awesome. Don't worry about me."

They rode ahead and I suddenly felt awkward with Damon. I wanted to yell at him. Ask him what he was really doing with Elizabeth last night. I didn't believe the, "she needs training tips," excuse one bit. I needed to know why he didn't chase after me when I left with Jesse, but the fact was I hadn't wanted him to. That fact made me sad as I focused on his blue eyes.

"Did you shoot your Gu's while you ran?" Damon asked.

"One." Who cared about Gu's?

"When?"

"Mile fourteen."

He arched an eyebrow. "There's our problem."

Our? We stopped on Nana's front lawn. "Do you want to come in for breakfast?" Where did that come from? I was mad

165

at him. Hurt. Embarrassed. Jaded. And wishing Jesse was the one who'd found me this morning. Who wanted Damon to come to breakfast?

"Not with the glares Tasha was giving me."

I hadn't noticed. Good friend that Tasha. "You probably deserve some glares," I muttered.

"Yeah. I probably do." He yanked off his baseball cap. "Could I call you later? Maybe we could go to dinner and . . . talk?"

"Elizabeth's not available tonight?" I asked.

"Come on, Cassie, that's not fair."

"You're right. Thanks for helping me through the wall." Turning, I marched up to Nana's front porch, humiliated he'd seen me like that and once again relieved that he didn't chase after me.

Nathan stared out the window of the rental car. He'd cautiously followed Cassidy on her run, grateful she was almost within the safety of Nana's home again. After several days of meetings in Salt Lake with the FBI, he'd made it to Cache Valley late last night and first thing this morning paid for a state-of-the-art security system to be installed while Cassidy was out on her run. Of course his mother nagged him about spending money. "We're fine," Nana insisted. "Nobody's gonna hurt our girl when I'm in this house. If you're gonna spend money on me put in some granite countertops or a dishwasher that actually works."

Nathan shook his head. Nana would never change. She had plenty of money, but still lived in this old house and donated most of her money to Nathan's charities.

Nathan watched Cassie lumber up the stairs and the redheaded boy walk dejectedly to his car. He couldn't help but chuckle. Good girl. She still knew how to put them in their place. He wrote down the boy's license plate number. It all looked innocent enough, but this was his daughter and he would make sure she was safe.

He wished he could run up the stairs after her. But he didn't dare. He knew the men who had accosted him in Mexico were either here watching for him or Clive Ramirez and Nick Panetti would send someone else to finish the job. Ramirez didn't tolerate sloppy work. If the men who'd failed to kill Nathan hadn't been disposed of, they probably had even more reason to get the job done right.

Nathan didn't know how long he had to play this cat and mouse game, but he had to keep Cassidy safe. Maybe with the FBI's help, he could flush out Ramirez's men before they found him. This marathon training wasn't helping his nerves, but he couldn't ask her to stop. From what Nana had said, this was the first time Cassidy had been passionate about anything since her mother's death.

Nathan slowly pulled away from the home he was raised in. In an ideal world, he'd rush inside and hug his daughter then share a hearty breakfast with those he loved. He frowned. Nothing was ideal about his life right now, but Cassidy was safe. That was something to be grateful for.

Week Eleven

I now considered a ten-miler an "easy run". As I flew over the pavement of Smithfield, I fingered the pepper spray in my shorts pocket and wondered why I hadn't heard from my father, Jesse, or Damon. But it was a glorious sixty degrees, the sunrise over the Wasatch Mountains was a puffball of red and orange, and all this running was making me feel great. I could worry after my run.

A black Chevy Tahoe pulled alongside me, idling at my same speed. Ice slid into my stomach. Bile rose up my throat. Warmth exploded through me as my heartbeat escalated and my legs took off through the field to the west. The only beacons of safety were some homes a hundred yards through this field. Someone there would have to protect me. Muscle Man and Greasy Beanpole were not capturing me again.

"Cassie! It's me. Stop."

I froze at the call from the man in the vehicle. I whirled to face him. "Daddy," I whispered.

My body lurched in his direction. My legs gave out. I collapsed onto the rutted field. My father jumped out of the driver's side door. He rushed to me and lifted me off the ground. I threw my arms around his neck and clung to him like a little girl waking up from a nightmare. "Dad?"

"Oh, Cassie, my girl, my girl." He kissed my cheek. His tears wet my face. We clung to each other. Cradling me against his side, he asked, "Are you injured? We need to get out of here before somebody sees us."

"Injured?" I asked.

"You fell."

I laughed, swiping at my tear-covered cheeks. "I couldn't believe it was you. Nana told me everything, but . . . it's just so hard to really believe it—you're alive. You're here." My dad was really okay. Seeing him made it all real.

"I am." He winced. "Cassie, I'm sorry we had to lie to you. I was trying to keep you safe and I was dealing with losing your mother."

I wished he hadn't brought it up. Feeling like he couldn't trust me was hard. "I'm . . . trying to understand." I found myself pulling away from him.

Dad kept his hand on my arm as if he couldn't stand to be disconnected from me. "We were protecting you, Cassie. You didn't need the stress . . ." He exhaled, not finishing his thought.

I shook my head. "Jared and Nana both knew. Didn't you think I could keep a secret?"

Dad grabbed me around the waist and ushered me into his side. "Sorry, babe, this isn't the time. We've got to go."

I looked up to see a large vehicle approaching from the north. Dad pulled me into a full sprint. We reached the Tahoe. He shoved me inside then scrambled over me and into the driver's seat.

"Dad, calm down. It's just a va . . ." The words died in my throat. A cargo van. I could clearly see the driver and the man in the passenger seat. "Muscle Man," I whispered, fear clogging my throat.

Dad jerked the key and gunned the engine. We flew past the van. Muscle Man's eyes locked onto mine as we passed. I glared right back. Dirty monster had no right to kill my mother.

Greasy Beanpole flipped the van around. The lumbering buggy pursued us like a sports car.

"Hang on," Dad yelled, pressing the accelerator to the floor.

After several attempts, my trembling fingers secured my seatbelt.

Dad zoomed through the neighborhoods surrounding the golf course. The van caught us. I spun around in my seat, peeking above the headrest to see Muscle Man's ugly face. He leered at us. Greasy Beanpole gripped the steering wheel with both hands, leaning forward as if intent on running our sport utility over.

Dad darted down the golf course hill. The van couldn't manipulate the corners as well. We turned onto the road leading up Smithfield Canyon. "Why are we going up a canyon?" I asked. "Drive to the police station."

Dad's hazel eyes twinkled. He tossed me his phone. "And let them disappear? We're going to trap them."

"Trap them or us?"

He careened around a corner. "Call the police. Once we get far enough up the canyon there will be no way out."

Yeah, and we'll be at Muscle Man's mercy.

I followed his instructions, begging Detectives Shine and Fine to set up some sort of roadblock and send a load of officers up the canyon as well. They said they'd come and do their best to bring support. I wasn't encouraged.

Beautiful houses and greenery blurred as we sped up the windy road. I kept watch behind. "I can't see them."

Then the road would straighten out and I could almost feel Muscle Man capturing us. "There they are," I screamed, clutching the armrest.

Dad nodded each time I reported, his focus on the road. We raced the length of a decent straightaway. The van didn't appear behind us. We maneuvered a few more tight turns and then Dad squealed onto a dirt road overgrown with trees, shrubs, and wild flowers. He parked behind a grouping of trees. I watched intently out my window. Seconds later, the van darted past us.

I caught my first full breath in minutes. "It worked."

Dad looked at me. "You're beautiful, Cassie."

I pushed buttons on Dad's phone. "Odd comment for a life or death situation."

Dad grinned. "True. I just can't believe how pretty you are. How much you look like . . ." He shook his head. Suddenly unable to meet my gaze, Dad dropped the vehicle into reverse, punched the gas pedal, and spun around. We raced out onto the road and back down the canyon.

I kept watch behind us, an easier task than responding to Dad's last comment. He slowed down, giving Muscle Man a chance to catch us. My heart withered at the thought. Within minutes, the van reappeared. "Here they come," I screamed, clinging to the armrest with sweaty fingers.

Dad smiled. "Perfect. If the police did what you asked, this could be our break."

We came to the spot where Canyon Road split into Upper and Lower. Several police cars barricaded the road. Dad slowed to a stop. I watched behind us for the van to appear around the next corner. Several seconds passed. "They were closing in on us," I muttered.

I jumped from the car.

"Cassidy," Dad yelled, climbing out his side.

Detective Shine and Fine strode to meet us.

"They must've turned around," I called in way of greeting. "They should be here by now."

Shine nodded. "We'll leave a car here and go find them." Fine was already running to their patrol car.

Dad and I waited a few minutes before trudging back to the Tahoe. Silence surrounded us as we sank into the captain chairs and studied the road. I prayed for Muscle Man's capture. "Where do you think they went?"

Dad shrugged. "Don't worry. We'll get them." He reached across the console and took my hand in his. "I'll make sure you're safe."

"I think you're the one who isn't safe. Why do they want you so bad?"

Anger filled his eyes. "Human trafficking is a billion dollar industry." He grinned, though I could still feel his disgust. "I cut into their profits."

171

I wanted to ask how he did that, but he went on, "Plus, Ramirez and Panetti both hate me." He shrugged. "Especially Panetti. You remember."

I shivered, wishing I didn't.

Dad stared at me. "Your mother was so proud of you. She bragged to everyone about her brilliant exercise scientist who was helping the world be healthier." He cleared his throat. "Are you still running your corporate fitness company? That was such a great concept."

I shifted on the leather seat and studied the empty road. When would Shine and Fine reappear, gloating that they'd caught Muscle Man? "Um, no. When the recession hit, the companies had to cut somewhere." I fiddled with my watch, flushing red. "Guess I was a dispensable product."

"Nana didn't tell me." Dad rubbed my arm. "That wasn't your fault."

Maybe not, but it sure made me feel like a failure. "But I'm starting a new personal training business for small groups. I've got a great gym who is already signing up clients, we start in October. They were nice to let me focus on the marathon first."

"That's great. You never were a quitter. You're so much like your mom—beautiful and inspiring." He smiled softly. "I wish she could see you now."

The words warmed me, but would my mom be proud of me? My new venture would be fun and help women get into shape, but she'd given her life protecting children. I needed to do more that she and I could be proud of.

Dad patted my head like he could read my mind. "There's so much more to you than your outward beauty."

"Thanks, Dad." I stared out the car window, hoping he was right. At that moment, Shine and Fine's patrol car reappeared. I jumped out of the Tahoe and rushed to meet them.

Shine shook his head at me. "The van's deserted up a narrow dirt road a couple miles back. No sign of the men."

I grabbed his arm. "You've got to find them."

He nodded. "Johnson and Rodriguez are searching the surrounding area on foot. We're bringing in more reinforcements. They couldn't just disappear."

I shivered. Dad wrapped his arm around me. Muscle Man had disappeared. When would he reappear?

Weeks Twelve and Thirteen

After several days of silence, Damon started calling repeatedly. I got pretty good at making up excuses or avoiding him. I still heard nothing from Jesse. Nothing! I could almost talk myself into truly disliking him, but my lips singed from his touch and I could still see the warmth in his eyes as he said he'd protect me.

My dad made me promise to train inside until they knew where Muscle Man and Greasy Beanpole were and he was certain I was safe. The little bit of time I'd been able to spend with my dad was so wonderful, I didn't put up much of a fight.

On Saturday, I was scheduled to for my third twenty miler. I'd run my last twenty miles on the treadmill and I really couldn't take anymore. I think I would've preferred fleeing from Muscle Man. When my dad called, I thought it was worth asking, "Please, can you have somebody follow me so I can run outside?"

"Sick of the treadmill?"

"More than you know."

"I just want to guarantee you're safe."

"But Muscle Man hasn't shown up for two weeks. He probably got fired or gave up."

"These men have been tracking me for years, sweetheart. You really think they're going to give up after one run-in with the police?"

It wasn't even a run-in. Muscle Man and Greasy Beanpole had evaded the police and our trap up the canyon. They could be anywhere. "Please, I can't hack the treadmill anymore. I'm getting injuries, and I won't be prepared for the marathon. Inside running is different than outside."

He paused for half a second. "I don't know, babe."

Ooh, I had him now. I'd achieved a pause. "I know it's asking a lot," I said, "but I really am about to lose my mind. Don't you trust my judgment?" It was a subterranean blow, but I had to take it. He was inches from where I wanted him.

"Cassie," Dad exhaled.

I waited. My arguments had been made, it was crucial not to push too hard.

The seconds crawled by. Finally, he muttered, "Okay, okay. I'll ask a couple of the FBI agents to follow you. What time?"

"Yes." I did a little dance in the living room. "Woo-hoo. Woo-hoo."

"Stop celebrating and tell me a time."

"Let a girl party for a second."

"Cassidy, this is not a party. Your life is on the line here."

I rolled my eyes. "Naw. It's you they want dead. They just like to threaten me to get to you." The second my flippant words were out, I regretted them. "Sorry, Dad. You know I'm thrilled you're still alive and I want to keep you that way."

"You make a man wonder," he said. "By the way, who was the boy that finished your run with you a few weeks ago? The one your Nana says you won't talk to anymore."

"Like you haven't already checked him out?"

"I'd like to hear it from you."

"Past history, Pops." I gritted my teeth. Here I was recovering from Damon and my long-misplaced father had to remind me.

"You sure? Nana seems to think you were pretty smitten by him."

"Smitten? Really, Dad. Smitten? When you can talk with my generation give me a call. I'll be ready at five-thirty in the morning."

"Five-thirty? Good heavens, Cassidy."

"Thanks, Dad. Love ya. Gotta go carb up and get my rest so your FBI buddies won't get too bored following me." I hung up the phone before he could change his mind and went to the kitchen to scrounge up some carbs. It was annoying that my dad thought he needed to pry about Damon, but honestly really nice that he was around to care.

A white Toyota Avalon waited outside my front door at promptly five-thirty. I waved and jogged to the car. Dad rolled down the window. "You sure we have to do this, Cassie?"

I frowned. "You shouldn't be out here."

He shook his head, his blond hair needed a trim. "It'll be fine. I wanted the chance to see you, even if it meant getting up before the sun." He sighed. "If I can stay awake."

It felt like a blanket straight out of the dryer had been wrapped around my shoulders. My dad was giving up sleep just to watch me run. "Like it's going to be so hard on you. You get to sit in a car and watch me kick my own butt."

He smiled. "You always have such a nice way of putting things."

I handed him a mug and his face split into the grin I'd missed so much these past two years. "Your famous hot cocoa?"

"I figured I'd butter up whoever was helping me out this morning." I shifted from one foot to the other. "Thanks for doing this for me, Dad."

"Anything for you." He took a tentative sip. "Ah. Just like I like it. Dark chocolate with a hint of cinnamon. I've missed you, sweetie."

"At least you knew I was alive." The words came out before I could retract them. "I mean, I missed you more because I thought you were dead."

His skin faded as if somebody had poured bleach on him, but he ignored the words I already regretted and started lecturing, "If anything looks suspicious, you're going to have to get in. You don't pause. You jump in the car. Do you understand?"

"Yes, Dad. Jump. No questions." I tried to sound sweet so both of us could forget about my previous words. "Follow me."

I headed west, through the fields and dairy farms. I remembered to eat often. The only downside of the run was the smell of manure and the guilt of knowing my dad was idling slowly behind me. I should've made him his favorite oatmeal chocolate chip cookies to go with the cocoa.

Even though I acted like I felt safe, I kept searching the road in front and behind for a van. Thankfully, the only vehicles we saw were tractors and an occasional Idaho truck—big wheels, fancy rims, and stinky diesel. A few groups of bikers passed us, but no Muscle Man or Greasy Beanpole.

I was headed back south from Trenton when I heard two bikers talking behind me. It always cracked me up that bikers didn't realize how their voices carried.

"Isn't she the one?"

My back stiffened. My ears opened wider.

"Yes, it's definitely her."

They were almost upon me. I flipped around to face them head on and beckoned to my dad. He was fifty feet behind them. The bikers were in front of him and approaching fast with huge grins aimed my direction.

"Hello there," the one started.

The howl of the Avalon's wheels cut off whatever the guy was trying to say. My dad squealed around the two men, jamming his car between their bikes and me. He flung open the passenger door and screamed, "Get in."

The men swerved, barely missing the car. They continued down the road. The first speaker turned and stared at us like we were insane. "I've heard of over-protective fathers, but sheesh."

The other one chuckled. Within seconds they were gone.

I squatted next to the open door, breathing heavily. "Sorry. They were talking about me. I remembered that you said other men might be assigned to come after us . . . Sorry." I was such a freak-out.

My dad wiped a hand over his face. "Don't worry." He forced a smile. "It woke me up."

"Me too."

"Do you want to get in?" he asked.

I shook my head. "Nah. I've still got about six miles to go." He shooed me with his hand. "I'll stay closer."

I nodded my thanks and started running again. My adrenaline pumped from the scare. I wondered if there would ever come a day that I'd react normally.

As we pulled back into Smithfield's city limits, Dad idled alongside me. "You have such a great stride, Cassie. I can't believe how fast you ran that twenty miles."

I grinned, wiping at the sweat on my forehead. "Thanks, Dad. You should've seen how pathetic I was a few months ago."

"You're anything but pathetic now."

I slowed to a walk for the last couple of blocks. It was almost more painful to walk then run at this point. We finally reached the house.

"Dad, do you think Muscle Man gave up?" I asked through his car window.

Dad's fingers tightened around the steering wheel. He gestured. "Can you sit with me a minute?"

I needed to stretch my legs but an opportunity to talk with my dad wasn't something I wanted to miss. I climbed into the car, wincing as I sat down.

"I'm afraid they'll never give up. They know where I am now. They know the FBI and police are watching for them. They may just be giving us a few weeks reprieve before they hit." He shook his head. "It's something Ramirez loves to do. Toy with his victims before he barbecues them."

"Barbecues them?" I shuddered. The sweat on my back

cooled to freezing.

Dad exhaled slowly. "It's just an expression he likes to use."

"This Ramirez guy is the slave trader?"

"Yes."

"He's in Mexico?"

"We believe he's based in Acapulco, but he imports slaves throughout South America. Mexico is where they transfer and distribute." Bitterness was so strong in my dad's voice and face I almost didn't recognize him.

I swallowed, brushing at the sweat on my forehead. "He just steals children and sells them?"

"Sometimes. Or they trick the children into going with them. There's a huge profit to be made in the sex industry in Mexico through the Internet and the vacation towns. The children who aren't as desirable get sold for labor. They also smuggle them into America."

"What?" My stomach soured and not from all the Gu's I'd eaten. "They seriously smuggle them into America?"

"Beautiful Hispanic girls do well in New Orleans' brothels," his scowl lines deepened, "and everywhere else for that matter."

I rubbed my arms for warmth. "And you've been able to stop them from being taken?"

Dad focused on the dashboard. "Prevention is nearly impossible, especially the victims imported from South America. We concentrate on retrieval." Dad smiled to himself. "We have sources that tell us when a shipment has been made or a village has been hit. We find the traffickers before they get too far. Sham and I work well together."

"How do you free the slaves?"

He shrugged. "Depends on the situation, sometimes we're able to free them without bloodshed, sometimes not."

"B-but?" My heart thudded against my chest. "You kill the slavers?"

"Sometimes. They deserve a lot worse. If you knew the things they do . . . If we don't take care of them." He shook his

179

head. "The government's corrupt. We used to turn the slavers over to them, but they'd release them within weeks. Sham and I stopped using the legal system years ago." He smiled again. "But we're a great addition to the anti-trafficking programs we work with, they just don't ask anymore how we retrieve the victims."

He didn't expound and honestly, I didn't want to ask. Slavery? Killing? I was so naïve. I thought my parents went to Mexico to use Mom's teaching degree and Dad's doctoring skills. My face flamed red. How selfish I must seem to my dad. Living in the land of the free and complaining because he'd been gone from me. I suddenly understood how my mom could sacrifice her life for such a cause.

"I want to help," I said.

Dad's head rotated so quickly he probably gave himself whiplash. "No, Cassidy. It's too dangerous."

"Stop protecting me." I wrapped my hand around his arm, begging with my eyes. "I'm not a little girl anymore. I could do a lot of good with all the money you left for me."

"I don't mind you donating some money, but I don't want you anywhere near the traffickers." He took a deep breath. "I still haven't forgiven myself for letting your mom get involved. But I could never tell that woman no." He blinked quickly then smiled at me. "You're more like her than you know."

Now I was the one blinking. I released his arm and hugged him awkwardly over the console. This obviously wasn't the time to fight him for the right to help in his cause, but someday soon I'd figure out a way to get involved.

"You're amazing, Cassie. I'm proud of you."

My throat felt thick. "I'm proud of you too, Dad."

He pulled back and looked at me. "What for?"

"For saving the world."

The wrinkles around his mouth and eyes deepened. I'd never thought my dad could age, but the past few years had obviously been hard. "One child at a time."

I let that linger as long as I could handle before I cleared my throat. "Tell me about the children."

A genuine smile crossed his face. "They're adorable." Then his eyes clouded. "The ones that the slavers haven't . . . damaged too much are so loving and grateful."

I nodded. He was still protecting me, not wanting me to know about the damage the slavers were inflicting. "I'd love to help the children," I said. "To even think of someone hurting Tate . . ." My voice trailed off as we both shuddered.

"I understand you want to help but I really can't stand the thought of you being anywhere near danger."

I didn't point out how much danger I'd been in right here in safe little Cache Valley. A plan started formulating in my mind of how I would help. "Are you coming in?" I changed the subject to ease my dad's worry lines. "I'm sure Nana will have breakfast ready."

"I wish. Nana is at the store." He pointed at a dark blue sedan parked a few houses over. "That's my replacement. They'll watch over you. I'm going to a hotel to get some sleep."

"I don't understand why you can't stay here with us."

He shrugged. "Not sure I do, either, but it's what the FBI is suggesting right now. I think they want to spread the bait around." He frowned. "Sorry. Not that you're bait."

I shivered again. "Glad to be so appealing."

Dad reached over me and unlatched the car door. "You'd better get inside. Don't worry. The house is clean. We haven't seen anything from Ramirez's men for the past two weeks and the FBI does a good job with surveillance. We'll be okay."

I nodded, though I didn't believe him. Muscle Man was out there, biding his time. "Thanks for going with me, Dad. I love you."

"Love you, too."

I climbed gingerly out of the car and up the porch steps. Nana really wasn't home. Surprising. First time in a while Nana hadn't been around to try and shove a huge breakfast down my throat. I whipped up a protein shake with powder, peanut butter, and bananas, grabbed a bag of crushed ice from the freezer, and shuffled to the bathroom. I filled my tub with ice and cold water, painstakingly removing my shoes and socks. There was no way I could undress completely so I eased into the tub in my running clothes. "Holy crap," I screamed.

The cold water bit at my skin. I forced myself to settle into the water until it covered the band of my running shorts.

Loud footsteps pounded up the stairs. Nana appeared at the open bathroom door, took one look at me, and sighed. "What are you doing now?"

"I-i-ice bath," I stuttered out. *Glad to see you too.*

"Why on earth would you sit in a tub of ice water fully clothed?"

"Too-too sore to take my clothes off. The i-ice," my teeth chattered, "will keep the swelling down."

Nana rolled her eyes. "Well, don't give yourself hypothermia."

She turned and strode down the hallway. I sipped my shake for a few minutes, staring dully at the ice floating in my bathtub. Within minutes, my body rolled with shivers. I forced myself not to think about how cold I was, pretending I was floating in the warm waters of Lake Powell.

I relaxed my head against the marble that framed the tub and closed my eyes. The ice really was helping. My legs and knees no longer hurt. After a few more minutes, the water seemed to be warming up. My shivering reached a controllable level then almost disappeared.

Jesse's face appeared in my head. Why couldn't I just forget about him? The man had too much nerve. Kissing me while giving me every excuse in the book not to date me.

"You have to let me see her," Damon's voice carried through the open doorway.

I sat up, blinking.

"She is in no condition to accept visitors."

"I'm not taking your excuses anymore," Damon's voice grew louder. "She's here. I know it."

"You're stalking my granddaughter now?"

They were coming up the stairs. I tried to move, but my limbs felt heavy. It was too nice in the tub.

"Where is she?"

"She's in an ice bath."

"How long has she been in it?"

"I don't know. I got home from the store about forty-five minutes ago and she was sitting in it."

"Forty-five minutes!" Damon flew into the bathroom, took one look at me, and pulled the plug.

"Hey," I protested weakly. "The water was warm."

He put his fingers into the water and drew them back quickly. "Cassie. How long have you been in here?"

"I don't know," I mumbled.

Damon turned on the water, adjusting the temperature until he was satisfied. My comfortable warmth drained away and burning water rushed onto my feet and legs.

"Ouch." I wanted to yell louder but I was just too tired. "Hot."

Damon put his hand in the water again. He plugged the drain and shook his head. "It's barely above lukewarm. You have hypothermia." He glanced over my reddened legs. "And probably frostbite as well."

The water stung. I tried to move away from it. Damon held me in place. "I'm sorry, sweetie, but you need to stay in this bath until your temperature gets back to normal."

"Don't call me sweetie," I muttered. I put up a futile struggle against his warm hands as the tub filled with scalding water. Gradually my toes and legs stopped prickling and the water felt cool. I stopped fighting him and Damon turned up the heat. Closing my eyes, I wished I could go to sleep.

"No, Cassie. You need to stay awake." He shook his head and mumbled, "Who but you would sit in an ice bath until they had hypothermia?"

"Hey," I protested. "The book says ice baths are helpful."

"For a few minutes. The book." Damon exhaled. "Why didn't you ask me?"

"You were too busy tutoring Elizabeth."

Damon glanced at Nana. "Where do you keep the towels? I think we can get her out now."

Nana had been surprisingly quiet throughout this exchange. She suddenly bustled to life. "You get out of here. I'll help her get her wet clothes off and she'll come talk to you in a minute."

I scowled at Nana.

Damon gave me one more look and stood up. "I'll be downstairs."

With Nana's help I stripped off my wet clothes and washed my face and armpits.

"How did Damon get past our watchers?"

She smiled. "I told them he was okay. He checked out on your father's scans. A financial planner with no ties to any of this mess. Exactly the kind of man you should be dating. Damon's not going to hurt you."

At *least not physically*. I shrugged into my robe. "I can't go down there like this," I said.

"You'll be fine. Just keep the robe tied."

"Great advice," I muttered. Painfully, I descended the stairs. I couldn't resist a softly muttered, "Ouch," on each step.

Damon must've heard me coming. He waited at the bottom of the steps and helped me into the living room like I was an invalid. "I'm sick of you avoiding me," he said, settling onto the couch next to me. "I'm not leaving here until you tell me why you won't return my calls."

I blinked at him. "You've called?"

He exhaled. "Cassie. Please talk to me."

I stared out the window, studying the patterns in the neighbor's brick. My dad labored to preserve children from slavery. I had an amazing life and an amazing man trying to make it better. I needed to forget about Jesse and concentrate on the man who wanted me. "Well, I guess I've been acting like a twelve-year old." It was as good of an excuse as any. I wasn't going to tell him that I'd been avoiding him on the hope that Jesse would call.

"Sixteen," Damon said.

I swung my gaze to his face. "Really? You think I've been that mature?"

A small grin appeared in his eyes. "I'm trying to be nice."

He was such a nice guy and as Nana said, "No ties to any of this mess." I really liked that. There was no reason I shouldn't give him another try. "Well, thank you. I appreciate it."

His gaze swept over me. I noticed my robe gaped. I gathered it and cinched the strap tighter.

"I like the outfit," Damon said.

"I think you'll like the one I'm wearing tonight even better."

A warm smile spread across his face. "Does this mean I'm taking you to dinner?"

"And ice cream."

Damon pulled me into his arms, gave me a quick kiss then jumped from the couch. "Your outfit tonight better be as nice as that one." He hurried to the front door. "See you at seven."

I sat on the couch, twisting my robe ties in my fingers. Why wasn't I more excited?

"Well, that was the easiest makeup I've ever seen," Nana said from the doorway. "Especially with how you've been acting."

I smiled. She didn't know why I was so confused. "I think he's a keeper. I can't imagine another man forgiving me so quickly."

Nana clucked her tongue. "Why do you think I told you to wear the robe?"

"Huh?"

"Look down," she said and disappeared through the doorway.

Damon decided we should try out the new Japanese restaurant. We opted to sit in a back room rather than watch our food be cooked in front of us so we wouldn't have to wait so long. Another couple were at a table across the room and two men sat in a booth not far from ours. The men didn't talk to each other. They alternated between staring at their menus and casting glances at us. My spine tingled. Were these guys FBI and part of my protection detail or friends of Muscle Man?

Finally I could stand it no longer and excused myself to go to the restroom. I could hide in there and call my dad. I walked briskly down the corridor to the bathroom, praying neither of the men or Damon would follow me. Footsteps sounded behind me, I increased my pace. Yanking open the bathroom door, I screamed as a hand wrapped around my waist. The man spun me into his chest, placing a hand over my lips.

"Shh, Cassidy, it's me."

I glanced up. Jesse. He smiled. Removing his hand from over my mouth, he gently traced my lips with his forefinger. I knew I should pull away. I couldn't do it.

"I didn't mean to scare you," he said.

I just stared at him. I couldn't talk with him touching me like that. Jesse lowered his head and replaced his finger with his lips. I melted into him for several wonderful seconds before remembering I was with Damon. Dredging up strength I didn't know I had, I pulled away from him. "Wh-what are you doing here?" Too bad I couldn't catch my breath, he had to know how his kiss affected me.

Jesse sighed, his dark eyes gazing at me like a puppy dog whose toy had been taken away. "I wanted you to know that I'm close by, watching out for you, even when I can't make contact."

186

I studied his chin. "That's nice, but I'm with Damon now. He can protect me *and* date with me without making excuses."

A growl resounded from Jesse's chest. "You have no idea who the good guy is, do you?"

"No," I snapped, "I don't and nothing you've done has convinced me it's you."

Jesse's hand trailed down the side of my face. "Really? Even when I do this?" His lips brushed over mine.

I tingled from my mouth to my heels. "All that does is confuse me," I murmured.

"Maybe I'd better try it again." He pulled me against him, working his magic on my mouth. I was ready for him to sweep me into his arms and carry me away on a white horse when he released me from the kiss. "I've missed you, Cassidy."

I took a couple of calming breaths, closing my eyes so I couldn't see him. "You don't even know me."

He gently massaged my back. "I know more than you think."

I buried my head in his shoulder, wishing I could be with him yet more confused than ever about who he really was and what he wanted with me. "I can't do this, Jesse. Damon is there for me. All you do is mess with my mind."

Jesse sighed. His lack of response did nothing to reassure me. I forced myself to pull away and walk around him. "I've got to get back to my date."

Jesse caught my arm. "I need you to trust me."

I turned to look at him. The sincerity in his gaze almost got me. "Sure. When you tell me all about yourself, why you're 'close by but can't make contact', and who you're supposedly protecting me from."

He shook his head. "You don't know what you're asking."

"Neither do you." I pulled from his grip, needing to escape before I threw myself at him again. I risked one last glance before I rounded the corner. Jesse watched me, his shoulders slumped, one hand reaching out to me. My breath caught. My feet stopped. Relying on all the self-control I possessed I turned my head and commanded my legs to carry me back to Damon. His welcoming smile did nothing to alleviate the ache I felt for Jesse.

I sat and buried my face in the menu. Feeling someone studying me, I turned, half-expecting it to be Jesse. It was the two mystery men. Seeing Jesse had distracted me from calling my dad. Should I claim to need the restroom again? I glowered at the men. The dark guy darted his eyes to the window, the one with bright blue eyes and prematurely grey hair gave me a wink.

Shivering, I turned back to my menu, maybe they were just a couple of buddies who liked Japanese food. "So, what looks good?" I asked Damon, the forced brightness in my voice obvious.

He didn't answer. I glanced up to see him glaring at my watchdogs and then looking back at me. "You know those two?"

My blood gelled. "Um, which two?" I turned my eyes to the other couple in the corner. "The girl does look familiar. Do you think she went to Utah State? Maybe I had a class with her."

Damon scowled. "I'm not talking about those two." He gestured with his chin. "I'm talking about the men you keep looking at that just winked at you."

I needed to stop worrying about who those guys were and act normal. We were safe for the moment. Surely, they wouldn't attack us in the restaurant. Thinking of going outside after dinner turned my empty stomach. I swallowed. Was Jesse still close by? Was he really watching out for me? "They winked at me?" Feigning surprise, I fluffed my hair. "Both of them? I knew I looked good tonight, but sheesh."

Damon smiled, though the lines on his face stayed tight. "You do look good. So you're telling me you don't know those men?"

I had to force myself not to look at them again or allow the terror of who they might be radiate from my face. "N-no."

"Why am I not convinced?" Damon cocked his head to the side, dissecting me with his eyes.

Luckily the waiter came at that moment. I started twenty-menu questions and distracted Damon by my annoying chatter after the waiter left and throughout dinner. I'm not sure why he let the scary men subject rest, but I was grateful.

We got up to go. The men threw down some money on their half-eaten meals and followed us out the door. Damon looked back over his shoulder at them like he was ready for a fist-war. I tugged Damon out of the restaurant and towards his car, fear rising in my throat. Were those two good or bad? I wasn't going to chance a confrontation to find out.

Damon kept looking over his shoulder. He hurried me to his Chrysler and settled me inside. I couldn't resist checking in the mirror. The men climbed into a white car.

Damon started the engine and gunned out of the parking lot. He studied his rearview mirror. "They're following us," he said.

I swiveled. Sure enough. They were observing the rules of trailing, two cars behind. "No," I gulped down the fear, digging the tips of my fingers into the leather seat. "They're just going the same direction as us." Where was Jesse?

Damon dropped the pedal to the floor and spun around a silver minivan. *Yes,* I thought, *drive faster, drive faster.* "They hardly even ate their food," he said. "When we got up to leave, they jumped. They watched you all through dinner like I was going to throw you down on the table and take advantage of you."

"Probably just over-protective old guys." I prayed that was the case, grateful Damon was trying to get us away from them.

"They looked our age."

"So, they don't have much of a life." I grabbed the "oh crap" bar. Damon was right. They were young and I was having a hard time convincing myself they were FBI.

Damon gripped the steering wheel with both hands. His eyes flickered to the rearview. "They're still behind us. Grab my cell phone." He gestured towards the console. "If they try anything we'd better call the police."

"Um, I . . ." Should we call the police? Could they protect us if these were Muscle Man's friends? Just then my cell phone played, "My Brown-Eyed Girl." I ripped it from my purse. "Hello?"

"Cassidy. Why are you running from the FBI? Is this Damon guy really okay?"

I exhaled and turned away from Damon. He was so caught up in the high-speed chase he probably wouldn't listen, but I covered my mouth just in case. "Why didn't you tell me? I thought they were with, you know . . ."

"Well, they're not," he snapped. "Make Damon slow down or they will pry you from that car in two minutes."

I cringed, though relief flowed through me. Damon and I weren't in danger. "Damon's okay," I said. "He was just trying to protect me. It would've been helpful to know that these guys don't know the meaning of discreet."

Dad actually laughed.

"Can I tell Damon what's going on?"

"No."

"Please. Wouldn't it be better if he was aware of the situation and could help us rather than give your buddies something exciting to do on a Saturday night?"

There were three long seconds of silence. "Bare essentials, Cassie."

"Got it." I closed the phone and grabbed Damon's arm. "Slow down."

He glanced at me. "Not until I lose them."

"Damon." I increased the pressure on his arm. "I know who they are. They're following me."

He stared at me like I had taken a hard hit to the head. "Why are they following you?"

"Slow down and I'll explain."

"How do I know they won't hurt you?"

"They aren't the ones who are trying to hurt me."

His eyes widened. "Somebody is?"

I pointed at the Kmart parking lot. "Pull off. I'll tell you what I can."

Damon turned off the road and slammed the car to a stop. He rotated to face me in the bucket seats. "You aren't telling me what you can. You're telling me everything." He looked around at the brightly lit parking lot and the white car that had pulled into a stall fifty feet from where we parked. "What's going on, Cassie?"

I understood his need to know what was going on, but did he have to be so demanding? I took a deep breath and began, "You know how I told you my parents were killed in Mexico?"

He nodded.

"So the good news is my dad's alive. But it also turns out he's got some nasty men trying to make sure he dies this time."

Damon's brow squiggled. He pulled my clasped hands apart and gently stroked the fingers of my left hand. "If they want your dad dead why are they after you?"

"They couldn't get to him, so they used me to flush him out. Dad escaped and came to America. Now we're trying to trap the bad guys before they kill him again." I took a deep breath, pulled my fingers from his, and folded my hands in my lap.

"Where is your dad now?"

"Hiding."

"Why isn't he staying with you and Nana?"

"To keep him safe."

"Where does he stay?"

I shot him a nasty look, shifting in my seat. "He doesn't tell me that. If they find him, he's dead."

His brows shot up. "What did your dad do to them?"

"Their boss," I corrected. "I guess Dad has seriously hampered their boss's slave trade."

"Slave trade?"

"Mexico is a lucrative spot for human trafficking. My dad fights the slavers. They want him dead."

Damon steepled his hands, rocking slowly back and forth. "Wow," he muttered.

"Yeah. Wow," I said.

I waited, wondering how long it would take to sink in. He wouldn't want to date me. Who would want to be around something this nuts?

When he didn't say anything for several minutes, I whispered, "Do you mind taking me home? If you don't want to, I understand. I can catch a ride with them." I jerked my thumb towards the men watching us.

Damon snapped from his reverie. "I'm not letting those idiots take you home."

I turned from his intense stare. "I didn't know if you'd want to be with me after—"

Damon pinned my shoulders against the seat, leaned across the console, and took advantage of my mouth for several minutes. When he pulled back he threw one more glare at the men. "They can watch you all they want. It's not going to stop me from being with you."

I caught a full breath. "Are you sure? I don't want to involve you in something that could get you hurt."

Damon grinned. "Every time I'm with you there are more surprises. Being hurt is a lot less risky to me than not being with you."

I smiled in return but something felt off. Damon truly seemed to like me but was there some other reason he kept pursuing me so hard? The question gave me chills that didn't quit long after he returned me safely to Nana's.

Week Fourteen

Al's eyes darted around the opulent office. He caught sight of several bottles of barbecue sauce decorating a side table and shivered. He'd never been invited to Ramirez's barbecues and hoped he never would be. Al shifted his weight from one foot to the other. Staring down at Clive Ramirez left him half-exhilarated, half-terrified. Being surrounded by Clive Ramirez's heavy hitters left him all-terrified.

Al risked a glance at the giants leering at his nine and three o'clock. There were two more behind him and who knew how many prowling the mansion. Would he live through this interview?

Ramirez looked up from his computer screen. He did not offer them a seat. "A million dollars. I've given you a million dollars and you have done *nothing* for me." He spoke between lips that were so fat they looked permanently swollen. With his tawny mane of hair, shock of freckles, and lithe body he was like a lion ready to spring and tear them apart. He was terrifying without any help from his cronies.

Suddenly the office door flung open. Nick Panetti stormed inside, his eyes darting around until they focused in on Al. "How can you keep failing to kill him?" He turned the force of his gaze on Ramirez. "Let me go get Doc."

Ramirez smiled slowly. "You had your chance years ago." He softly tapped his fingers on the desk. "From what I understand, Doc's beautiful daughter got the best of you."

Panetti's eyes narrowed. "I'll grab the girl. Nathan would come begging to trade his life for hers."

Ramirez held up a hand. "Please wait for me in the living room."

Panetti whirled and stomped from the room, slamming the door.

Ramirez arched an eyebrow at Al as if waiting for him to grovel. "Sir," Al began. "We are the ones who discovered Nathan Christensen is still alive. You have to let us have another chance at killing him for you."

Ramirez's eyes traveled lazily over Al, a predator savoring the moment when he'd rip out the jugular. "I *have* to?"

"Well, um, we would appreciate it," Al stuttered. Terry turned to him with bright eyes. He also knew they were steps away from an ugly death.

"You would *appreciate* it." Ramirez laughed dryly. "Yes, I'm sure you would." Ramirez clicked something on the computer screen then looked back up at them. He obviously didn't need to stand taller than someone to intimidate them. "You shot Nathan and his wife two years ago. Nathan miraculously survived. I paid you for that blunder, as well as this one."

He stared until Al couldn't resist tugging at the collar of his button-down shirt. Why had he dressed nice for his own funeral?

"You captured Nathan last week and he got the better of you. You chased him up a *canyon*," he paused to emphasize their stupidity, "and barely escaped the local police. I'm sure you've heard the expression, 'Three strikes you are my barbecue meat?'"

Ramirez's worshippers chuckled. Terry turned white as a burial shroud. Al wasn't sure if he should drum up a sniveling reply or remain still for the pronouncement. The laughing stopped and silence reigned until he didn't know if he could take it anymore.

"I will allow you one more chance," Ramirez said. "Do you know why?"

Al shook his head, allowing himself to breathe again.

A thin smile turned Ramirez's fat lips. "You've got one more chance because you know what will happen if you mess up." He paused, his puffy lips widening. "No mistakes this time. I have others who are steadily getting closer to Nathan's family. If they succeed in flushing him out first . . ." He stared until Al couldn't meet his eye anymore.

Al grabbed Terry's arm. "We understand." He pulled Terry backwards out of the office, supporting his sagging partner.

The canyon wind bit at my bare legs. I bounced at the starting line of The Top of Utah Marathon. Damon stood by my side with Hot Redhead lurking next to him. She leaned into a hamstring stretch. I tried not to gawk, but no one looks that good with their bum to the world.

"You promise not to try and stay with me today?" Damon asked.

I sighed. "If I must." I lowered my voice. "As long as you promise to ditch Hot Redhead."

Damon chuckled. "Done. You know I prefer brunettes."

I grinned. "That's good news." I looked around. Serious runners hedged me in on all sides. I doubted anyone else was stopping eight miles short of the finish line and hadn't paid for the race. I was the only one without a number and timing chip. I stuck out like a hot-pink dress at a funeral. "Are you sure this is okay?"

Damon squeezed my hand. "I know one of the sponsors. I explained you needed a safe training run."

I shook my head. "And convinced him to let me do a partial race?"

"I showed him your picture on my cell phone." Damon winked.

Damon was such a nice guy, always helping me with my training. I'd been a little leery of him after our last date, but my dad had made sure Damon wasn't involved with Muscle Man or any of the other scary guys chasing my dad. What a relief.

A man with a megaphone spent a few minutes pushing the crowd behind the starting line then he raised a pistol, shot the thing, and we were off.

I didn't attempt to stay with Damon and surprisingly, neither did Hot Redhead. For some unknown reason, she stuck to me like peanut butter on toast.

We cruised down Blacksmith Fork Canyon. The road was lined with mountainous walls and loads of trees. The sun crested the ridge behind us. The rays from the sun and the exertion from my run finally warmed me up. Every few minutes I glimpsed my bike-riding protectors, the same two agents from the other night. Safety was a wonderful thing. I wanted to enjoy the scenic run and relish how great my legs felt chopping up the miles, but Hot Redhead's presence torqued me. "Damon's up there." I pointed down the twisting road then shooed her with my fingers. "Run along now."

She smiled. "Maybe I'm not interested in Damon."

My stomach tightened. My head darted to the side. "Okay, now that terrifies me more than anything else you've said or done."

Elizabeth laughed. An actual laugh. It was as pretty as the rest of her. "I'm not interested in you, either. I'm just making sure you stay away from Damon."

"How you gonna do that?"

Elizabeth strode down the road like a champ but she didn't give me any more information.

I concentrated on the excruciating pace Elizabeth set. Darn my pride. "So you just can't stand Damon liking me?" I asked after several miles of silence. The day was really warming up or maybe it was my frustration with Hot Redhead, sweat dribbled down my chest, soaking my sports bra.

That made her smile again. "Someday you'll understand my purpose."

I stared at her. I didn't like the way she was talking. All mature.

We'd just passed the aid station at mile thirteen and shot out of the canyon onto Nibley Hollow Road when Elizabeth got it into her head to engage me in civil conversation. "Tell me about yourself."

I stared at the beautiful homes spaced along the roadside, towering two-story estates seeking anonymity behind lush trees and bushes. "If you don't mind, I'm trying to enjoy the scenery."

"Can't we make an attempt at being friends?"

"I think that poop went down the septic line a long time ago."

Her delicate brow wrinkled. "He said you have an interesting way of phrasing things."

My head whirled. I stared into her clear green eyes. "Who said that?" It didn't sound like something Damon would say, but maybe. A smile grew on my face. If Damon said it that would mean he talked about me when they were out to dinner.

"No one." Elizabeth focused on the pavement.

"Who said it?" I stared her down until she finally returned my gaze. "It was Damon, wasn't it?"

She nodded. "Okay, yes, Damon said it. When we went to dinner."

"Aha." I gloated. The surge of triumph sending power into my legs. "Damon was talking about me during dinner with *you*." I could hear his voice at the start of the race. *You know I prefer brunettes.* Oh, I was really beginning to like that man.

Elizabeth tossed her long, red hair but didn't say anything for a few more miles. We approached mile sixteen and my legs were starting to feel it. Just two more miles and I would be done.

"You never did tell me anything about yourself," Hot Redhead said.

I rolled my eyes. "I never could figure out why you cared."

"Come on," she goaded me. "It's a way to pass the miles."

I focused on regulating my breathing, but she just kept waiting and giving me these prodding glances. "Well, I'm a loan processor, but I'm going to quit soon and work in my field of expertise." I puffed out my chest. "I have a degree in exercise science." Elizabeth stared so I kept rattling, "I was born in Smithfield. I've lived with my grandma since my parents . . ." She didn't need to know everything. I'd told her four sentences too much and she was still looking at me like my monologue disappointed her.

I straightened my elbows and shook my arms out, pinpricks danced along my forearms. "What is it you want to know?"

"Why you act the way you do."

A couple of runners passed us. I bowed my arms again and increased my pace a bit. "What do you mean? I act perfectly normal. You're the crazy one."

Elizabeth arched an eyebrow. "Don't think I'll comment on that one. Okay, different question."

"You're killing me, here," I said, pushing a sweaty strand of hair behind my ear. "Can we stop all the chitchat and just run?"

She flipped her ponytail off her neck. "If someone was threatening to kill someone you loved, what would you do?"

I stared at her like she'd grown blackheads and carefully enunciated each word, "You are crazy."

"Answer the question."

My sweat ran cold. "Stay away from me." I upped my pace, tripping over my own foot. I sprawled on the ground and people rushed up to me.

"Are you okay?"

"What did she trip on?"

"Oh, sweetheart, you're bleeding."

I grunted and swept the rocks and blood from my palms and elbows. Elizabeth helped me off the ground. "I didn't mean to scare you Cassidy."

I arched an eyebrow. It seemed everyone was either scaring me or trying to protect me. Which crowd was Elizabeth in?

198

Week Fifteen

I stared at the numbers on my computer screen. I was supposed to be getting loan documents ready for a hefty-sized refinance. "Come on, Cassidy," I muttered, "think about the bonus you'll get when this closes."

My cell phone rang. I quietly retrieved it and glanced at the caller I.D. Jared Christensen. Eyes darting behind me, I checked for my ever-watchful boss. He wasn't staring through the connecting window he'd installed last summer so he could monitor my every move. He must be in the break room heating up Lean Cuisines. I repeatedly explained that ten Lean Cuisines were more calories than a Big Mac, but he said these were approved by his wife.

I flipped open the phone. "Hey, Jared, can I call you ba⁻"

"Cassie!" Jared screeched in my ear. "It's Raquel. She's been in a wreck."

I jumped from my chair. "Is she okay? The baby? Tate?"

"Tate was at a neighbor's. Raquel's a mess. They don't know about the baby yet." He let out a sob.

I grabbed my purse and keys from under the desk, clutching my keys so tightly they dug into my palm. "I'm on my way."

"I'm scared."

I faltered. Raquel injured? Jared scared? My world tilted. "It'll be okay." Such an empty promise, but all I had.

"Hurry." The phone disconnected.

I scurried around the desk and plowed into my boss's bulk. "Oof!" Chicken and veggies flew from his hands, showering both of us. "Cassidy," he squawked. "Watch out."

I didn't stop to apologize.

He grabbed my arm before I could dodge away. "Where do you think you're going?"

"My sister-in-law has been in an accident."

"You can go." He pointed at the floor. "After you clean up this mess." He jabbed a pudgy fist at the computer. "And after you send the Roberts' loan off."

I stared at him. The Roberts' loan was more important than Raquel? "I'll finish it up tomorrow." I tried to pull away from him.

He tightened the pressure on my arm. "You walk out that door, you might as well never come back."

My jaw dropped. I'd done amazing work for him and every other loan officer in this company. "You would seriously do that to me?"

The lines around his eyes deepened. "You know how important this loan is."

"My family needs me."

He clasped my arm tighter. "Decide."

I shook free from his greasy fingers. I was destined for better things than this job anyway. "Good luck with the Roberts."

I ran around him, squishing carrots and zucchini into the carpet and ignoring his sputters and protests. The drive to the hospital was less than a mile. Not short enough to keep the tears at bay. I prayed and blinked and tried to drive a straight line. What if Raquel didn't awaken? What if the baby had been injured? My poor family couldn't take any more heartache.

Jared and I were in limbo. The hospital staff moved Raquel from the emergency room to the intensive care unit.

They decided not to life-flight her to a larger hospital in Salt Lake. We took that as a good sign. Dr. Magona, a tall man with pale, receding hair and an inability to meet our gaze, found us in the waiting room and explained what was happening.

"Is the baby going to be okay?" I interrupted his boring speech.

His gaze flickered to me then settled on the wall behind me. "It appears the fetus escaped any significant injury during the accident, but would benefit from more time in the womb."

"What about Raquel?" Jared asked. "Do you think she'll be . . . okay soon?"

Dr. Magona shook his head. "It's too early to tell. She's still unconscious. We've set her tibia, fused L4 and L5, and stabilized the broken ribs. It doesn't appear that the spinal cord was damaged. The biggest concern right now is the swelling on her brain. Her body is trying to heal itself and still provide for the fetus. Once the swelling recedes, she may awaken. She may not recover until after the baby is delivered. She may . . ." He shifted uncomfortably and thankfully didn't finish the third option.

"Why not just take the baby now?" Jared asked.

"The baby will benefit from every extra day in the womb, especially his respiratory system." The doctor clenched his clipboard. "We feel the safest route for both baby and mother is a wait and see approach."

Jared looked like he wanted to argue, but he didn't. The doctor left. Jared and I were granted a few minutes each to visit Raquel's room. Jared came out with red-rimmed eyes and gestured to the double doors of the ICU. "Go wake her up for me, will you, sis?"

I tried to smile. "I'll do my best." I picked up the phone, gave the nurse Raquel's name, and waited for her to buzz the door open. Trudging slowly through ICU, I dreaded seeing my sister-in-law. Maybe I should just turn around. What could I do that would make it better?

Then I was in her room and there was nothing to do but

look at her sad form, her stomach pitching the blanket like a teepee. I raced to her side and grabbed her hand. It was so cold. I almost dropped it again, but forced myself to hold on.

"Hey, El," my voice whispered into the stillness broken only by beeping monitors. She looked awful—bandages and casts, pale skin and bruises.

"So . . . I have this new idea. I think you'll like it." I talked because I didn't know what else to do. I told her all about my new plan to help children in impoverished countries be healthier with clean drinking water, healthy foods, and incorporating physical fitness and some fun into their lives. "It's like combining two things I love, being healthy and helping the children. Perfect that I quit my job today so I can focus on my personal training business and my new charity work." I looked down at her. I always told Raquel everything to hear her advice and because she always supported me, but obviously she wasn't responding to these ideas.

"I promised Jared I would wake you up. Rambling isn't working, maybe I should sing." I took a deep breath. "'Oh, Lord, it's hard to be humble, when you're perfect in every way.'" I warmed up and really got into it. "'Can't wait to look in the mirror, 'cause I get better lookin' each day.'"

"What are you *doing*?" a voice hissed behind me.

I jumped and spun to face the intruder. A fuzzy-haired woman with a long nose and no lips stared at me.

"Um, sorry. My brother told me to wake her up. El likes it when I sing."

The nurse folded her arms across her starched blue scrubs. "She needs to rest, missie, so pipe down."

Missie? I marched up to the woman and said, "My brother told me to wake her up so I'm going to sing until she wakes up." I leaned in until she could smell my watermelon-flavored gum. "I'm going to sing my flipping heart out."

The nurse backed up a step. "You've only got thirty seconds left of your visiting time."

"Then I'll make it good." I shut the door, stunned at how I was standing up to authority today. I finished my song, albeit in a quieter tone. When I heard the door crack I gave Raquel a soft kiss on the cheek. "I'll be back soon." I swung the door open wide and said to the stern nurse, "Thank you for taking care of her."

She gave me a nod. I pranced out of ICU but reality hit as I neared my brother. Raquel was in trouble. My singing wasn't going to make a difference. My dad waited for me, his arm circling Jared's shoulder.

I ran to hug my dad, but fear laced the embrace. "What are you doing here? You can't risk yourself like this."

Dad's face contorted in anger. He stuck his chest out. "Let them shoot me. I'm not going to hide away while they hurt my family."

My heart constricted as my dad's last phrase sunk in. "Hurt your family? You think Muscle Man did this?"

Dad cracked his knuckles, his lips thinning into a grimace. "The police said it was a hit and run. Eyewitnesses described the same men that chased you and me."

Jared's angry expression matched my dad's. "They think they're some kind of trained killers. Just wait until I get a hold of them."

I nodded. "They'd better hope it's you instead of me."

I punched F4 on the vending machine, knowing the Snickers wouldn't fix anything, but it was preferable to dying of hunger.

"Need some nourishment so you can run the halls of the hospital?"

I whirled to face the owner of that deep voice. The candy plunked to the bottom of the machine. All I could see was Jesse. My breathing became irregular. He filled out his scrubs in a way I'd never seen. "You actually are a doctor."

Jesse grinned. "Every once in a while I dress up as one. What are you doing here?"

For a brief moment I'd forgotten about Raquel lying in a hospital bed. I swallowed and turned away, bending to retrieve my Snickers. "My sister-in-law was in a wreck," I mumbled.

Warm fingers encased my upper arms and gently spun me to face him. My candy fell to the industrial carpet. I didn't pick it up. Jesse's eyes were so full of concern I had to study his chin to avoid bawling for the tenth time today.

"How serious?" he asked.

"It's bad." I sniffled.

"Who's her doctor?"

"Magona." I allowed myself to look up at him. His dark-chocolate gaze melted me. I swayed, grateful he held on.

Jesse pulled me against his chest, rubbing my back and murmuring comforting words, "Magona's one of the best. She'll be okay." Holding me close, he ushered me down a quiet hallway before continuing to give me a hug for the memory books.

Tears spilled over. Jesse gently kissed the wetness off my cheek. I trembled, turning my face towards his and taking advantage of his mouth, desperate to stay close to him and forget about everything else. The salt of my tears mingled with the sweet taste of Jesse.

A few minutes flew by in this wonderful position before Jesse whispered against my mouth, "I know this isn't the time, but I've got to tell you." He paused then the words rushed out, "I don't want you around that redheaded guy."

I leaned away from him and glared, had he really just interrupted that kiss and his opportunity to comfort me because of some issue he had with Damon? "That is the dumbest interruption of a kiss I've ever heard. I'm sick of you warning me. If you have some reason I shouldn't be with Damon, spill it."

Jesse's jaw clenched. He released his hold on me. "I can't give you a specific reason. It's just a feeling."

I could hardly breathe, the loss of his embrace was like a physical pain. Through sheer force of will I converted my craving to touch him into anger. "A feeling? I've had feelings too." I poked a finger into his chest. "About *you*, but you've done nothing to make it work."

"Oh, Cassidy." His eyes warmed, but unfortunately he didn't reach out to me with those brawny, tattooed arms. "I want to be with you, but you don't understand." He jammed a hand through his dark hair. "I've been . . . busy."

"Busy?" I guffawed and folded my arms across my middle. "If you want to be with me, why don't you act like it?"

Jesse studied the beige walls. "If there's anyone less worthy of you than Damon . . . it's me."

"What kind of garbage is that? Grow some confidence."

Jesse exhaled. "Confidence has nothing to do with it." Shaking his head, he looked at me as if it were the last time he would get the chance. "You don't understand. I can't tell you what I'm about," his mouth twitched, "but I wish you'd listen to me and stay away from Damon."

I couldn't handle the begging in his gaze and I wouldn't give him the satisfaction of saying I'd stay away from Damon. My eyes dropped to his chest. A small nametag was attached to his scrubs. "Dr. Jesse *Panetti?*" My body chilled.

His throat bobbed as he swallowed. "Yes."

I focused on his eyes, but now he was staring at the top of my head. He couldn't possibly be related to *that* Panetti. "Are you related to," my voice cracked, "N-Nick Panetti?"

"Oh, Cassidy." He shook his head, clenching his fist. "He's my father."

I shrunk into myself. "No. You can't be. Your dad tried to," I blinked several times and managed to whisper, "kill my dad."

205

Jesse closed his eyes for a minute. "Yes, he did."

I backed away several steps. Jesse's strong fingers wrapped around my arm. He wasn't hurting me, but I definitely couldn't escape.

"Cassidy, I am nothing like my father. Nothing. I'm on Nathan's side." If I'd thought his eyes were begging me before, now they were on their knees pleading. "I would never hurt you or your family."

I jerked my arm away. Thankfully, he released me so I didn't have permanent damage. "How can I believe that?" I whispered. "Now I know who your father is, he's still trying to hurt my dad."

Two male orderlies walked down the hallway. They cast furtive glances our way. Jesse nodded as they passed, waiting until we were alone again before saying, "I know exactly what my father is doing. Why do you think I'm trying to protect you?"

"So that's why you're always around?" My heart sunk. He was here to protect me, not because he cared. "Stalking me. Showing up to help me all the time. Warning me against Damon?" I gasped. "Wait. Is Damon one of . . . you?"

Jesse's jaw hardened. "No. I just don't like the guy."

I couldn't process all this awful information. "Please, just stay away from me." I wished I actually meant it. How could I have fallen for a Panetti? The son of the man who had tried and was still trying to kill my dad?

"Cassidy." He reached out a hand, but thankfully didn't touch me. "You trusted me until you knew my last name."

"No." I shook my head. "I never trusted you." I felt wetness building behind my eyelids. "I just wanted you."

Jesse's hand didn't stop this time. He caressed my cheek. I leaned into his hand, wishing I could fling myself into his arms but knowing now Jesse and I couldn't be together. Finally, I accumulated enough strength to jerk my face away and pivot from him.

"You're going to trust me, Cassidy," he said to my back.

I didn't look at him. One dose of those eyes and I might cave. "I doubt that very much," I said, before dragging myself away.

"How long do we have to wait and watch?" Terry whined. "We're on a time limit here. Give me a sniper rifle and I'll kill him already."

"You gonna march into that hospital and plug him? There are probably FBI all over the place." Al nodded at the emergency room exit door. They'd seen Nathan sneak in a few minutes ago, but they'd been two seconds too late and missed the opportunity to grab him.

"You're just brilliant, Ter. Why don't you just ask the police to cuff you and put you away until Ramirez's men come for you?" Al blew all his air out. "You've got to think. That was such a stupid hit you did on the daughter-in-law. Someone could identify us. We're lucky we could change vehicles and there weren't any police around. Ramirez isn't going to be happy if he hears about this mess."

"I had to do something. You think you're so smart. I'm sick of worrying about the FBI catching us." Terry's voice rose to a heinous wail. "Ramirez is going to kill us!"

Al gritted his teeth and clenched his fists. "No, he's not."

The air in the cab of the Chevy truck was charged with tension. Al considered turning Terry over to the authorities and finishing the job himself. Two million dollars all his own. It almost made him smile.

"I'm sorry," Terry muttered. "I'm sorry."

Al watched his partner. Terry knew when he'd pushed too far.

"I know this isn't your fault," Terry continued. "I just want it to be over. Let me shoot the doc when he walks out that door."

Al exhaled. The apology helped, a little bit. He gestured out the window. "We have to ship the body back. The FBI and local police have been watching for us the past few weeks. You shoot him and try to retrieve that body and you'll be arrested in seconds. Do you really want to screw up our last chance?"

Terry gulped. "Do you really think Ramirez barbecues people who fail him?"

Al shrugged, ignoring the lurch in his gut. "I think people talk."

"I've heard it from more than a few people. Some who've been at his parties and been forced to eat the barbecue. Maybe we should just grab the girl again and use her as a hostage."

An idea formed in Al's mind. A genuine smile appeared on his face. "Maybe. She could be our ticket." He clapped Terry on the shoulder. Terry winced. "Good idea. Cassidy Christensen is going to help us kill her dad."

I grabbed my dad and dragged him away from the family. When we were far enough away that no one could see or hear us, I turned and faced him. "I just saw Jesse."

Dad's eyebrows rose. "Jesse?"

"Panetti." Saying the name gave me chills. How could Jesse be that monster's son? How could I still long to be with him?

Dad took several breaths before muttering, "How do you know Jesse Panetti?"

"I met him several months ago. He just always seems to be there when I need him."

My father's face paled. "They told me he'd had contact but they promised it was minimal."

Contact? I blushed just thinking about the contact Jesse and I had shared. "Dad . . ." I had to admit the truth, about my feelings anyway, no way was Dad going to find out from me just how close I'd been to Jesse Panetti. "I really like him." My cheeks warmed. "I'm sorry. I know that's wrong, but I still do."

Dad was shaking his head, not looking at me or answering. Was he disappointed in me or terrified of me being around Jesse? "Dad." I grabbed his hand. "Who is Jesse? Who is he really?"

He focused on my face. "He's a double operative, just like his father was. He's very smart in what he does. I can't believe he'd risk himself to become involved with you."

The tears that hadn't stopped since Raquel's accident spilled over again. Dread enveloped me. I felt heavier than Nana's roll dough. "He works for his dad?"

Dad shrugged. "I don't know."

I stared in disbelief.

"I really don't, sweetheart. My contacts in the FBI believe Jesse is on our side. He provides them with information about the whereabouts of the slaves and has been instrumental in freeing many, but he still hasn't delivered his dad." He shook his head. "We thought Jesse's dad was on our side. I met him here at the hospital. We became friends and then joined together to eradicate human trafficking. A few years later Panetti showed his true loyalties and stuck a knife in me."

All the times Jesse had been there to help me flashed through my mind. Our dads had originally been friends, just like Jesse had claimed to be my friend. "The FBI claims Jesse is helping them," I said, "so he *has* to be on our side."

Dad smiled sadly. "The fact is he's double-crossing his dad and Ramirez. He might not survive long enough for you to worry about."

I felt like my dad had just jabbed a knife in *my* gut. "But what if I . . . care about him?"

Dad's head jerked up. "Stay away from him, Cassidy."

I glared. Now that I knew what Jesse was doing, his absences and confusing statements all made sense. He truly was trying to protect me, risking himself to do it, and now my dad was telling me to stay away from him?

Dad placed a heavy hand on my shoulder. "Don't do this. I'm not just being over-protective. Jesse Panetti is dangerous. Even if his intentions are good, he's still dangerous to you because of the risks he's taking. Promise me you'll stay away from him."

Could I really promise that? When I first discovered Jesse's last name I thought it would change how I felt about him, but I was wrong. I still wanted to spend every minute with Jesse, figuring out who he really was and developing a real relationship.

"Cassidy." Dad squeezed my shoulder. "Honey, you've got to promise me. I don't ask much of you, but I have to ask this. Promise you won't seek out Jesse Panetti."

"For how long?"

"Forever!"

I shook my head. "Not going to happen."

"Oh, Cassie." He sighed, staring at the floor for several minutes before saying, "At least stay away from him until we figure this mess out."

I'd never seen my father so desperate for me to agree. I could at least give him a little reassurance. I'd already told Jesse to stay away from me, I needed time to sort out my feelings, and I'd never forgive myself if something happened to my dad or Jesse because I'd been obstinate. I swallowed once and muttered, "Okay." Silence reigned for several minutes before I asked, "What about Damon? Jesse keeps warning me away from him."

"Damon?" Dad rolled his neck slowly from one side to the other. "All our information shows Damon is exactly who he says. He has no connections to Ramirez or Panetti." He frowned. "But Jesse may know something I don't. Stay away from Damon until I give you the go-ahead."

I nodded. Blackness clouded my mind. My father was taking away the two men I was interested in. The thought of never having Jesse touch me again cloaked me with despair.

Dad gave me a minute before wrapping his fingers around my hand. "Here I thought I was protecting you and you've been in contact with Jesse Panetti." He shivered as he said the name. "Anybody else I should know about?"

He said it half-jokingly but there was someone. "Hot Redhead keeps bugging me. I think she just wants Damon but there's something weird about that chick."

"Hot *Who?*"

I waved a hand. "I call her Hot Redhead. Her name is Elizabeth."

"A pretty redhead?" Dad's brow furrowed. He released his grip on me. "Named Elizabeth?"

"Uh-huh." I studied him, wondering why I'd felt the need to unload more stress, but he seemed surprisingly relaxed in the face of another bad guy.

Dad smiled. "Don't worry. I'll take care of Hot Redhead."

"But how can you—"

Dad cut me off. "Honey. Your marathon's a week from today."

My stomach jumped. "Uh-huh."

"Are you ready?"

"Yes, but . . ." I had to be the bigger person. "I'm not going to run it." I gestured towards Raquel's room. "With everything that's happened, I just can't do it. I can't be the reason that Muscle Man gets you."

"I want you to run it. You've worked so hard." He exhaled slowly. "Too many times I've kept you in the dark because I thought it would protect you." He glanced up at me. "You're so strong now, Cassie. I should've let you know I was alive. I'm sorry."

I swallowed, blinking quickly. I gave my dad a hug. "Thanks. I know you were just trying to protect me."

Dad cleared his throat then continued, "I want you to understand the situation. Four FBI agents will follow us to St. George. Two will follow you throughout the marathon, two will stick with me. They'll also alert the local police to be on the lookout, but that force will be overwhelmed by the marathon."

"Tell me the truth. If I run this marathon am I putting you in more danger?"

Dad shook his head. "No." He barked an insincere laugh. "Some of the FBI believe it's a great way to force a showdown. Like you're some kind of dangling carrot." He glanced up at me. "I'm not going to let anything happen to you, but I'm afraid they're right. There will be so many people, so many unknowns. This will be the best opportunity Ramirez's men have to strike. Are we brave enough, Cassidy?"

I looked at my dad's strong chin, his hazel eyes, his mouth that used to laugh so easily. I closed my eyes and pictured Raquel bruised and beaten. My brother watching his beloved wife in anguish. Poor little Tate afraid and crying for his mom. Was I brave enough to run this marathon and bring Muscle Man out to fight? If I didn't risk it, was I betraying Raquel, my dad, and my mom's memory?

"I'm not afraid," I lied.

Dad chuckled, pulling me against his side. "You never are."

How I wished that were true.

Week Sixteen–better known as Marathon Day–yikes!

The parking lot was awash with hundreds of headlights cutting through the steady downpour. Runners spilled from vehicles and sloshed through puddles, trying to beat each other to the bus loading station. *Save it for the race*, I thought. Four-thirty was too early to act this competitive.

My stomach hadn't settled since I'd awakened at three-thirty. Dad tried to force-feed a banana and piece of whole wheat bread down me at our hotel. I chomped on and attempted to swallow the mushy banana and dry bread, but my stomach rebelled. I spit most of it in the garbage can.

Dad escorted me from the Honda Accord, his car-of-the-day, towards the loading area for runners.

"I don't think you should be out here." I glanced around the busy parking lot. "So exposed like this."

Dad's grip on my elbow tightened. His smile didn't reach his eyes. "I'm fine." He pointed at two men, the same agents who had followed Damon and I from the Japanese restaurant and rode bikes through the Top of Utah Marathon. "They'll be watching over you. My agents are close by as well."

We stopped next to a crowd of runners. Despite the soaking, I wasn't quite ready to jump into line. I studied the darkened parking lot, making sure Damon wasn't there. "Will my guys be on bikes?"

He nodded. "They won't be able to stay as close as I'd like but . . ." He forced a smile. "You'll be okay. We're not afraid

213

anymore, right? Thanks for your little pep talk back at the hotel."

"That talk was for me." I bent down and retied my shoelaces for the third time, nothing felt right this morning.

Dad took off his raincoat and shielded both of us, ushering me into the bus line. "Let's get you out of this rain."

Shivering, I checked the crowds of people for Muscle Man. "I'm going to be in it for the next few hours."

"It'll ease up. It never rains for very long here." Dad rubbed my arm. "You've got your cell phone?"

I patted my shorts pocket. "Right here."

"Jared or I will call if something happens with Raquel, so don't worry." He stayed with me as the line snaked forward. "You have some food and water?"

I lifted a plastic St. George Marathon bag, designed to leave clothes at the starting line. "Right here."

Dad gave me his stern father look. "You'll eat something before you run."

"Once my stomach settles."

The line slowly slipped towards the school buses spewing black smoke into the pre-dawn air.

Dad turned to me. "I won't be able to see you until Mile 21. They said unless I'm volunteering I'd have to drive so far out of my way to see you earlier that I'd miss you at the finish line."

My stomach dropped. I suddenly felt like a little girl going to her first sleepover and leaving the comfort of my parents and my canopy bed. An awful gnawing inside made me wonder if I'd see my dad again.

I grabbed him and squeezed. "Be careful, Dad."

He returned the hug. "You be careful." He pulled back and studied my face for a second. "And have fun."

I forced a smile. "Should be a real party."

"Load up," a man yelled.

There were only a few people in front of me in line. I reached the steps. "I'll see you at 21," I yelled.

"I'll be there," he called back.

The tide of people swept me up and onto the bus. As I trudged towards the back a large palm encircled my waist. I jumped and spun, my nervousness increasing when I saw Damon grinning at me, his chiseled face shadowed by a baseball cap.

"H-hey, where'd you come from?" How had he just happened to be on the same bus as me?

Damon walked me down the aisle and ushered me into a seat. I stared out the window, trying to locate my father. Damon peered over my shoulder. "Who are you looking for?"

"My dad."

"I missed him," Damon muttered.

I turned away from the crowd. Dad had already disappeared. It bothered me immensely that Damon cared that he'd missed him.

"Is he meeting you after?"

I nodded, biting my lip and clutching my clothing bag with sweaty palms.

Damon smiled. "It will be nice to finally meet your dad." He pushed my sweatshirt back a few inches and tugged on one of my Princess Leia braids. "This is cute."

I rolled my eyes. "No, it is definitely not cute, but I promised El I'd run in Princess Leia braids. It's for her." My stomach churned. Dad had never told me whether he'd found out more information about Damon. With the week we'd had with Raquel I had hardly thought about Damon. But Dad had said Damon's initial check came up clean. Unlike Jesse who was a definite no. Would I ever feel Jesse's touch again? Should I be trying to ditch Damon?

My FBI guys loaded up last with their bikes. I didn't dare stare at them and make the connection obvious, especially since Damon might remember them from the Japanese restaurant, but I was so glad to see them on the same bus.

The bus lumbered away. I endured the dark, bouncy ride and Damon's questions about why I hadn't returned his calls.

He couldn't refute my excuse. He knew how important Raquel was to me. A smattering of rain and a whole lot of wind greeted us as we descended from the bus. My stomach danced. I shook from cold and nerves. I just wanted seven a.m. and that gunshot. I couldn't handle much more waiting.

My phone rang. I snatched it from my shorts and turned my back on Damon.

"It's going to be today, Cassie." Jared was never one to waste time. "The doctors are prepping her for surgery in a few hours."

"Today!" I stomped my feet. "You kidding me?"

Jared blew out a long breath. "The baby's heart rate is decelerating. It's too dangerous to keep him in any longer. They think his lungs are developed enough and if not . . ." Jared paused.

I held my breath and prayed through the entire pause.

"A lot of babies have been in NICU and recovered okay." He made another shaky sound. "I wish you were here."

Damon watched me without saying anything.

"I should come home," I said. "You need Dad and me. Don't you? Don't you need us?"

"No," Jared said. "I've got Nana and Tasha is coming soon."

"Well, that makes me feel all reassured."

Jared gave me a small chuckle. Damon smiled at me. His large hand massaged my upper arm. I smiled in gratitude. He was always so nice to me.

"You run that race," Jared said. "You've trained too hard. El was so proud of you. You kick it for her and the baby."

Tears squeezed from my eyes. "It's just a stupid race. Raquel and the baby are a billion times more important."

There was silence on the line. "You listen to me, sis. Raquel has always believed in you. She's just been waiting for you to succeed. She knew you wouldn't quit. You're going to run that race for her and the doctors are going to deliver our baby and El's going to recover." He coughed, sniffed, and continued, "I'm proud of you. You do it for her."

216

The phone disconnected. Jared had exceeded his emotional capacity.

I stared at my cell phone and wondered why I was hundreds of miles from the most important people in my life. I met Damon's gaze. "Raquel's having her baby."

He squeezed my arm. "Then this will be a doubly special day."

"How much time do we have left?" I asked. I didn't want to talk about the situation at home and be drained from emotion.

"It's twenty to seven."

"Um, I'm embarrassed to admit this, but . . ." I did not want another accident in a race and I needed some way to call my dad without Damon listening.

He grinned at me. "You want to check out the décor in the port-a-potties."

"I hear they're very spacious."

"Uh-huh." He grabbed my hand and tugged me through the crowd waiting for the privilege of using a stinky bathroom.

"I don't want you to have an accident while I'm running with you."

I stuck out my tongue. "Very funny." A door opened and I ran in. I texted my dad while I peed, not daring to call and have Damon hear.

"Damon's here. What do I do?"

The answer was almost immediate. "Stay away from him."

"Is he with Muscle Man?"

"Nothing to confirm that but I'd feel better if you weren't with him."

"Ok."

I pushed send and slipped out of the port-a-potty. Damon stood by the door waiting for me. How in the world was I supposed to ditch him?

"We'd better get going," he said.

I bobbed my head. He followed me up to the road. A gunshot signaled seven a.m. had finally come. We surged through the starting line with a flowing mass of people. It was inky dark, rain pattering our faces. I pulled my visor down farther and darted in and out of people, trying to ditch Damon. His long legs ate up any distance I created between us. With the darkness and lack of visibility I felt like I was having an out-of-body experience. The first mile passed so quickly I could hardly believe it.

"7:07:21," a man called out as we sailed through mile marker one.

Probably a bit faster than I should be running, but my marathon pace was no longer the biggest concern. Ditching Damon was easier said than done. I didn't have the stride of a 6'2" man with legs longer than a giraffe's neck. "I know you've trained for a faster pace than this," I told him. "I won't feel bad if you go ahead."

"I'd feel bad, I want to be with you."

What did I say to that? "Um, thanks."

"I've already qualified for Boston. Let's get you there."

Could Damon really have some other agenda? I glanced around and saw my bike riders fifty yards behind us. With the FBI there and Damon acting completely normal, I was having a hard time wasting energy trying to escape him.

We ran into a headwind but the rain started to taper. An hour later, the sky lightened a bit and the crowd thinned, even if I wanted to hide from Damon I couldn't. I prayed for the wind to stop. When that didn't work I prayed that I wouldn't feel it so much. After several miles I noticed that either the storm was abating or my prayers were working. We sailed through the miles and I felt great. To get past the boredom I shoved in my iPod and imagined my nephew coming into the world.

I approached the aid station at mile thirteen. My heart thumped with excitement. I was halfway through. Then reality hit. My legs were tired. This weather bit the big one. I still had no idea how to escape Damon. And I was only halfway through?

218

The volunteers were in the street calling out, "Gu, gu."

I grabbed one, ripped the top off and squeezed it into my mouth. I could hardly swallow the lump, but I knew I needed the energy boost.

"Gatorade, Gatorade," the next table of volunteers called out.

I shook my head and kept going. I wanted water to get this awful sludge out of my mouth. One of the volunteers raced up to my side. "Gatorade," she said, shoving the cup into my hands.

"No," I said, trying to push the cup back into her hands.

She encroached upon my personal space. "You need this Gatorade."

I stared at the tiny, thick-skulled woman. I couldn't see much from underneath the low-riding baseball cap, but her shape looked like. "Hot Redhead?" I asked.

She glanced up at me then. Her eyes large and intense. "Get away from Damon."

"I'm trying."

She pushed me away, nodding in Damon's direction. "Find a way."

Clutching the paper cup of Gatorade, I gulped it down then tossed it. I started jogging again. Glancing back through the mist, I saw Elizabeth watching me. How did she know about Damon? What did she expect me to do?

"Did you get a Gu down?" Damon was by my side.

I jumped and let out a little scream.

Damon laughed. "You okay?"

I nodded and started running down the road. Damon stayed right by my side. I turned my iPod up so he wouldn't try to talk me and mulled over Elizabeth's warning. Damon was a better runner than me and we were in the middle of a race. The safest thing to do had to be to finish the race or at least make it to my dad. If Damon or Elizabeth were working with Muscle Man they probably wouldn't try anything with all the other runners around.

"How are you doing?" Damon yelled to be heard over my music.

I took out one of my earbuds. "I thought this marathon was downhill."

Damon laughed. "It drops in elevation, but there's still some uphill along the way. You okay?" He took off his hat, shook the rainwater from it, swiped his face clean and replaced the baseball cap.

"Just peachy." I nodded towards his watch. "Are we on pace?"

"A bit ahead even."

I took a long breath, trying to act normal, trying to forget about Elizabeth's warning but it just reinforced my dad saying to get away and all the times Jesse had warned me. "I'm going to slow down. You keep going."

Damon shook his head. "If," he smiled, "or actually, when you hit the wall, we're going to need some extra minutes to get through it."

"The only reason I'm going to hit the wall is because you're killing me," I muttered. "Seriously." I slowed my pace. "You keep going, I need a minute."

Damon grinned. Taking me by the hand, he pulled me along with him. "I'm not leaving you."

I retrieved my hand from his grip but kept at the same pace. I could keep forcing him to pull me along, make a scene and hope the FBI came to help, or get to mile twenty-one where my dad was waiting with more FBI help.

We passed the aid station at mile nineteen without much more than a drink of water, but my heart started lightening. The FBI bike riders were still within sight and I'd almost made it to my dad.

Just when I thought I had the marathon licked, my legs stopped responding to my commands to rotate and my vision darkened. Damon grabbed onto my elbow and yelled in my ear, "It's okay, Cassie. It's just the wall. Keep moving and you'll get through it."

"Can't," I muttered.

Through my pain, I felt the buzz of my cell phone. "Phone," I said. "Get it."

Damon yanked the phone out to oblige me and flipped it open. "Hello?"

I listened through the haze and kept putting one foot in front of the other.

"The baby's here? How's Raquel?" He paused and then, "Oh, that is awesome."

"Give me." I reached out for the phone but Damon dodged me.

"Cassie isn't doing so well. I'll have her call you at the finish line. Congrats." Damon closed the phone. "Raquel had the baby. The little guy is doing great. Jared says he looks just like him."

I managed a smile. My nephew was here. He was safe. "Raquel?" I asked.

"She's doing well. The doctor was excited about the way her body handled the operation. Her brain waves look good. They think she may recover more easily now."

I felt a surge of adrenaline rush through me. My brain cleared. I saw aid station twenty-one up ahead. My nephew was here. He was doing well and so was Raquel. If they could get through what they'd been dealt. I could get through this dang marathon. I sailed into the aid station, stole a caffeinated Gu, downed it and a cup of water, then started again.

"You're past the wall," Damon said, sticking to me like cellulite.

"Thank heavens." We were on a downhill bend sinking into St. George from the northwest and I could see my dad in the middle of the crowd.

"Cassie!"

I found enough energy to raise my hand and turn his direction. Damon brushed close to me. "Your dad's in trouble," he whispered in my ear.

I looked over my dad's shoulder. Muscle Man and Greasy Beanpole were closing in on him. "Dad!"

He took a step towards me, smiling. Muscle Man and Greasy Beanpole sandwiched him, lifting him off his feet, and rushing back through the crowd. I screamed, running after them. Damon raced next to me. The FBI got caught in the throng of people at the aid station. They ditched their bikes and struggled through the crowd.

I almost tripped on a man lying in the street. I looked down. Blood oozed from his motionless chest. "Damon," I screamed.

He grabbed my hand, pulling me along. "Worry about your dad."

Muscle Man and Greasy Beanpole shoved my dad into a tan cargo van. Seconds later the van was squealing away.

I raced after them. Damon grabbed my arm. "This way!"

"They've got my dad," I panted.

"I know." He yanked his keys from a small pocket of his shorts and clicked the unlock button. "My car is right here."

I stared at him. The FBI were almost through the crowd. Should I wait for them? Did they have a vehicle close by?

Damon pushed me into his car, making the decision for me. I crawled over the console as he leaped in and started the engine. We gunned away from the FBI. I glanced back to see the gray-haired agent shaking his head at me and dialing furiously into his phone.

I turned forward. The cargo van was careening away but Damon floored it, keeping them in sight. I shivered, wet from the rain and my sweat, scared of what was going to happen to my dad.

"Why was your car parked here?"

He shrugged, not looking at me.

I reached for my cell phone then remembered Damon had pocketed it after he'd talked to Jared. "Give me my cell phone so I can call the police."

Damon careened around a corner. "I don't have your cell phone."

"Yes, you do."

He held up a hand. "I don't know what you're talking about. Can you please let me drive so I don't lose your dad?"

My questions kept growing but the one thing I didn't want to do was lose my dad so I shut up and held on. We followed the van around the north side of the bluff and into sandstone hills frequented by bikers and runners. Damon stayed far enough back that I hoped they didn't notice us.

The van stopped. I prayed for some movement so I could see that my dad was still alive. It didn't happen. A sinking feeling in my gut got deeper as I glanced at Damon's face. He didn't look like himself, his expression a mask of determination and anger. He reached over me and pulled a gun from the glove box. I leaned away from the dull black pistol, my breath coming in short gasps. I sat there panting, my throat so dry I didn't know if I could verbalize any of the questions I had. Who was Damon and what was he doing?

Damon leaped from his car. I jumped out, following him as he ran around the van and yanked the side door open. Muscle Man sat inside with my dad next to him. He was still alive. I wobbled with relief. Dad's eyes jumped from me to Damon. "Oh, Cassidy. No!"

Muscle Man grinned. "I don't think anyone told you sweetheart, but you're dessert."

Post-Marathon Party—I Wish

I glanced at Damon. He stared at me with a slight smirk on his face. Was he a part of this?

Greasy Beanpole came around from the driver's side, brushing against me and bending to unlatch the second door. I shrunk back, revulsion sweeping through me.

Muscle Man stood, shoving my dad from the van. Damon pushed me out of the way and jumped onto Greasy Beanpole. At the same time my dad dove at Muscle Man's ankles, tripping him.

What the heck? Why didn't anyone tell me about the pre-arranged signal?

Damon pummeled Greasy Beanpole into the van floor while my father and his huge rival wrestled in the reddish-brown mud for control of the gun in Muscle Man's hands.

I came at Muscle Man from behind. He easily threw me off and circled my dad's esophagus with his arm. His shiny black pistol dug into my father's temple. Dad stopped fighting. Muscle Man whirled to glare at me. "Stop right there, Cassidy."

"No, *you* stop," Damon said from the van door. He pushed Greasy Beanpole in front of him, a gun pressed against the smaller man's neck.

Muscle Man laughed. He stood, dragging my father up with him without moving his finger from the trigger. "You think I care about Terry? Do me a favor and shoot him, save me a million bucks."

"Al," Greasy Beanpole whined.

"Shut up," Muscle Man yelled.

"All we're going to accomplish here is a blood bath," Damon said, his voice level and reasonable, eons from where I was emotionally. An hour ago I'd tried to ditch him and now he was saving us. I didn't care who he was as long as he saved my dad. "I shoot your buddy. You shoot Nathan. I shoot you. Either way you end up dead."

Muscle Man smiled. "You *wish* it would play out like that. Preppy little college boy. You ever shot somebody in your life?" He stared. Damon didn't look away. Finally Muscle Man shook his head. "I shoot Nathan, then I kill you. You may get a lucky shot off and plug Terry but then I still walk with two million dollars and Cassidy." He smirked. "Why do you think I let you follow me? I wasn't going to leave without the girl."

"No!" my dad screamed. Muscle Man jammed the gun harder into his head.

I clutched myself to try to stop the trembling and the need to vomit. Muscle Man had waited for me. I glanced around, hoping someone would come to our rescue. The van blocked our view of the road but I couldn't hear any vehicles approaching.

"The girl is kind of a pain. Let me kill her for you."

The voice came from the back of the van. I spun. Elizabeth strolled casually towards us with a gun extended.

I snapped. "What are you doing? Put that gun away, you psycho!"

"I don't think so, Cassidy." Elizabeth was as calm as she was beautiful. She even looked good with her red hair plastered to her skull from rainwater. "I've tried to do things the right way, but you," she jabbed the dull black metal in my direction, "keep getting in the way."

"Okay, crazy woman." I tried to ignore the deadly weapon pointed at me. My legs were shaking and I couldn't blame it on the twenty-one miles I'd just run. "What are you going to accomplish shooting me?"

Her eyes met my dad's and then gestured to Muscle Man. The world stopped rotating. My stomach dropped. Hot Redhead was on our side. Where did that put Damon?

225

Muscle Man stared at her. "Who are you? How'd you follow us?"

"I put a tracking device on Damon's car."

"She's after Damon," I told him, maybe I could at least distract him while Elizabeth and Damon figured out what to do with their guns. "Think about what you're doing, Elizabeth," I said. "There are a lot of men looking for a beautiful girl like yourself. Why waste your life shooting me just because Damon thinks I'm cooler than you?"

Elizabeth tossed her hair over her shoulder. "You're not cooler than me."

"Of course I'm not," I said, trying to sound soothing, but my voice was quavering too much. I clenched my hands, praying my dad and I would somehow live through this. "Just put the gun down, Elizabeth. We'll get you a good psychiatrist and someday soon you'll meet someone even better than Damon."

My eyes flickered to him. Damon watched with a bemused smile as Elizabeth and I argued. He kept the gun pointed at the whimpering Greasy Beanpole, his strong grip not allowing the criminal to move.

"I want Damon," Elizabeth insisted.

"Enough of this high-school drama," Muscle Man interrupted. He moved the gun from my dad's head to point it at Elizabeth.

It was the opening she needed. I heard the retort of a pistol. I screamed. Muscle Man sunk to the earth, taking my dad with him. The gun fell from Muscle Man's fingers. I sprang to my dad, pushing at Muscle Man's bulk to free him. Elizabeth joined me. Together we rolled him off. Dad struggled to his feet, bringing Elizabeth and me up with him. We all stared down at the motionless monster.

"Hot Redhead! You shot him." I shook my head in disbelief, stomach twisting at all the blood pooling on the right side of Muscle Man's chest but at the same time so relieved that he wouldn't touch me again.

226

Another shot recoiled through the air. I jumped from my dad's arms and spun to see Damon shoving Greasy Beanpole into the dust. "Damon?"

He kicked Greasy Beanpole with his running shoe then smiled at Elizabeth. "Thank you. These two have definitely served their purpose."

Elizabeth glared at him. "No loyalty for your own."

Damon laughed. "Al and Terry were great. They kept an eye on Cassidy whenever I had to focus on another job and got Nathan to come to Utah without me having to compromise myself. Too bad they didn't know who I was." His blue eyes were cold as they met my gaze. "There was no way I was going to share this reward with them."

"What reward?" My insides froze. Jesse had tried to warn me. But Damon had seemed so genuine, so nice. He couldn't be . . .

Damon's gun swung to aim straight at my father. "The two million dollars."

I grabbed my dad's arm. Elizabeth pointed her gun at Damon. "I *knew* it! The FBI swore you were nobody, but I knew something was off."

"Why didn't you say something?" my dad's whisper was harsh and unforgiving.

Elizabeth didn't look at him. "I did say something. The FBI thought I was crazy. I even checked out his background and spoke with some clients."

Damon grinned. "Nobody would guess that I work for Clive Ramirez." His finger tightened on the trigger. "Better make sure the truth doesn't leak out from any of you."

"No," I breathed, staring at Damon. He wouldn't shoot my dad, would he?

Elizabeth's arm stayed steady. "He's Ramirez's crony, Cassidy."

"Oh, no." The world spun. I would've fallen if my dad hadn't held me up.

"Damon is one of the best covers I've seen," Elizabeth said.

"That's because I'm Damon. Great cover when you don't have to fabricate anything."

"Then how did you get involved with Ramirez?" Dad studied Damon carefully.

"My mom met Clive in Acapulco years ago. She always had a different man around. I hated most of them, but Clive and I really hit it off. He was like the father I never had. He's been training me for years and over the past six months I've done such a good job that he's trusted me with important hits." He grinned. "Like this one."

We were so close together, Damon couldn't possibly miss when he pulled that trigger. But maybe I could distract him. I inched closer to him. Elizabeth's eyes flickered to me before she asked another question. "Why'd you kill the man up the canyon?"

Damon half-smiled, inclining his head to Elizabeth. "I didn't know if anyone would put that together." He shrugged. "Paul Ethington. He was supposed to be keeping an eye on Nathan's family. He was the one that informed us Cassidy had signed up for the Health Days Race and made sure she won the St. George Marathon. Then Ramirez found out he was feeding info to the FBI. I was sent to take him out and become involved with Cassidy so when Nathan came home I could take care of him easily."

"You k-killed that guy?" I stuttered, clinging to the van door with slick fingers and picturing that body in Smithfield Canyon. My stomach was in my throat.

Damon glanced at me. "I was going to move him after the race, but then you found him."

"You knew Al and Terry were going after me today?" Dad asked, his voice calm, his gaze studying Damon. How could he look so unafraid when I wanted to fall on the ground and beg Damon not to kill us?

Damon chuckled. "Clive told me their plans. They were going to wait until Cassidy reached mile twenty-one and distracted you. They were pretty organized," he admitted. "They took out the FBI agents watching over you seconds before they grabbed you. They made it easy for me. I simply had my car at the right spot, grabbed Cassidy, and followed you."

My eyes narrowed. "I can't believe I fell for your act." No matter how scared I was I wouldn't let him hurt my dad. Just another step and I could jump on him. Could I move fast enough to knock the gun away? If I could distract him, Dad and Elizabeth could take him out.

Damon's eyes searched mine. "I am sorry about this, Cassie. It started out as a job, but I really grew to enjoy you. You entertained me while I waited for the right time to kill Nathan."

I was like an apple Damon had enjoyed a few bites of, and then dropped into the dirt and kicked to the side of the road. Rage boiled in my chest. Damon had tricked me, betrayed me, and now he was going to shoot my father. The arm supporting his gun steadied, focusing directly on my dad. I could barely see through my anger. I lowered my head and barreled into Damon's chest. He stuttered off balance but didn't go down. The gun discharged.

I heard a loud, "Oomph," and a body slamming into the mud.

I swung at Damon with both fists. He grabbed at my arms with one hand, trying to steady his gun for another shot. I didn't dare look to see if he'd killed my father, I kept pummeling him. The gun was ripped from Damon's grasp by lean fingers. Fingers that I recognized. "Jesse!"

Jesse gave me a brief smile before tossing the gun into the brush and slamming his fist into Damon's face. I jumped away from the fight and spun to see if my dad was okay.

Dad knelt on the ground, sheltering Elizabeth with his body.

229

She'd taken the bullet for my dad. I hurried to them. A hand grabbed my foot, toppling me onto my dad and Elizabeth. Strong arms yanked me back and pulled me against Muscle Man's side. No! He couldn't still be alive. The right side of his shirt was drenched in blood and mud. My throat tightened as my pulse reverberated in my skull. "No," I screamed, flailing at him with my fists.

Jesse's head whipped around, his eyes round and terror-filled. "Cassidy!"

Muscle Man tried to pin my arms and hold me with his left hand, lifting a gun in his bloody right hand. "It's over, Cassidy," he whispered.

Jesse jumped off of Damon and came running. My dad released Elizabeth and scrambled towards us on his knees. I freed my arm and grabbed Muscle Man's fingers, squeezing with every ounce of strength I'd gleaned from years of weight lifting. Muscle Man cried out in pain, his weakened right limb unable to support the gun and the pressure. The gun clanked to the dirt. I slammed my fist into the bloodiest part of his chest that I could see. He released me and I flew back into the dirt.

My dad pounced on Muscle Man, holding him down. Jesse grinned at me. "Well done."

Over Jesse's shoulder I could see Damon stomping towards us covered in dirt and blood from their fight. "Jesse!"

He whirled. Damon spotted his pistol underneath a sagebrush and swept it from the ground. Jesse leapt at him before he could bring it up and shoot. They bounced onto the ground, Jesse trying to hold onto Damon's wrist and slam the pistol from his fingers. My dad had Muscle Man pinned. Elizabeth sat up, looking half-dazed. I could barely haul myself off the ground, but I wasn't going to let Damon hurt Jesse. I stuttered across the few feet and slammed the heel of my running shoe against Damon's fingers and the gun.

He howled in pain, letting go of the pistol. Jesse pushed him into the mud. Policemen and FBI agents spilled around the van. They rolled over Muscle Man and cuffed him. To his credit he didn't cry out in pain, just glared at me. Some other officers hauled Greasy Beanpole away, which was really gross considering he had to be dead.

Damon screamed in protest as they pulled Jesse off of him and cuffed Damon. "I'm clean. He's the one you want." He pointed at Jesse. "Check my credentials."

Luckily the policemen didn't buy his story. I prayed he'd rot in a prison cell. Jesse folded his arms across his chest and watched them haul Damon away.

I glanced over to Hot Redhead and my dad. She leaned against my dad's shoulder. "I'm fine, Nathan. It just grazed my arm." She pressed at a bloody wound on her upper arm with delicate fingers.

Dad ripped off his T-shirt and covered the wound with it. The relief in my dad's face shocked me for a second. Did he have feelings for . . . I couldn't complete the thought. It was like a betrayal to my mom to even think it. My jaw was on the grass. "So Hot Redhead *is* one of the good guys."

Elizabeth smiled at me. "My name is Caroline Farnsworth. I've been following you for your dad since he discovered Ramirez knew he was alive and was coming after him again."

"Dang, girl. You're not only a pretty good shot, you're the best actress I've ever met."

She arched an eyebrow. "I definitely made some mistakes with this one so I'm glad it all worked out." She shook her head. "For some reason I wanted you away from Damon, even though everyone swore he wasn't anyone to be concerned about."

"So that's why you acted so nuts."

Her beautiful smile returned. "I was trying anything I could to keep you safe. I didn't want you training for this marathon or being around anyone I had any doubts about."

"Thanks," I murmured, still struggling to see her as a good guy, especially with my dad wrapping his arm around her shoulder.

A strong arm encircled my waist. "Are you all right?"

I smiled up at Jesse. "I am now. How did you know to come?"

He grinned. "I told you I'd protect you."

Hot Redhead and my dad both frowned at Jesse.

"You were almost too late," Hot Redhead said.

My dad whirled on Elizabeth. "You *told* him to come."

She focused on Jesse. "He's been very helpful with Cassidy's protection." She squirmed at my dad's frown. "It wasn't like I was in contact with him, but I saw him watching over her a few times and I called him today after I contacted the FBI and police."

"I don't want him anywhere near her!" Dad turned the force of his glower on Jesse. "Who gave you permission to come and blow your cover?"

Jesse pursed his lips. "I don't need permission when Cassidy is in trouble."

Dad's eyebrows arched. His fists clenched. "She is *my* daughter."

"Yes, sir, and you know how much I respect you, but Cassidy is a very capable not to mention beautiful woman who can make decisions for herself."

I blinked, warmth rushing through me. "Um, we'll be right back." I gave Dad a smile and tugged Jesse away from him, maybe Hot Redhead could keep him busy for a minute. Dad seemed a bit more interested in her than he should've been. She couldn't be more than five years older than me and my mom hadn't been gone that long.

When we were out of earshot I whirled to face Jesse. "So you are a good guy?"

He chuckled, reaching up to brush at a wet lock of hair that had escaped from my braids. "I like to think so."

I trembled from his touch. I wanted to throw myself into his arms, but I had to know what was really going on. "How do I know you're not just pretending to help the FBI."

Jesse took a deep breath. His fudge-colored eyes searched my face. "I think you know I wouldn't betray you."

I swallowed. Yesterday I wouldn't have guessed that Damon would betray me. But Jesse had a point. There was no way to deny how he'd always made me feel. I couldn't question what my own gut was telling me. "But how are you involved in all of this?"

"When my dad sold himself to Ramirez a few years ago he wanted me with him. I refused so he," he coughed and looked down, "he blackmailed me."

Blackmailed? By his own father? I wanted to ask how he'd blackmailed him but Jesse kept talking, probably so I wouldn't ask.

"He wants me to work with him but obviously my commitment level is in question so my assignments are gruntwork, usually moving shipments of slaves." He scowled. "I do all I can to make it easier for them and protect them from the worst of the slavers."

"You have to be a part of it?"

He studied the red mud on my shoes. "I've found a way I can help. The slavers all think I'm one of them." He opened his hands. "Most people looking at me would believe it too. After a few drinks they tell me about other shipments, other hiding and exchange spots for the slaves. I have to be careful what information I share with the FBI. If the children I am working with get rescued and I don't get arrested or killed, nobody would believe my cover." He studied me. "I also have access to some of my dad and Ramirez's conversations because I've figured out some of my dad's passwords. This morning I found some communication about Damon. I hurried here as fast as I could."

My brain spun as I processed all he was telling me. "You didn't know who Damon was?"

His eyes widened. "You think if I would've known I would've let him anywhere near you? I've never met him or Ramirez and the FBI claimed he was clean."

"Then why did you keep warning me about him?"

"I wish I could say I had some kind of intuition." Jesse ducked his head. "But the truth was I didn't like seeing you with anyone else."

I grinned. "Answers like that will probably win my trust faster than anything."

Jesse chuckled. "I'll have to remember that. You told me you'd trust me when I took you on a real date. How does next weekend sound?"

My insides warmed. I didn't care what my dad thought. I'd give anything to have this man in my life for a long, long time. "Why wait?"

Jesse opened his arms. I fell into them. "You're all I've thought about, Cassidy," he whispered against my cheek.

I rotated my face to his, kissing him for several wonderful moments before a familiar throat clearing pulled us apart. "We might have to start that real dating thing after I convince Daddy-o," I whispered.

Jesse sighed. He glanced at my father then turned back to me with a grim smile. "That's going to take some doing."

One look at my dad's face told me it would take a miracle.

Monday morning I paced the hospital hallway with baby Thor in arms. Jared refused to discuss names without Raquel, so I dubbed the cute little man Thor. I bounced the baby to sleep, my legs still feeling the after-effects of the marathon. After the initial questioning had settled down, Jesse had talked the FBI and my dad into letting me finish the marathon. He ran by my side through the last five miles. I had a pathetic time of 5:35:41 but I'd finished, and spending an hour chatting with Jesse had been the best part of the whole experience.

I gazed down at my nephew's knob of a nose, soft cheeks, and distinctive rosebud lips. His eyes were, of course, closed. He slept too much, but besides that Thor was perfect. I was smitten.

The little guy had done amazing, only staying on oxygen for a few hours after his birth. He was all checked out and ready to go home. If only Thor's momma would recover and come with us.

"Can I take Baby Thor in to see his mom before we go home?" I asked the nurse at the ICU counter after she buzzed all of us in.

The petite blonde wrinkled her nose. "Thor?"

"It's just temporary," I said, but my feelings were injured. What was wrong with Thor?

She gestured toward Raquel's room. "Just for a few minutes."

I pointed at Dad, Jared, and Tate. "Can we all go in?"

She nodded. "Keep it short."

The boys followed me into Raquel's room. Tate was strangely muted when he visited his mom in the hospital. I could sense how much it hurt him to see her like this.

I hugged the baby closer. "Hey, El. I've got a really cool reason for you to get better." I pivoted so she could see his cute face if she opened her eyes.

She mumbled something incoherent.

"I named the little guy Thor and it's going to stick if you don't snap out of this head injury and change it." I leaned close, whispering in her ear. "Come on, El. Thor needs a Momma hug and a Momma kiss and you definitely need to see how cute he is."

Her eyes remained closed. Her breathing soft and slow. Not even a mutter. I kept close, hoping to see some change. I didn't realize I was squishing the little dude until he let out a wail.

"Oh, crap. Sorry, Thor." I straightened. The plug had fallen out. I retrieved it from the blanket, reinserted, and started to bounce. Thor spit the pacifier back at me and hollered his frustration.

"Auntie," Tate reprimanded. "Don't hurt my bro."

"Sorry, Tater." I bounced and sang and looked to Dad and Jared for help, but they weren't paying attention to my distress. They both focused on Raquel. I turned in that direction. But the voice came before I made eye contact, "Cassie, is that . . . my baby?"

"El!" I screamed.

The baby screamed louder.

Jared attacked Raquel first, followed closely by Tate and my dad. After seconds of impatient charity, I gave the screaming baby to my dad and got my own hug.

Jared elevated her bed and Dad gently laid the baby on her chest. Raquel cuddled him against her chest, kissing, cooing, and soothing. He calmed immediately. Tate crowded into her other side, beaming.

"Hey," I said. "Thor wouldn't do that for me."

Everyone laughed.

Raquel kissed Tate's cheek again, but couldn't take her eyes from the baby. "Thor?"

Jared couldn't take his hands from his wife. He stroked her cheek. "It's just a Cassie-name. We'll think of one together."

Raquel smiled. "He's beautiful."

Everyone murmured their agreement. Even the crowd of nurses in the doorway seemed reluctant to break up the reunion.

"How about Nathan?" Raquel said.

Jared grinned. "Tate and Nate. I like it."

I glanced at my dad. He was smiling and wiping at tears.

I sighed. "Can I at least call him Thor?"

Raquel shook her head. "Only when I can't hear you."

My dad put his arm around me. "Don't you like the name Nathan?"

"Well, with two of you around, it might get confusing."

His smile fled. "Well, who knows how much longer I'll be around."

I jerked from his hug. "Really, Dad."

"I fly back to Mexico in a few days."

We all protested, but Dad stood firm. Finally, he said, "But I don't see any reason why Cassidy couldn't come visit me soon. I can help you get started volunteering in the *safe* areas."

My eyes widened. I'd decided I was going to help the children with or without his blessing but it really meant a lot that he was supportive of me. Now if I could just get him to approve of Jesse.

My dad rushed off to meet with the FBI, again. Damon and Muscle Man were in custody but not talking. The FBI hoped the little bit of information Jesse had about his dad's whereabouts and some background research on Terry and the other dead guy might turn something up.

I left Jared and Raquel with their cute boys and slowly meandered the hospital halls. A large hand covered my elbow. "Glad to see you home safe," a deep voice murmured.

I whirled into Jesse's inviting chest. Placing my hands on his pecs to give me some distance didn't help. It was all I could do to not squeeze the well-formed muscles. "I've missed you."

Jesse grinned. "Any luck on convincing your father that you need me in your life?"

I swallowed, my stomach churning. "He doesn't want me near you."

He inhaled sharply. "And what do you think?"

I bit my lip. "He may as well have sentenced me to life in my room." I turned away from his grin. I gnawed harder on my lip. Jesse had answered some of my questions about his dad and his involvement in anti-trafficking while we finished the marathon on Saturday, but there was one question I'd been too scared to ask. My palms were wet but I forced myself to be brave. "Who assigned you to watch out for me?"

"Nobody." He stared into my eyes. "I intercepted the information that you would be at the Health Days Race and several of Ramirez's men were going to try to use you to get to your dad." He shrugged. "It made me mad so I decided to interfere. But then once I met you . . ." He pressed his lips together. "Sorry, but I couldn't stay away."

I had to hide a smile. "You always showed up just when I needed you."

"Most of my work as a physician is nine to five like yours so I could keep a close eye on you morning and night when I was in town."

My insides warmed at the thought of him watching over me. "So how do I know that you really like me?"

"Oh, I like you." Jesse smiled, his cheek crinkled irresistibly. I wanted to reach up and caress his cheek. "You're going to have to learn to trust that I'm telling you the truth about that and everything else."

I knew my dad didn't want me talking to Jesse, let alone learning how to trust him. But how could I help myself? I wanted to feel his arms around me, learn the history behind each tattoo, know exactly why he ticked the way he did. "I guess now you'll be fulfilling your promise to spend every minute by my side. You've got a lot of work to earn my trust."

Jesse threw back his head and laughed, but when his eyes met mine they were much too serious. "Oh, Cassidy. You are exactly what I've been looking for. Nobody can make me laugh the way you do."

I grinned, liking the way this was heading. I reached out my hand. He took it.

"Which means I'm concerned enough about your safety I wouldn't dare spend every minute with you," Jesse said.

I jerked my hand away. "That was so *not* the way you should've finished that statement."

Jesse shook his head. "I'm sorry, but I can't stand the thought of what could happen if my dad finds out how much I care about you."

Cold and warmth instantly enveloped me. The thought of seeing Nick Panetti covered me with chilly dread while Jesse saying how much he cared was like a warm blanket.

Jesse took my hand again and tugged me down the hall. "Come on."

"Where do you think I'm going with you?" I glanced over my shoulder, checking for my dad. I felt like a teenager sneaking away with the leader of the motorcycle gang.

"To the cafeteria. Maybe if I buy you a donut you'll forgive me next time I have to disappear."

"I'll forgive you when you stop disappearing."

Jesse pulled our clasped hands towards him and brushed his lips over my fingers. Stopping in the middle of the hallway, he tenderly kissed me. I clung to him, committing to memory each movement of his lips, the feel of him against me. He released my mouth, running a hand down the side of my face. "For *you*," he said, "I might have to make an exception."

"I don't know what kind of exception you're talking about," I hadn't stopped tingling from his kiss, "but if you keep looking at me like that, kissing me like that, and making me want you that bad, you'd better either start dating me or stay far away from me."

Jesse laughed with his entire body. "Maybe when I can talk some sense into your dad and guarantee that dating me won't threaten your life."

"Sounds like we've got a long road ahead of us."

He smiled. "For you, it'll be worth it." He inclined his head. "Let's go buy you that donut."

We sauntered towards the cafeteria. I clung to his hand. I didn't even like donuts, but it might be the only chance I had to be with this man. And to watch him grin at me like that? I'd eat a dozen.

The End

Cami Checketts is an idealist who dreams of helping children throughout the world but can hardly keep up with her four boys. She's one of those crazies who enjoys running and probably won't be able to walk when she's sixty.

Cami loves to visit with book clubs and fitness groups in person and via Facetime. She doesn't love public speaking but will prepare a fabulous speech or discussion if you promise to provide refreshments with a high chocolate content.

For more information about her books., please refer to her book blog – http://camicheckettsbooks.blogpost.com and http://fitnessformom.blogspot.com for fitness articles and exercise advice.

Made in United States
Orlando, FL
22 June 2023

34413442R00137